the Silence of monsters

Jay Crownover LLC
www.jaycrownover.com
The Silence of Monsters © 2024 by Jay Crownover

All rights reserved. No part of this publication may be reproduced, distributed, or transmitted in any form or by any means without prior written permission.

A letter of copyright has been applied for through the Library of Congress.

All rights reserved. Printed in the United States of America. No part of this book may be used or reproduced in any manner whatsoever without written permission, except in the case of brief quotations embodied in critical articles and reviews. For information, address Jay Crownover LLC: email at Jaycrownover@gmail.com

Publisher's Note: This is a work of fiction. Names, characters, places, and incidents are a product of the author's imagination. Locales and public names are sometimes used for atmospheric purposes. Any resemblance to actual people, living or dead, or to businesses, companies, events, institutions, or locales is completely coincidental.

eBook Cover Design by Beautiful Book Covers
www.etsy.com/shop/BeautifulBookCovers
Cover Design by the incomparable Hang Le
www.byhangle.com
Editing and Formatting by: Elaine York, Allusion Publishing
www.allusionpublishing.com
Copy Editing by: Bethany Salminen, Bethany Edits
www.bethanyedits.net

the Silence of monsters

jay crownover

Dedicated to:
All the ordinary girls who don't have
to be told they're extraordinary.

From Jay's Desk

I'm in my Soap Opera/Old Money Era!

No really, this book is supposed to have BIG K-drama, telenovela, and old school soap opera vibes. With a splash of *Phantom of the Opera* thrown in for good measure. This story is intentionally over-the-top with the family drama and a rich boy/poor girl trope. And because some characters go to the extremes in terms of love and hate, I do want to drop a **trigger warning** for those who are sensitive to mental health issues and suicidal ideation.

There's a character I hope you all hate with the fire of a thousand suns. The way they speak and refer to other characters dealing with mental illness is purposefully offensive. It shows the scorn and dismissal they have for a subject that should be handled with care and consideration. They have neither. If you've read any of my books prior to this one, you are probably very familiar with the passion I have for portraying mental health issues in a realistic and honest light. I hope my intent comes across as positive. This character is so far removed from my personal POV that they were difficult to write. So, reader, beware if this is a hot spot for you. The same character uses suicidal ideation in a manipulative and scheming way, not as a legitimate cry for help. Like I said, this character is meant to be hated and irredeemable. In the real world, suicidal ideation in any form is not a subject anyone should take lightly.

If you are struggling with thoughts of self-harm, please reach out to someone. Reach out to the crisis lifeline. 988 Suicide & Crisis Lifeline

I'll go into more detail about my inspiration in the afterword if you're the type who is curious about more than the story in front of you. For those who are sticklers for dialect and regional specifics, even though this book takes place on the East Coast, in theoretical New England/New York, I kept the dialogue simple and with minimal accents. I was thinking about finding a narrator for audio, and I was worried picking someone who could do a regional accent so specific would slow down the delayed process. (My audiobook provider is six to eight months out with production.) That's literally the only reason the Hallidays don't sound like they're from Connecticut or New Hampshire. In my head, all the Hallidays sound like my friend Dianne, who was born and raised in Manchester, New Hampshire. For the Halliday estate, I was picturing something like Taylor Swift's house in Rhode Island, only older and more sprawling.

I hope you enjoy my emo billionaire and his very ordinary (extraordinary) love interest as much as I do. This book took on a life of its own, and I can guarantee you won't see the end coming. I sure didn't!

Love & Ink,
Jay

Chapter One
channing

There was an old grandfather clock resting against one wall of the crowded antique and curio shop. No matter how often it was sent out for repairs, it always ran fast. The ticking of the hands perfectly matched the rapid beat of my heart and the unforgiving throb at my temples. The chime rang bright and clear, but it was always ten minutes before the hour.

I rubbed the center of my forehead out of frustration while the teenager standing across the counter nervously spun a diamond ring around her index finger. Those diamonds were a gift from her uncle, which meant they were undoubtedly real. And there was no practical reason for a thirteen-year-old girl to own such a pricey piece of jewelry. She couldn't even keep track of her cellphone. Which was why she'd shown up at the shop where I worked with no warning.

"You have to call home and let them know where you are." I blinked back the headache trying to ruin my day and watched my one-and-only niece through narrowed eyes. "If you don't call your uncle, he's going to report you missing. That's going to get both of us in trouble." I sighed and reached out, squishing her still round cheeks together so that she had no choice but to make a cute, kissy face. She still had enough baby fat on her face that I could see the carefree, sweet little girl she'd been lingering on her delicate features.

"If your grandma tells law enforcement that I kidnapped you, I don't know that either of us will convince them otherwise." I squeezed her cheeks harder until she jerked her head away. Her green and gold eyes were so much like her mother's. I always felt my heart twist painfully when our gazes locked. "Running away from home is dangerous, Winnie. You're fortunate nothing happened to you while you were traveling to the city on your own." I tried to sound stern and authoritative. However, I was neither of those things, and the warning fell flat.

The teenager rolled her eyes at me, but I could tell the mention of her grandmother made her nervous. "I told you; I lost my phone. I'll call Uncle Chester and let him know I'm safe and that I'm with you. Don't make me go back home right away, Aunt Channing. I hate it there."

Winnie's eyes welled with tears, and I could tell she was really at the end of her emotional rope. I swore under my breath and walked around the counter so I could give my niece a hug. She shuddered when I wrapped my arms around her and dropped her forehead to my shoulder. I patted her back and told her, "Don't call your uncle *Chester*. You know how much he hates it."

She sniffed loudly and muttered into the fabric of my shirt, "That's what you call him."

I barked out a dry laugh and tapped her on the back of the head. "I call him that because he and I are sworn enemies." And as my sworn nemesis, there was little I could do to come out on top when it came to Winchester Halliday. The man was gratuitously wealthy, obnoxiously well connected, and had far too much power for one man. The only thing I could do to let him know I wasn't afraid of him or envious of his gilded cage was to annoy him to death by treating him like he wasn't in the top one percent of society. Using the part of his name he despised never failed to get under his skin.

I pulled away from the hug and reached into my bag that was sitting haphazardly on the counter. "I'll call your Uncle Win. Let me tell the boss I have to leave early. I'll take you to my apartment and feed you while we figure out the next step." I sighed again and reached out to smooth her tangled hair back off her face. "You have to go back, Winnie."

There was no room for false hope when dealing with the Hallidays.

I could tell Winnie was going to cry, so I shuffled her to the small break room at the back of the store while I went in search of my boss.

I liked my job because it was easy and interesting. I enjoyed researching all the odds and ends that came through the door, and it was fun telling some customers that they had found buried treasure. It was also the job I'd held onto the longest while living in the city. My boss was a retired history professor who had a fascination with all things dark and macabre. It was like working for Dracula. He was an intense character, but pretty easygoing. When I told him I had a family emergency and needed to leave, he didn't bat an eye. When I mentioned I might need to take a few days off to deal with a personal issue, all he did was tilt his head and tell me to let him know if I needed his help with anything. I promised him I would keep him in the loop. Then, I found a quiet corner to call Winnie's uncle, my only brother-in-law, who just happened to be my second least favorite person in the world.

The grandfather clock chimed, making me jump. The ticking sounded like a countdown to something inexplicably dangerous. I closed my eyes and mentally braced myself as the phone rang.

I wasn't kidding when I told Winnie her uncle and I were enemies. The only person I hated more than him — was her grandmother. All the Hallidays, aside from my niece, were awful. Somewhere along the line, the entire family had foregone humanity and basic decency. I wouldn't put it past them to have made a pact with the devil. Why not exchange their souls for unlimited money and power? It's not like they would ever need them. The entire family never showed grace to those they didn't consider beneficial to them. I definitely had nothing to offer the likes of Winchester Halliday, so there was zero guarantee he would answer my call. If he didn't, I would just have to bite the bullet and call his mother, Colette Halliday. Even though I'd rather eat glass than speak to Winnie's grandmother.

Luckily, a deep and impatient voice answered the call. "What do you want, Harvey? I'm very busy."

From the time we first met, Win called me by my last name. Sometimes I wondered if he didn't know what my first name was. My fingers tightened on the cellphone as I took a deep breath to calm my nerves. "Do you have any idea that Winnie is missing?"

Win swore, and I heard him snapping orders to whomever was in the room with him. "I've had people out looking for her for the last four hours. She had a piano lesson after class today. She called and told her instructor she was sick. I didn't realize she was missing until her teacher called to check on her and asked how she was feeling." He swore again and I could hear the frustration in his tone. "I've been trying to keep my mother from calling the FBI. I trusted my people to locate her in a timely manner. I should've known she was with you."

There was no relief in his tone. Only irritation and impatience.

"She showed up at the store where I work out of the blue. I wasn't expecting her. Winnie told me she had a friend drive her to the train station. She lost her phone on the train. When she got to the central station in the city, she walked around until she found someone who had an idea where my store was located. I'm going to take her home with me for now." I snorted and snapped at him, "She's begging not to go back to your house, Chester."

"She's a teenager. She doesn't know what she wants." I heard the rustling of fabric as he moved. "I'm sending people to your place to get her. They'll be there in a couple of hours."

"That's a bad idea. If you send your black-suit brigade to drag her back against her will, she might run again when she gets the chance. Next time she might not come to me. What are you going to do if she really disappears and gets herself into a dangerous situation? Back off for a couple of days. Let me talk to her. I'll bring her home when she's not as upset and irrational as she is right now."

"No. She has school and lessons. Unlike you, Winnie will follow through with her responsibilities. You're the last person she needs to spend time with." His words were biting and harsh, but they were nothing I hadn't heard from him before. He always made his disdain for me and my lifestyle abundantly clear.

"You're being unreasonable, Chester. She came to me for a reason. You and your mother are more concerned with turning her into a perfect Halliday than you are with her wellbeing. I understand wanting Winnie to be responsible and accountable, but she's just a kid. Let her have a childhood." And some fun. I didn't add the last part because I wasn't certain that Win knew what fun was.

When Winnie was younger, I still lived near Halliday Cove. The Halliday family founded the small, coastal town back when their ancestors landed on the coast. I was allowed to see my niece more frequently back then, even though Colette tried everything in her power to keep the little girl away from her relatives who weren't named Halliday.

However, when Winnie got older and started exhibiting troubling behavior and major signs of distress, Colette called a child psychologist. The specialist recommended it would be best if Winnie could have contact with her mother's side of the family to benefit from spending time with people who knew and loved her deceased mother. Among them, I was the only living relative who wasn't deemed a risk to the little girl.

As Winnie got older and her issues stabilized, the Hallidays, namely Colette, once again did whatever they could to cut me out of my niece's life. In the last few years, I'd only seen her a handful of times. Each visit, I could tell she was turning more and more into a copy-and-paste version of Win. The similarities made sense since he was her primary guardian, but I wanted more in life for her. Win was miserable. I didn't want Winnie to see the world in the same bleak, boring way he did.

Win scoffed on the other end of the call. "Of course, you think I'm depriving Winnie of a proper childhood because I want her to be accountable and responsible. She should end up like you, bouncing from job to job? Do you want her to treat getting married and divorced like it's a hobby? Do you want her living paycheck-to-paycheck because she has no financial awareness like you? You're a terrible role model, Harvey."

I wanted to reach through the phone and wrap my hands around his neck. Not because he was incorrect, but because he was just so arrogant and dismissive about my existence. I hated how he talked to me, and how he looked down on me.

"At least I'm not unhappy day in and day out. It doesn't take a genius to tell Winnie is terribly upset. You're raising her. It's your job to make sure her life is full and celebrated. She's a human being, not a robot. And not your pet." She would never be a Halliday clone if I had a say in the matter. I kept the last part to myself. Because if there was one line I wouldn't cross with him, it was anything to do with his mother.

I was never sure if Win was so touchy about his family because they were the only people he loved in the world, or because he hated them as much as he loathed everyone else. The man was an iceberg, which made him very tough to read. In all the years I'd known him, I don't think I'd ever seen him smile or laugh. It was no surprise Winnie felt like she had to run away from that suffocating atmosphere.

I leaned my head back and banged it on the wall in frustration. "If you won't let her stay with me for a few days, then the very least you can do is come and get her yourself. If she's feeling trapped and frustrated, the last thing she needs is to get hauled back to the Cove by your goons. Stop treating her like a subordinate and start treating her like your niece."

I hung up the call before I said something I might regret.

Mostly, Win and I stayed in our respective bubbles and didn't interact. We had no reason to. And since we easily enraged each other, there was no point. It was never far from my mind that if I spoke to the man the way I really wanted to and told him what I honestly thought about him and the way he was raising my niece, he could ruin me. The Hallidays had the means and mindset to crush the life out of anyone who wronged them with a mere phone call. Getting on Win's bad side was never the best idea. Since I lived there permanently, I walked on eggshells around him to make sure I never pushed my luck so far that there was no coming back.

When I went back to the break room, I found my niece munching on snacks and holding a can of soda. It looked like my boss did his best to cheer her up and make her comfortable while I argued with Win.

I took a seat across from the teenager and forced a smile. "I talked to your uncle. He's worried about you."

Winnie snorted and rolled her eyes. "I bet he didn't even know I was gone. He's always working. He's so busy, I haven't seen his face for more than a couple of minutes in months."

I cursed the man silently and reached out to bop the end of her nose. "You need to tell him you want to spend time with him. Running away doesn't solve the problem."

"You can't tell me you believe that Uncle Win listens to anyone. You know him better than that."

I let out a rough laugh. "You're right. I don't think he cares what anyone has to say. But you aren't *anyone*, Winnie." She was his family, a Halliday, which made her special.

Winnie made a face, showing she did not believe a word of what I just said. She took a drink of the sugary soda and set the can down on the table in front of her. "I'm sorry I showed up here unannounced. I remember where your old apartment is, but last time we talked, you told me you moved. You always move. I didn't know where to look for you, Aunt Channing." I wasn't sure if she knew how much she'd just sounded like her uncle. I could hear Win in her accusatory tone.

"I'm sorry. I should've made sure you had my new address." I moved more often than the average thirty-five-year-old woman.

I jumped into new relationships with both feet and a blind heart. I always optimistically believed whomever I was with would be *the one*. Which left me without a roof over my head once the relationship ended. I didn't get married and divorced like it was a hobby, as Win suggested. However, I had two ex-husbands. I married and divorced both when I was too young to know better. After the trauma of those relationships, I now changed boyfriends as frequently as others changed the oil in their cars, trying to find my idea of happily ever after. My New Year's resolution for this year, after I hit my mid-thirties, was to stay single until my birthday. So far, I managed to stick to it. For the first time in forever, I was living on my own, in a place I could afford with my sole income. It was the most responsible I'd felt in a long time, which made Win's dismissive words toward me even more infuriating.

"Come on." I shook off the dark mood that always followed conversations with Win and focused on my niece. "Let's go to my apartment. We can figure out a way to handle your Uncle Chester on the way."

Winnie laughed and followed me out of the fun, quirky store. "He hates it to death when you call him that."

I grinned down at her. "I know." I wrapped my arm around her thin shoulders as we walked toward my small apartment. "Do you want to tell me why it was suddenly so bad at home that you left without telling anyone?" She had always lived a life controlled down to the minute. The tradeoff was that she grew up with privilege only a handful of people would ever experience. Winnie had the very best of everything at her fingertips. Even if I didn't like Win and his mother, I couldn't argue that they gave Winnie a wealth of opportunities and experiences. As a teenager, she'd already been to Rome and Paris. I rarely ventured far from the East Coast.

She sniffed and looked down at the dirty sidewalk. "I hate it there. There are so many rules. There's no privacy. Their expectations are too high. I failed an advanced math class, and Grandma told me she was looking into private schools overseas for me. I don't feel like playing the piano. I don't want to learn ballet. I don't even know what a cotillion is, but she's making me attend classes for one.

I'm tired, Aunt Channing." She gave her head a small shake and muttered, "Plus, I think that house is haunted. It gives me the creeps."

I pulled her into a tight side hug and dropped a kiss on the top of her head. "That is a lot." It was too much. I agreed with her. "What do you mean, you think the house is haunted?"

My older sister and Win's younger brother had passed away in a fire that ravaged their wing of the Halliday estate when Winnie was just a baby. I always thought it was an awful idea for the remaining family to rebuild and move on. They acted as if the tragedy had never happened. Of course, they would never leave the sprawling, opulent property that had been in their family for generations. It didn't surprise me that Winnie felt spooked about staying under the same roof where her parents died.

"I keep hearing things. Thumps and bumps that sound like someone is hiding in the walls. And I swear, the other day when I was studying, I could hear someone singing. I looked in every room and wandered around the entire estate, but I couldn't find where the sound was coming from. Grandma told me that I was making excuses to avoid studying. Uncle Win told me the house is hundreds of years old, so it's going to make noises."

I begrudgingly nodded in agreement. "I think your uncle is probably right. Old houses like that make strange noises. They moan and groan and even whistle. That's how they speak their history. I don't think you have anything to worry about."

Winnie sighed and shrugged her shoulders at my reassurance. She changed the subject so fast that I had to scramble to keep up with her.

"Grandma wants Uncle Win to get married. She keeps telling me he's getting too old to start a family. She's harping on him to settle down and have kids. He never responds to her, so she started inviting all these different women over for these fancy dinners and ambushing him with blind dates. Dinnertime was the only time Uncle Win would put down work and spend some normal time with me. Now, he rarely comes home before midnight. It's so awkward and uncomfortable. I just want a regular family."

"I hate to break it to you, kid, but there is no such thing as a regular family."

Just look at mine.

My older sister was gone. My mother was institutionalized. My father was God knows where, shacked up with God knows who. Even though he and my mother were still very much married. I'd mostly been on my own since I was a teenager. Which is why I let myself fall in love so easily. I was always trying to fill in the holes in my heart that my fractured family left behind.

"You're too young to realize that all the privilege you have now is going to ensure not only you, but whomever you bring into your life, have a promising future. It's much better to have too much than not enough, Winnie."

She sniffed again and wrapped her arm around my waist. "But all I want is my mom and dad."

Her words stabbed into the center of my chest. I felt tears sting my eyes as I pulled her closer. "I know, sweetie. I wish more than anything that's something I could give you."

Even with all the money and connections in the world, it was impossible for Winchester Halliday to bring the dead back to life. If he could, he would resurrect his younger brother in a heartbeat.

We were equally helpless to give our niece the thing she desperately wanted above all else. That was the *only* commonality we shared.

Chapter Two

win

I looked around the dingy hallway with contempt. It led to the apartment where my niece was waiting. The walls and doors were paper thin. I could hear arguing, sex, and laughter filtering out of the different units. I frowned when I caught sight of a rat scurrying from one dark corner to the next. The man standing to my right stiffened, and I heard him swear.

I lifted my eyebrows and glanced at my long-time head of security. "I'm sure you stayed in worse conditions when you were in the military."

The other man grunted and wiped the look of disgust off his face. "I did, Sir. I can't imagine your niece running away from home and purposely coming to a place like this. It doesn't make any sense."

I grunted in agreement. Rocco Drach hadn't lived a life of leisure before enlisting in the military. He was a man who worked hard for what he had and appreciated that he could now afford the finer things in life. I hired him to work for me the day I took over as the CEO of the family business, Halliday Inc. Aside from my younger brother, who was devastatingly no longer part of my life, I didn't trust anyone more than the former military man. Rocco had been right next to me while I did my best to ensure Winnie was raised properly after my brother's death. He was instrumental in helping me keep my mother's machinations at bay where the young girl was involved. I had no doubt the intimidating bear of a man was genuinely puzzled at Winnie's current conduct. She was usually a docile and well-behaved young lady. He had no idea how attached Winnie was to her aunt. No one could see the influence Channing Harvey had over my niece the way I did. The Halliday estate might be Winnie's house, but Channing was her home. It didn't matter what I gave the little girl, because whatever Channing offered her was always better.

"Even if it was a tent under a bridge somewhere, Winnie would want to be there if that's where Channing was. This isn't the first time Winnie's tried to sneak away and see her aunt." I gave the older man a look out of the corner of my eye. "Which is why your team is supposed to know where she is and who she's with. Keeping my niece safe is your number one priority."

It wasn't normal for a thirteen-year-old to need a full security detail; there was nothing normal about your life when you were born a Halliday. I wouldn't risk my niece's life just because she had the same last name as me. I couldn't protect my brother. The least I could do was make sure his daughter was never in danger. I promised as much when I was named her godfather. Winnie was all I had left after my favorite person passed. My little brother's time was cut too short. I refused to let a repeat happen with his daughter.

When we reached the door to the apartment, I could hear raucous laughter and female voices. One was young and had a soft accent. The other was husky and full of character. Channing wasn't a smoker, but her voice sounded like it was crafted by cigarettes and whiskey. It was easy to identify anywhere. As was the raspy laugh that followed something my niece said. I lifted my hand to knock on the door, but paused midway when I heard Winnie ask, "What did my mother like to do? I know Grandma won't let me drop all my lessons, but maybe she'll consider letting me do something I'm truly interested in if I ask the right way. I need to figure out what it is I might like. Right now, everything feels so pointless and boring."

"Hmmm... your mom liked to paint, and she liked to dance. She liked to sing. She fronted a band for a short time before she met your dad. She liked a little bit of everything. I can't think of one thing she stuck with for longer than a few months, though. She wanted to experience everything life had to offer."

"Oh." The disappointment was clear in Winnie's voice. "My piano teacher always tells me I'm a natural, and that I have inherent talent. I thought you were going to say she played an instrument."

Channing's voice softened. "You must've gotten that from your dad. If I remember right, your dad played the piano and your Uncle Win played the violin when they were kids."

"I can't picture Uncle Win playing a violin. I feel like he was born wearing a suit and tie. All he cares about is work." Winnie giggled, and I felt a bit of pressure in my chest.

I couldn't recall the last time I heard my niece laugh. She was always somber and serious when we interacted. Channing's warning that Winnie needed to be allowed a childhood scratched annoyingly at the back of my mind.

Even under the threat of death, I couldn't and wouldn't admit the lackadaisical woman might have a point.

I knocked on the door and waited impatiently for Channing to answer. Rocco swore again as another rat hustled down the hallway. He turned pale and gave me a helpless look. If I wasn't so worried about my niece and frustrated by what was happening at home because of my mother, I would've teased him relentlessly. I'd witnessed Rocco face off against any number of opponents with ice in his veins and nerves of steel. I couldn't believe a fuzzy little rodent was his undoing. He looked like he was seconds away from pulling a gun on the critter.

The door swung open, and I automatically looked down at Channing. She wasn't a short woman. She wasn't tall either. In fact, everything about her was in the middle of two extremes. She wasn't heavy, but she wasn't thin. She wasn't loud, but no one would ever mistake her for being quiet. Channing wasn't someone who took herself, or anyone else, too seriously. However, she was far from easygoing. I never claimed to know her very well, but I'd paid close attention to her since both she and her sister disrupted my regimented life when we were all kids. She might come across as ordinary. However, Channing was anything but. She could do what no Halliday ever could. Love. She loved effortlessly in a big, bold, unforgettable way.

The redhead looked at me in surprise, her gaze darting past me to watch Rocco. I usually traveled with more than a one-man security detail. The look on her face clearly showed that she didn't think I would take her advice and come for Winnie on my own.

"Are you going to let me in?" I asked curtly. It was evident she didn't want to permit me to enter.

Channing swished the end of her long ponytail over her shoulder and moved to the side. Her hair was strawberry blond, the same as Winnie's. Her eyes were a hazel brown-blue-green combo, whereas my niece's were a green and gold swirl. There were enough similarities; it was obvious Winnie took more after the Harvey side of the family than the Hallidays. The similarity irritated my mother to no end every time she looked at the young girl.

Channing waved a hand covered in silver rings toward the interior of the tiny apartment. My niece jumped to her feet when our gazes locked. She clasped her hands together nervously and darted her gaze between me and her aunt.

The apartment was cramped and old. But it was spotlessly clean. There were no signs of the furry visitors in the hallway. Thank goodness. The décor was bright and eclectic. The couch where Winnie had been sitting was an ungodly shade of lime green that would be offensive anywhere else. It felt oddly fitting in Channing's home.

"I'm sorry I left and snuck away to the city. I didn't mean to leave my phone on the train. I was going to call you once I found Aunt Channing's store and ask if I could stay with her for a few days. I didn't intend to make you worry." Winnie gulped and tightened her hands into fists. "I wouldn't have had to run away if you would let me see Aunt Channing when I asked."

Channing and I exchanged a look. Her eyes were filled with accusation. My look in return was filled with dissatisfaction. I never denied that I purposely limited Winnie's access to the woman I publicly deemed an unfit influence. The reasons to keep them apart were far too complex for a teenager to understand. They were so complicated I wasn't certain I understood them half the time. At the core of the problem was the fact that nothing good, aside from Winnie, ever came from mixing the Harveys and the Hallidays together.

I hated it when my brother Archie fell in love with Channing's older sister, Willow. I was beyond upset when he told me he got her pregnant and was planning to marry her despite our parents' objections. It was a terrible idea from the jump. My mother would never let him have a moment's peace if he defied her.

The Harveys were like a family from a nostalgic blue-collar sitcom. Each was a character in their own right. My family could never understand or be bothered with their issues. My parents were a union orchestrated between two powerful families. Love and happiness had no place between husband and wife. No one on my brother's side of the situation would lower themselves by being sympathetic toward the young couple. What they did, instead, was try to buy Willow off and threaten the rest of her family to keep their daughter away from Archie. My mother was relentless in her quest to break up the two of them.

Unfortunately, Willow and Channing's scumbag father took the money my mother offered and disappeared. A revelation that only came out after my brother returned home with his wife and daughter. There was no way my mother was going to let Willow forget the kind of horrible person her father was. She was ruthless with her criticism.

The Harveys had no place in the world of the Hallidays.

After Archie and Willow died in the fire, I assumed I would never have to deal with them again. Little did I know Winnie was going to be the string that tied us together for eternity. I vastly underestimated how desperately she was going to need a connection to her mother's family — Channing, in particular.

"We can talk about visitation after we get home. It's late, and you have school tomorrow. We need to leave as quickly as possible." I glanced at Channing. She was frowning at me, but didn't say anything to contradict my orders.

"I'm not going." Winnie crossed her arms over her chest and braced her feet. I could tell she was gearing up for a battle tonight, and I might have to haul her out of this apartment over my shoulder. "I'm staying with Aunt Channing unless you promise you'll let me see her whenever I want. I hate the estate. I hate school and all the extra things Grandma makes me do afterward. I don't want to go to a private school in Switzerland." She started crying and her face turned red. "You're never home, and you never listen to me when I try to talk to you."

Winnie started sobbing in earnest, and Channing rushed around the ugly couch to wrap her in a tight hug.

I frowned and exchanged a confused look with Rocco. "Boarding school in Switzerland?" This was the first time I'd heard anything about it.

Channing glared at me over the top of our niece's head and mouthed, "Your mother."

Of course it was my mother.

I was her primary guardian. I had full legal custody of Winnie, but my mother often acted like she was in charge of dictating the direction of Winnie's life. I was all too familiar with the way Colette Halliday micromanaged and steamrolled through every situation.

Winnie was right. I'd been working far more than normal lately because I shared her hatred of being at our house. I'd chosen to run away, too. It was hypocritical to blame my niece for doing the same thing.

I sighed and reached up to loosen my tie. I rushed to Channing's apartment as soon as I hung up from her call. I still had a meeting tonight that I'd moved to a video conference after I decided to get Winnie myself. I hadn't had time to eat anything or think about this entire situation rationally yet. It was easiest to blame Winnie and

Channing. It was much harder to look at the history of prejudice and judgment between our families and realize that the fault was related to a much bigger, lingering issue.

"No one is sending you to boarding school." Winnie currently attended one of the best private schools in the country. My mother threatening to send her away was nothing more than her being petty and mean. She ruled through intimidation. I often wondered if she was so stern because she married into the Halliday empire. It wasn't one she conquered with her own prowess. My mother's family was well-off but came nowhere near the prestige and power the Hallidays held in the palms of their hands. It always seemed like she had more to prove since she didn't start out with the same legacy Winnie and I had, even if we were all part of the same family. "I'm sorry that I've been so busy at work. I'll do better. I promise I will listen to whatever you have to say."

My niece sniffled, but she didn't stop crying. Channing gave me a pointed look as she continued to soothe her.

"Your aunt and I will discuss things on another day. We'll see what we can do about seeing her more often. Right now, you need to focus on school. If you don't want to do all the activities your grandmother signed you up for, we can figure that out. But you can't just do nothing. You're more ambitious than that. Those activities not only give you skills that might be useful in the future, they teach you about time management and how to stick to something challenging. When you get older, you can't just quit something because you don't enjoy it."

Channing scoffed loudly. "That's bullshit. One of the best parts of being an adult is quitting things that don't bring you joy. Why should you force yourself to stick with something that sucks when there are a million other options out there to explore?"

I wanted to roll my eyes at the naïve comment. "Maybe in your world people can jump from one thing to the next with no thought to the consequences. That isn't an applicable mindset for normal adults."

I'd never wanted to take over the family business. I had no interest in real estate development or land management. I despised towering skyscrapers that felt like glass and steel coffins. I loathed that I was so busy running the company, I missed everything happening with my family. My commitments were skewed from the minute I was thrust into society. I had different ambitions for myself before I even understood that what I wanted to do with my life was never my choice.

Though my mother forced me to learn to play the violin as a child, I loved it. I was better than good at it. I foolishly aspired to be a classically trained musician and play with a renowned orchestra. My future, never being my own, was the hardest part of being a Halliday.

Shortly after the fire and death of my brother, my father, who had a chronic heart condition, passed away. The old man's health had been on the decline ever since Archie returned home, which was something my mother happily blamed on my brother's young bride. If I'd refused to take over the role of CEO when my mother started pressuring me, it wasn't only my immediate family who would have suffered. Thousands of employees and shareholders would lose everything. There wasn't a single point in my forty-three years of life where I'd ever had the option to walk away from something I didn't enjoy. I had to stick with it for the greater good. Like it or not, so would Winnie. She was next in line to take over everything.

"If being a normal adult means being miserable every single day, I'll pass. Just agree to let Winnie see me once a month, and we can resolve this situation without further issue. Stop being so uptight, Chester."

I gritted my teeth when Channing used my most hated nickname. I refused to react, because that's what she wanted. "This is far from resolved. Winnie ran away from home. She put herself in danger. She came to the city without permission and lost her phone. If something happened, she wouldn't have a way to contact me or call for help. She hasn't been making good decisions lately. I expect more from her."

"Your expectations are exactly why she's making dangerous choices to have a taste of freedom. You and your mother need to lighten up. She's just a kid."

I opened my mouth to continue arguing. Channing was the one person who snapped my patience in half without trying. The words never made it out because Rocco tapped my shoulder and reminded me that we still had to drive back to the Cove, where I had another video conference scheduled. If we didn't leave now, we wouldn't get home until dawn.

"Kids need to know they can't always get what they want, especially when their last name is Halliday. A lesson that's much easier to learn when you're young. We have to go. Come with me, Winnie. Don't make me haul you out of here in an uncouth manner. We're both better than that."

I could tell Winnie didn't want to leave. She was still crying. Channing whispered something into the girl's ear, and she decisively pulled herself together enough to move next to me. She waved to her aunt and followed me out of the apartment like a prisoner who was walking toward her execution. I wanted to offer a hug or some gesture of solace, but it was obvious my niece was angry at me and wouldn't appreciate me touching her.

On the way to the blacked-out SUV, my phone rang. I glanced at the screen, and when I saw it was my mother calling, I wanted to throw the phone into the nearest gutter and forget about it.

Rocco helped Winnie into the car, and I motioned for him to give me a minute while I answered the call. If I ignored her, she would keep calling me, and the people around me, until she got the information she was looking for. The woman was exhausting.

"Did you find the girl?" My mother's accent was similar to Winnie's, but her tone was sharp enough to cut through skin and bones.

"Of course I found her. We're on the way back to the Cove now."

"She was with that horrid woman, wasn't she? That family has always been a problem for us." I could hear the scorn dripping from every word she spoke.

I rubbed my forehead and tried to ignore the tension pulling at the back of my neck. "Winnie is part of that family regardless of how you feel about it, Mother. The more you try to erase Channing's existence, the more curious Winnie's going to be. The more you disparage her mother and her mother's family in front of her, the more she's going to seek someone who has a different opinion."

"They destroyed your brother. I will not let them ruin that little girl as well. They're all crazy."

I swore under my breath and reached deep for the last scraps of my patience. It was hard to fight back against those claims when my mother knew that Channing's mom had been institutionalized, and her sister had shown obvious signs of mental instability throughout her relationship with my brother.

I pushed back with something that couldn't be disputed. "You don't get to decide who is allowed in Winnie's life; I do." And while I didn't have high expectations for Channing Harvey, I knew she would never harm my niece. Anyone with eyes could see she loved the young woman with her whole heart. I couldn't say the same thing about my mother. She looked at Winnie like she was a chore that needed to be checked off a lengthy list.

My mother went quiet, and I heard her breathing change. She was angry at me and wanted to argue. She knew me well enough to know that if she started something, I'd hang up on her and do the opposite of whatever she asked to spite her. She drove me up a wall and pushed me to where I hated my behavior.

"You need to come home on time for dinner tomorrow night. I have someone I want you to meet. Her family is in the architectural and engineering field. I think you'll have a lot in common. She's a very nice young lady and appropriately attractive. It's time for you to settle down, Winchester. You and Winnie both need a quality woman in your life to take care of you. If you get married, I won't have to be the only one trying to keep Winnie on the right path. You have an opportunity to give her the closest thing she'll ever have to the normal family she wants so badly."

A muscle in my cheek twitched as my molars ground together to the point my jaw hurt. "I told you, stop trying to set me up. Stop inviting women over to the house. It makes both me and Winnie uncomfortable. I'm in no rush to meet anyone, let alone walk down the aisle."

Getting married was the last thing on my mind. I wouldn't even bring my worst enemy to my mother's front door. I paused for a second as a vague idea took shape in the back of my mind. My worst enemy was upstairs in that shithole apartment, and she disliked my mother almost as much as I did.

"Winnie and I are on the way home. We'll get back late. Don't wait up for us." I blew out a frustrated breath. "And stop threatening her with boarding school. She's not going anywhere without my say-so."

My mom huffed an offended breath and hung up the call. She didn't tell me to drive safely. She didn't ask if Winnie was all right. I was used to her indifference and manipulation. I hated that my mother subjected Winnie to the abhorrent parenting I silently endured. The poor girl lost her parents. She deserved more than being forcibly molded into my mother's maniacal image of what a perfect young woman from high society should be.

I couldn't walk away from all the things I hated in my life. Channing was right. I should enable my niece to have the luxury of doing everything I couldn't at her age.

The woman was smarter and more insightful than I'd ever given her credit for. I refused to end our longstanding feud for many reasons. It was the one thing in my life that forced me to feel things I'd long forgotten. The only time I felt alive was when I went head-to-head with the abrasive redhead.

When you were forced into a life you never wanted, it was best to turn off your emotions to maintain your sanity. I excelled at forgetting how to feel anything — unless I was dealing with Channing Harvey.

Chapter Three
channing

"How was your latest run-in with the sexy-as-fuck billionaire?" I met the curious eyes of my best friend in the mirror in front of me. Salome Clarke owned the salon a block over from the antique shop. We'd run into one another several times on our way to and from work and struck up a friendship, as well as a stylist-client relationship. I wouldn't trust anyone else with my hair, or my secrets.

I made a face at my reflection and told her, "He was surprisingly less awful than the last time we were in the same room. He didn't treat me like I was the hired help this time. For all his faults, I can't deny that he really seems to love Winnie and wants to do what he thinks is best for her."

Salome lifted her pierced eyebrow and swung her long braids over her bare shoulder. She was a knockout. Before she decided she wanted to be her own boss, she'd made a name for herself in the modeling industry. Sometimes her beauty still took me aback, even though we saw each other at least once a week.

"What's best for that girl is for someone to get her away from that wicked witch disguised as her grandmother. Lady Halliday won't rest until she fully indoctrinates your niece into the one percent." *Lady Halliday* was the snarky nickname my sister came up with for the stern matriarch when she first started sneaking around to date Archie.

I blew a wet piece of hair out of my face and silently agreed. "The funny thing is, I don't think he likes his mother any more than I do. But she's the only family he has left, aside from Winnie. He tolerates her nonsense because he doesn't have much choice." And he was never home. He was chained to a desk, building the Halliday brand bigger and stronger to appease the woman. He hardly had to deal with her because he was so busy at her behest.

Salome snipped at the ends of my hair and frowned. "Isn't there an unclaimed Halliday out there in the wild somewhere? Why doesn't Win drag him home and give his mother a real project?"

I laughed and looked down at my phone when a text message flashed on the screen. Win bought Winnie a new phone, but she was grounded and could only use it for an hour a day. She told me he let her quit ballet and drop the courses for the cotillion. However, she had to find a new activity to fill that time, and whatever she picked, she had to stick with it for a full year. She messaged me every day asking for recommendations. It was obvious she was looking to connect with something her parents might have loved doing.

I tried to recall the different things Willow enjoyed when she was a teenager, but it was difficult. Our family wasn't destitute, but we weren't anywhere near what one would consider wealthy. We lived a comfortable life. My dad was a fisherman and my mom ran a bakery. I didn't grow up with everything I wanted at my fingertips, but I never felt like my childhood lacked anything. My parents let Willow and me try, and subsequently quit, a variety of things throughout our youth. Willow decided when she was seventeen, going on eighteen, that what she liked most was Archie Halliday. The two met when our mother sent her on a rush delivery to the Halliday estate. She encountered Archie by chance, and once they started talking, there was room for little else in my sister's life. I couldn't tell Winnie that, considering how badly her parents' love story ended. To divert her attention from the past, I kept throwing out random suggestions for activities she might like, hoping something would stick. Today I suggested she try working for the yearbook committee or the school newspaper. I thought she might enjoy photography since it was a way to preserve precious memories. Things she was sorely lacking.

I looked back to the mirror and noticed Salome was waiting for an answer about the missing Halliday brother.

"There is a half-brother. He's young. I think he's only in his early twenties. Supposedly, Colette and Win only learned about him when he was mentioned in the will when Win's father died. Win's always working, so I believe he was in the dark. But Colette doesn't let anything having to do with that family slip by her. Winchester Senior had a year-long affair with a woman who worked for one of their properties. He left the kid a substantial number of shares in Halliday Inc. and a shit ton of money. He would've become a multimillionaire overnight if Colette hadn't taken him to court as soon as she found out about him. She seemed pretty well prepared for a battle that was supposed to be a surprise. I'm sure she was beyond furious when the court ruled in the kid's favor. Win has never mentioned him publicly or privately, but Colette never misses a chance to remind everyone he is *not* a Halliday. He will never be welcome in her home."

"She is such a miserable bitch."

I chuckled because Salome wasn't wrong. I blinked as she fluffed the long layers that framed my face. The new blond highlights brightened up my whole look and made the strawberry in my hair color stand out. When my bestie finished playing with my style, I always felt extra pretty. She would never let me leave her salon if I didn't feel like a solid ten. She always said that I was a walking, talking representation of her talent, so I had to serve self-confidence and sex appeal.

"Winnie mentioned that Colette is pushing Win to get married. It's a regular revolving door of social elites at their estate these days. Apparently, he hates every second of it, but Colette won't stop. According to my niece, he's been arguing with Colette every day. I've only seen him lose his temper a couple of times. She must've finally tripped over his bottom line." I was used to being the target of his anger. It was a novel experience to know it was directed at someone more worthy of his wrath for once. When Salome removed the protective cape, I shook my head and lifted my hair off my neck. "I don't think he's interested in marriage regardless of the woman or the matchmaker. I've known him since he was an Ivy League college student. Even back then, he was more focused on school than he was on dating."

It was honestly a shame. Win was very handsome and distinguished now, but when he was younger, he was straight up HOT. He was still tall and lean with a swimmer's build. Back then, he wore his dark hair long, and it curled cutely at the ends. There was a roguish charm about him that was like catnip to anyone when he was young and still had a hint of recklessness. When he was in his early twenties, his stormy gray eyes were clear and bright because the world gave him everything anyone could ask for and he hadn't experienced a great loss yet. These days, those silvery eyes are as sharp as the blade of a knife. They cut through all opponents with no remorse. Nowadays, his hair, while still dark and thick, sported a trendy, short style with silver and white strands scattered throughout. He wasn't fully salt and pepper yet, but the day was clearly coming. Win was still an undeniably attractive man. If he wanted to find a wife, he could rely on his appearance alone to get the job done. Especially when that face came attached to not just a historical family legacy, but also a generational wealth few would ever experience. The only reason Win was single was because he wanted to be.

The beads and charms threaded throughout Salome's hair clicked and jangled as she moved to sweep up around the chair. Our years of friendship meant she wouldn't let me pay her. We usually traded taking each other out for drinks or dinner as compensation, but I still wanted to leave her a tip. I transferred her money via an app so she couldn't refuse like she always did.

I joked as she reached for a hug, "Do you want me to see if I can get you on the long list of potential bachelorettes? Don't you think it would be nice to marry a billionaire?"

Salome snorted a laugh and pulled on the ends of my freshly cut hair. "Something tells me that even if Win fell in love with me at first sight, Lady Halliday would find a million-and-one reasons to keep me from marrying into her distinguished family. I don't think a woman like her is interested in diversifying the family bloodline. I'd end up like Meghan Markle."

I couldn't hold back a laugh at the comparison. "You're probably right. Winnie's half Halliday, and that's barely acceptable to Colette. I wouldn't want anyone I care about to have to live under the same roof as that woman. That's a fate worse than death." I shuddered at the thought as my friend laughed off the silly suggestion. Win wasn't Salome's type, even if he was handsome and rich. She preferred artistic types. She liked men with creative passion and drive. Win was an iceberg. I was pretty sure the only thing that ever got him hot and bothered was the smell of money or closing a big business deal. "I'm off today and tomorrow. Text me if you want to grab dinner or a drink when you're done with work."

The stunning woman gave me another hug and promised to let me know if she was free in the next few days. I hoped Win would let me see Winnie more regularly, and I could introduce her to my friends, and maybe even the other members of our small family. My father didn't have any interest in anyone other than himself, and I was no longer in contact with him. My mother, on the other hand, would benefit greatly from getting the chance to meet Willow's daughter and see that she was growing up so well. All her doctors and caretakers told me it would do wonders for her mental state. After my sister died, and the Hallidays did everything in their power to wipe my family off the face of the earth, my mother had a major psychological breakdown. She'd always struggled with her mental health. When she was a young woman, she'd been diagnosed with schizophrenia. Medication and behavioral therapy helped for a while, but once the family fell apart, so did she. It was a condition Willow and Winnie both dealt with in varying degrees because it tended to run in families. The illness was yet another reason for Colette Halliday to blame my family for the misfortune that befell her own.

When I stepped out of the salon, it was raining. I swore and held my purse over my head to preserve the fresh cut and color. My apartment was fifteen minutes away. My options were to run, call for a ride, or find somewhere to wait out the weather. I picked the third option. I ducked into a coffee shop just as the sky turned dark and it started to really pour. I shook myself like a dog at the entrance and glanced down when my phone rang. There were raindrops on the screen that blurred Win's name. I frowned deeply, thinking the only reason he had to reach out was Winnie. He wouldn't call me unless it was an emergency.

I found a seat where it wasn't too busy, wiped the phone on the leg of my jeans, and answered his call.

"What's wrong?" I tried to sound calm, but I could hear the tremor of anxiety in my voice. "Did something happen with Winnie?"

Win didn't answer at first. He cleared his throat and told me Winnie was fine. I could picture him shifting into serious business mode by his tone. "I want to discuss something with you. I'm in the city on business. Can we meet up?"

"Does it have to do with Winnie?" I couldn't imagine anything else he would want to talk to me about in person.

"It involves Winnie in a roundabout way."

I sighed and looked around the coffee shop. "Why can't we discuss it over the phone? Why does it have to be in person?" I had a hard time controlling my emotions when I was in the same room as Win. It was hard not to be overwhelmed by his oppressive aura. He made me defensive without even trying and we never brought out the best in one another. It always felt like a losing battle when we were face-to-face.

"It's a sensitive subject. I don't want you to hang up on me without hearing what I have to say." Win sounded calm and reasonable. I couldn't explain why I suddenly got goosebumps and an icy shiver ran down my spine.

"Fine." If I didn't agree to meet him now, he would corner me and force me into a conversation in the future when it was inconvenient for me. There was no denying a Halliday when they wanted something from you. "I'm at a coffee shop near my apartment." I told him the name and cross streets. "I'm only staying until the rain stops. You have until then to find me. I have no intention of letting you back into my place until you agree to let me see Winnie regularly." It was petty to say that. We both knew I couldn't keep him out of anywhere he wanted to be. I felt like I needed to establish some sort of boundary, or I would be completely powerless against him.

"I'll be there in ten minutes. Wait for me." There was no mistaking that he was giving me a direct order.

I wanted to leave out of spite. Instead, I ordered a drink and waited impatiently for Win to arrive. Absently, I wondered if he'd ever been in a local coffee shop before. He seemed more the type to drink specialty imported stuff that the average person couldn't afford. I laughed to myself, trying to picture him drinking something with whipped cream and candy-flavored syrup. He would never do anything as undignified as licking whipped cream off his face. Actions like that should be reserved for low-life, common folks like me.

I wrapped both hands around the coffee mug and watched as a black SUV pulled to a stop in front of the shop. Several men in dark suits climbed out and Win followed shortly after. He said something to the tall, stern man who was always next to him, and a hurried conversation ensued. I wished I could read lips because both men looked annoyed by what the other was saying. There was another nondescript man standing next to Win who was rapidly texting. It was the tensest entourage ever. Eventually, Win won the argument and walked into the shop and toward my table. He was by himself, which must've been what they were fighting about. Win never went anywhere without his security detail or his assistant.

He looked at the table, then at me, and frowned. I waited for him to complain about the location or the cleanliness, but he said nothing. He stared at me for a long, drawn-out moment. His fog-colored gaze was so intense I had to battle the urge to squirm in my seat.

"What's going on? I can't imagine anything dire enough that you would lower yourself to meet me on my home turf. That isn't your style at all, Chester."

He narrowed his eyes at me and reached out so he could tap the tips of his fingers on the table he looked unwilling to touch a moment ago. "I have a business proposition for you, Harvey."

I couldn't hold back a bark of laughter. "Seriously. What do you want to talk to me about? Is Winnie really okay? Please tell me you've seen the error of your ways and realize it's much better to let her have a relationship with me than to fight me every step of the way."

He gave a slight hum of acknowledgement. "I think there is a way for you to be more present in Winnie's life, while I make sure that your interactions are appropriate and won't harm our niece."

I scowled at him and set the coffee mug down with enough force that some of the liquid inside splashed onto my hand. I shook my fingers, secretly hoping the droplets would land on Win's pristine white shirt. "You want me to have supervised visits?" I bristled at the thought. He considered me immature and unreliable, but he had to know I'd never do anything that would put Winnie in danger. Considering his lack of trust in me, it made sense for him to view supervised visits with Winnie as a reasonable compromise. No doubt he wanted me to come to Halliday Cove to see my niece. My stomach turned at the thought.

"I'm considering something slightly more binding and beneficial to both parties than supervised visitation." He paused and his gaze sharpened on mine. "I want you to agree to a contract marriage with me, Channing."

It was a good thing I'd put the coffee cup down, because I would've dropped it. My jaw fell as if it were unhinged, and a thousand buzzing bees swarmed in my head. I lifted a hand and banged on my ear, thinking there was no way I'd heard Win correctly.

"Contract marriage? *You* want to marry *me*?" I felt like I couldn't breathe. "In what world do you envision something as insane as that? Have you been working too hard lately? Has your mother finally driven you beyond the brink?" I laughed so loudly that several people in the coffee shop turned to look in my direction. I put a hand over my heart and used the other to wipe away tears of mirth and disbelief.

"You aspire to be in Winnie's life, and I can make that happen. I want my mother to get off my case about getting married. Anyone else will want a sizable payout. All you want is time with our niece. You're the lesser of all evils at this point." He really sounded like he was in the middle of a business negotiation. There wasn't a single ripple within his icy façade. He made it seem like his suggestion wasn't the most outlandish thing I'd ever heard in my life. "You've been married more than once. What's adding another one to the list?"

It took every scintilla of self-control I possessed not to throw my coffee into Win's indifferent face.

"I loved both the men I married. I feel the opposite way about you, Chester. And as much as I long to be part of Winnie's everyday life, there is nothing on God's green earth that will get me to agree to being legally tied to you or living within spitting distance of your mother. You must realize how heartless it is to use Winnie as a bargaining chip for something like this." I laughed again, but this time there was no humor in the sound. "I don't know why I ever expect you to have human feelings." I stood and glared down at the unfazed man. "*Never*. I will never agree to marry you. With a contract, or without. I value myself more than that."

I stepped around him to get away from his insulting offer, but his hand wrapped around my wrist and pulled me to a halt.

A frigid shiver raced up and down my spine as our eyes locked. "I had a feeling you were going to react like this. You've never been able to see a golden opportunity when it's right in front of you. I wanted to start by asking, but don't think for a second that I won't force you to do what I want, Harvey. This is the simplest, most effective way to get us both what we want." He had the audacity to sound like he was doing me a favor.

I reached down and pried his fingers off my arm. I tried to calm my racing heart so I didn't smack him. Not only was his security detail nearby, but I wouldn't put it past him to press charges for assault. He played dirty.

"What happens when Colette finds out about your brilliant plan? She won't do anything to you because she needs you to keep Halliday Inc. afloat. But me..." I pointed at my chest. "Can you even imagine what she'd do to me? We both know what she drove my sister to. If I agreed to your ridiculous idea, your mother wouldn't rest until I'm buried next to Willow. No, thank you. I need to be alive to make sure Winnie knows how the other half lives and doesn't lose herself completely to you god-awful Hallidays."

I practically ran to the door. It was still raining outside, but I barely registered the weather. I was jogging at full speed toward my apartment. I clearly heard Win call after me, "Remember that you knowingly decided to do things the hard way."

I always knew he was a ruthless man.

But I had no idea just how brutal he could be, until I became his target.

Chapter Four

win

"There is a woman at the entrance of the building demanding to see you. She doesn't have an appointment, and security is threatening to have her arrested for trespassing."

I glanced at the employee who dared to interrupt my phone call. Channing must've been creating one hell of a scene, because entering my office without an invitation was forbidden. No staff member, regardless of job title, would risk their job by disrupting me. I looked at my cell phone and saw a message from Rocco. He handled the security of the office in the city as well as in my private life. He was warned well in advance about Channing's eventual arrival. Having her arrested was a last resort. I had no qualms about letting her sit behind bars for a few days if it took me one step closer to my goal.

"Let her up to my office and clear my calendar for the next hour." I gave the assistant curt orders and turned back to the call I'd put on hold while I dealt with the matter at hand. "Yes, I'm sure I want to purchase the building. I don't care that the asking price is more than the property's value. I'm not interested in making a profit. I'm buying it to make a point."

The building manager on the other end of the call could hardly hold back his excitement. "Most of my clients who rent the space have been there for many years. If you want them to vacate the building before you take ownership, just let me know." He didn't hesitate to throw the people who'd kept the building profitable all these years under the bus. There was no loyalty when it came to making money.

I gave a dissatisfied hum. "Don't worry about that for now. I'll address the current residents in the future." I had no desire to move anyone out of their business, as long as Channing agreed to my proposition. If she kept pushing back against my wishes, not only was I going to kick her best friend out of her salon, I was going to make sure she couldn't find an affordable spot to relocate anywhere in the city. Just as the mahogany door to my office was thrown open, I hung up the phone and watched as a furious Channing stormed to my desk.

Her cheeks flushed rosy red, and fury made her eyes bright. She was breathing hard, and I could see little marks on her hands and wrists where she'd obviously struggled with someone. No wonder the security staff didn't want to let her enter the building. She appeared a bit savage.

The corner of my mouth hooked up in a slight grin as she glared daggers at me. If looks could kill, my mother would be planning my funeral.

"Next time you want to see me, make an appointment like everyone else. You're lucky my security didn't have you hauled off to the closest police station." I leaned back in my leather chair and motioned for her to sit down. She looked like she was ready to crawl over my desk and strangle me with my tie. "Calm down, Harvey. Let's have a civilized conversation."

She picked up the heavy, engraved nameplate that sat on my desk and chucked it directly at my head. I dodged to the side; it hit the shelf behind me with a *bang* and knocked everything to the floor.

"Civilized? Do you even know what that word means?" Channing's chest heaved, and I could clearly imagine her breathing flames in my direction. "What you've put me through in the last month is anything but civil. You're the devil, Chester. I always thought your mother was the only truly evil member of your family, but you're a chip off the old block. I had no idea you could be so cruel."

I shrugged and watched her carefully to make sure she didn't launch anything else at my head. "I warned you what would happen if you decided to do things the hard way." My tone was dry and disinterested, even though she looked like she was on the verge of exploding.

"You're right. *I* made the choice. *I* rejected your offer." She pointed to herself, eyes blazing with unfiltered fury. "I understood exactly what was happening when I got an eviction notice overnight. It didn't surprise me when my boss suddenly let me go. He's a nice man, but he has a business to run. Profit over personnel makes sense. I'll admit that having my identity stolen made things extra tricky these past few weeks, but none of that was a shocking consequence after saying 'no' to a Halliday." She slammed the side of her fist on my desk and leaned closer. Channing gritted her teeth, and I could see her entire body shaking with suppressed emotion. "My dad is a jerk, so I wasn't too bothered when the cops suddenly picked him up on a bunch of old warrants and sent him to jail. It's not like I had the money to bail him out, even before my identity was stolen." She reached out to grab the front of my jacket, but I quickly stood up behind the desk to evade her grasp. "I could've navigated it all. It's not like I've never had to rebuild my life from the ground up before. But then you went after my mom. How fucked up do you have to be to mess with a mentally ill person, Chester? My mom doesn't have the ability to understand complex situations. She doesn't adapt to change well. She is more like a child than a grown woman. It's equivalent to picking on a kindergartener. I hope you're proud of yourself."

Channing looked at me like I was something vile stuck on the bottom of her shoe. However, I remained unfazed by her ire. In fact, I predicted her reaction. I'd started my method of harsh persuasion by only targeting her, knowing that she was a resourceful woman and wouldn't break so easily. When I moved on to manipulating her friends and family, I did it to purposely push Channing past what she could tolerate. Her loyalty to those who mattered the most to her was her downfall.

I fixed the knot of my tie and walked around the desk, so we were standing face-to-face. I was a good three inches taller than her. It was easier to be intimidating when I could loom over and look down on her.

"There is no bottom line when it comes to getting what I want. I told you that already. Don't underestimate me. This is just the tip of the *hard way*. Things will only get worse the longer you refuse. Your mother isn't the last of this." Was it unethical to buy a long-term care facility, just so I could threaten to shut it down? Yes. Did I care about morality when it came to getting what I wanted? No. I pointed to the open file that contained the marriage contract on my desk. "Your friend should have a plan for what to do once I shut her salon down. Be sure to let her know you're the reason she won't be able to find a new space for a reasonable price anywhere in the city."

Channing swore at me as she grabbed the paperwork. She threw it at my chest, and the contract inside fluttered harmlessly to the carpet.

"You can't move my mother from her care facility. I won't allow it. That's the only place she's known for the last decade. If you force me to take her somewhere else, she might have another breakdown and fully lose track of reality. I won't risk her health." She lowered her head and her strawberries and cream-colored hair swung to cover her flushed face. She put a hand over her heart like she was trying to hold it inside her chest. "I'll do whatever you want, Chester. Leave the people I love alone."

My eyebrows shot up. I didn't expect her to acquiesce so quickly. I made a mental note that her mother was clearly her Achilles' heel, and her best friend was her tipping point. It was always good to know the exact spots to disable an enemy.

I reached out and patted her shoulder in a conciliatory manner. "Don't act like I'm taking you to the gallows. I told you this is a business transaction. Both parties will benefit from it." I was ruthless when making deals, but I was also fair. I didn't play dirty unless I had no other choice. Whether Channing could see it or not, my mother's unrelenting demands had backed me into a corner, forcing me to take extreme measures to circumvent her.

Channing let out a long breath and shoved my hand off her shoulder. She lifted her head and our eyes locked. I felt like she was trying to stare a hole through the center of my forehead.

Sounding defeated, she asked, "How long do you plan to keep up this charade?" She blinked hard and tilted her head. "I'm thirty-five. If I want to settle down and start a family of my own, I don't exactly have forever to make that happen. If you want me to play this game with you for too long, you're really going to ruin my future." There was a hint of devastation in her tone.

I was hit with guilt. I quickly moved to recover my composure. Initially, my plan was five years. By then Winnie would be close to graduation, and it was a significant amount of time so my mother wouldn't try to rush me into another relationship. I wanted a clause in our contract that Channing didn't have to sleep with me, but she wasn't allowed to sleep with anyone else, either. But I'd given little thought to what those five years might mean to Channing. I never considered her future, which irked me, because I hated that mine was stolen the minute I was born. I ignorantly believed if she was going to start a family, she would've done it before now. She'd had plenty of time and opportunity, but she wasn't a Halliday. She didn't come from my world, where you got everything you wanted without question.

I could split the difference. "Two-and-a-half years, with an option to extend the contract to five." I motioned for her to sit down, and once she was calm enough to sink into one of the big leather chairs, I propped a hip on the edge of my desk and stared down at her. "I'm not asking you to do this and not get anything out of it. Once we separate, I'll compensate you for your time. You give me a number and we'll negotiate to a place that makes sense financially, for what you have to give up for that length of time. I'll fund your mother's stay at her facility for as long as you want to keep her there. And you will get as much time with Winnie as you want. You get to be there for her and watch her grow up. Isn't that what you've wanted this entire time?" I thought it was a win-win situation, but she still looked like she ate something sour.

"You're over-simplifying things. I don't need or want your money, and I can take care of my mother. I've been doing it since I was a kid. I *do* want to play a bigger role in Winnie's life, but not under your mother's watchful eye. This is an absolutely bonkers idea to protect you from Colette. Have you given any thought to how you're going to save *me* from her? She hates me. She hates my family. You couldn't have forgotten what she thinks my sister did to your brother? Are you seriously suggesting that I live where Willow died? That's too much to ask."

There was no escaping my mother's accusations. Of course I remembered.

The only reason I moved home to the family estate was because my mother was so unpredictable after the death of my brother and father. When she found out about my father's affair and the existence of my half-brother, she became fully unhinged. I had to stop her from hiring a hitman to take out the innocent young man. I had to prevent her from downing an entire bottle of sleeping pills with a bottle of French champagne. She never said she wanted to kill herself, but the intent was clear. I foolishly believed my mother was asking for help. There was a bleak period where I was certain only Winnie and I would be around to carry on the Halliday name. I felt like a failure when it came to keeping my family together.

Belatedly, I was aware how manipulative my mother's actions were. She used my fear against me, because she was the only parent I had left. I felt it was my responsibility to take care of her and mitigate the damage she could do to others. One of the reasons I wanted to do this with Channing was because of just how tough and resilient she was. She'd been able to handle every curveball that was thrown at her since she was a kid, and she handled the loss of her sister far better than I'd dealt with the death of my brother. Additionally, she was one of the few people who was not intimidated by the Halliday name. No one else stood a chance of going up against Colette and making it out unscathed. She was my only option.

"It is asking a lot. But you can handle it." I truly believed that.

Channing wasn't Willow.

When my younger brother fell in love with her older sister, both sets of parents were vehemently against it. My parents went to drastic lengths to keep the young lovers apart. Archie was miserable as a Halliday, and much like his daughter had done, he ran away from home so he could breathe and be with the person he loved. Channing was young back then, so she probably didn't know exactly how hard things were for her family after they defied mine. The way I manipulated her was a very ugly part of our families' history repeating itself.

My brother lived a vagabond lifestyle after he ran off with Willow. He only brought her home after she was pregnant with Winnie. They'd decided they needed to be responsible parents, so Archie had to reprise his role as heir. I still got a tickle in my throat when I recalled my brother's huge smile and bright eyes when he told me he was naming his daughter after me.

I wanted to believe my father and mother would adjust their prejudice when they allowed my brother to come home with his young family. Instead, they alienated my brother's bride and made his life a living hell for defying them in the first place. I told Archie he should take Willow and leave again. I promised I would help him and make sure they still had a good life, but he stubbornly maintained that we were family. He was unwilling to give up his place in the legacy. He had no desire to relinquish his inheritance and ready-made position in the company. And more than that, he didn't want his daughter to miss out on what could be hers. While he was away from home, he learned how hard normal people had to work for what they had. He was determined that his wife and daughter would never suffer just to merely exist. All the Hallidays were selfish in one way or another. My younger brother was no different. He was convinced that my parents would eventually embrace Willow and Winnie.

They didn't.

Willow was isolated.

She was tormented.

She was belittled and mocked.

At every turn, she was made to feel inferior.

It drove a wedge between her and my brother. Willow wanted to leave. He wouldn't let her.

I often wondered if he'd known there was a history of mental illness in Willow's family. Would he have taken her feelings more into consideration? There was a bomb with a long fuse moving through the lavish manor. When it ignited, no one was spared from the explosion's shrapnel.

I was overseas on a business trip with my father when the news came. My little brother was dead, and so was Channing's sister.

The investigation showed that the fire was set deliberately. An accelerant was purposely placed all around the main bedroom. It was revealed that both Willow and my brother were drugged with sleeping pills when the fire started. Because of all the antique furniture and old wooden fixtures, the flames gobbled up that wing of the house before anyone could save it, or the people inside. According to the experts, it wasn't clear who set the fire. But with the Harveys' mental health history, the blame automatically fell to Willow. Especially since she'd arranged for Winnie to be out of the house that night. I think the reason my mother still hated Channing was because Willow took Winnie to her before she ended her, and my brother's lives. It was clear that Willow felt her sister was a better choice to care for Winnie than the rest of us. If their mom hadn't had a serious breakdown and needed around-the-clock care in the wake of Willow's death, there was a high probability Channing would've gained custody of Winnie. It was no secret Willow wanted her daughter raised by her family and not her husband's.

It was a tragedy. Just like the fact my mother had buried my brother before my father and I made it home. It was an entirely preventable catastrophe. It *was* cruel and heartless to ask Channing to walk into the lion's den when she knew exactly how hungry the beast inside would be. However, the woman hated me. It wasn't like there would be a point in our relationship where I could change her opinion. It was better that I kept up a front of loathing and distaste, even if I didn't think Channing was the monster Colette made her out to be. My mom appreciated that we shared a common foe, so I always pretended to hate any Harvey as much as she did.

I picked up the contract and offered it to her. "This is the barebones agreement. Read through it and make the changes you think are necessary. I'll adjust the required time limit."

She took the file with shaky hands. I heard her gulp as she looked at the document as if it might bite her. "Even if I agree to this, we aren't going to fool anyone. Your mother knows we don't get along. Winnie knows we don't like each other. I told her we were sworn enemies a couple of weeks ago. Your entire inner circle is going to think you being with someone like me is a joke. They're going to think I'm only with you for the money."

I dipped my chin in agreement. "You're right about all of that. I don't care if my mom thinks it's fake. She can't keep hounding me to get married if I already am."

Channing laughed, but there was no humor in the sound. "All she's going to do is harass you until we divorce. You're just trading one headache for another."

"She won't." I pointed at the document she couldn't seem to look away from. "If I initiate a divorce before the contract term is complete, you will receive a portion of my shares in Halliday Inc. My mother will never let that happen." The only thing she loved in this world was this company. It felt like she'd been trying to take it over since she was a child. Her singular goal in life was to become a Halliday.

"And if *I* initiate a divorce before the contract expires?" Channing asked in a strangled voice..

"You'll have to pay for a breach of contract. You won't be able to afford it. Don't think that's an option, Harvey."

She stared blankly at the papers in her hand for a long moment before she lifted her head to glare at me. "I really hate you, Chester. I would give anything to have never met you."

I couldn't hold back a chuckle at her sudden surrender. I thought she would call me every name in the book and throw more things at my face before she relented.

"You've always hated me from afar. Now you can hate me up close and personal. Think of it as an upgrade."

She scowled at me, and I thought it was cute. There was a slight tingle under my skin that made me pause and consider why I wasn't reacting the way I always did when I closed out a difficult business deal.

I liked to win, but something about this victory felt different. Money was typically what I gained after a hard round of negotiation. There was an idea creeping into the back of my mind, whispering that this triumph held something much more important. When I could drop the heartless façade that was second nature to me, I would give some serious consideration as to why I felt like I had both won and lost this battle with the feisty redhead.

Chapter Five
channing

"Slow down, Champ. I haven't seen you drink like this since our wedding day."

My favorite ex-husband reached across the bar and took away the rocks glass from which I'd just chugged a mouthful of bourbon on ice. I wasn't much of a drinker. The exception was when I couldn't quite get a handle on my emotions. My feelings were swinging from one extreme to the other ever since Win extorted me. Every inch of my being wanted to tell him to shove his proposal and contract as far up his uptight ass as possible. I felt deep down that I had no way to avoid his unwavering determination to force me to do exactly what he desired. If I didn't have to worry about him going after the innocent people around me, I would walk away and never speak to him again. Winnie would be eighteen in five years. I could hold out until it was her choice whether she wanted me in her life or not — maybe. Win blocked every avenue of escape.

I lifted my blurry gaze to the familiar face of the man I once loved. Roan Goodwin saved me from my first disastrous marriage that I'd fallen into when I was barely a legal adult. He kept me together when my life was at its lowest point, and I'd first learned what it was like to lose something you loved with your whole heart. We were too young and impulsive when we tied the knot. It was a marriage of convenience in a different way. It didn't take long for us to realize that we made better friends than lovers. Our union was short-lived, but our friendship had endured long after our divorce. After Salome, Roan was the person I trusted and confided in the most. I called him my hero, but he always reminded me that I saved myself.

"I hate him." I tried to snatch my glass away, but Roan intercepted me and handed me a glass of ice water as a replacement. "I really hate him. He's the devil. That entire family, except for Winnie, deserves every awful thing they've done to others returned to them tenfold." I was full-on pouting and feeling very sorry for myself.

Roan reached across the bar and gave me a consolatory pat on the top of my head. "Didn't you tell me that when you were younger, you had a crush on Win?" I scowled at the handsome blond man and whipped my head to the side to knock his hand away.

Unfortunately, the movement was too fast, and I was too full of booze. The combination nearly dumped me off the barstool. Roan caught my arm and hauled me upright while he shook his head. He was a bartender at this bar back in the day, and now he owned it. I met him when I came to watch my first ex-husband's band play here. My first ex was a narcissistic nightmare who had serious control issues. He practically kept me under lock and key while he roamed around the country with his shitty punk band. I couldn't take a breath without reporting it to him. Meanwhile, he was sleeping with a different person in every city where he was lucky enough to land a gig. Roan was the person who pried me away from the first ex's clutches when I thought there was no escape. He taught me how to value myself and the love I had to offer. Roan took care of me, even when I was married to someone else. It was no surprise that he was doing the same thing now that I was facing another toxic marriage.

"I never said that. I've never liked him." I shook my head, and the room spun.

Roan chuckled and moved down the bar to take another customer's order. If he didn't want me to have another drink, no one would serve me. I begrudgingly sipped the water he put in front of me and tried to remember if I'd ever seen Win as anything other than a demon.

"Before Colette cracked down on her son and your sister dating, the two of you used to make deliveries to their house for all her fancy rich-lady parties. You told me you begged Willow to take you with her because you hoped Win would be home from college. I remember it always made you upset when he wasn't there. And when he was, you were mad he ignored you."

I scoffed and traced a trail of water on the surface of my glass with my fingertip. "He's so manipulative. I can't believe he wants me to live with the woman who drove my sister to suicide." I smacked the side of my fist on the top of the bar and then swore as pain radiated up my wrist. "Do you think that's his plan? Is he hoping for me to do something as drastic to remove me from Winnie's life permanently?" I started breathing fast and felt my heart race at the thought. "Does he want me to die?"

Roan moved back in front of me and spread out his hands so he could lean on the bar, putting us eye-to-eye. "Men like Win Halliday don't need to play elaborate games to get rid of someone. If he really wanted to harm you, he wouldn't have waited this long. And he wouldn't do it himself. He's always put Winnie first. If something were to happen to you, there is no telling what that might do to her mental state. He would never risk it after he saw what happened with your mom and sister. My guess is that he knows you're tough enough to stand up to Colette. From everything you've said in between drinks, it sounds like he needs you right now."

Salome told me nearly the exact same thing when I'd called her to complain. She was more biased in my favor, but she still reminded me that Win would never act so outrageously without a reason. I lifted the back of my hand to rub my nose and blinked back the sudden burn of tears. "I don't want to get married again if it's not going to last. I promised myself if I ever committed to marriage again, it would be the real deal. I want to spend my life with someone who wants to keep me forever. I want a man who loves everything about me."

Roan lifted a hand and pinched my cheek, which made me forget I wanted to cry. I batted his hand away and happily took the bowl of spicy bar mix he slid in front of me. "Channing, you should know by now nothing is certain when it comes to matters of the heart. *I wanted to keep you forever.* You know I love everything about you. We thought we were going to share our lives until we grew old and gray. Our marriage didn't work out because we were both so busy pretending to be exactly what the other person wanted, we forgot to be who we really were. Sometimes what we think we want isn't what's best for us. You've got to get the fantasy of a perfect marriage out of your head. Otherwise, no one is ever going to meet your expectations, and you'll keep running through losers trying to find an illusion."

I licked the leftover seasoning from the bar mix off my fingers and tried not to get depressed at his very accurate dissection of why we couldn't last.

"If no one can meet my expectations, then I should stay single. I'm tired of settling for leftover scraps of love and affection." And I didn't want to be in a situation where it felt like my feelings and future were being unmercifully extorted. "I'm not convinced Win even has a heart. I'm pretty sure all the Hallidays are born with a big black hole that sucks away the warmth and care they might have for another person. It's making me crazy that I can't tell him to go fuck himself."

Roan chuckled and pushed away from the edge of the bar. "You can tell him that, but it won't make a difference. As long as he knows you're willing to do whatever it takes to keep your mother safe and Winnie in your life, he has you exactly where he wants you. When you have such an obvious weakness, men like Win have no problem using it against you."

I frowned and leaned back on the barstool. "She's not a weakness. She's my mother. She's family. I'm all she has. Why are you trying to make this situation seem less heinous than it is? If I hadn't given in to Win's demands, he would've come after you, too, Roan. He could've snatched this bar out of your hands in the blink of an eye. Even if the building isn't for sale, he'll find a way to get the city to shut it down. There would be no way for you to stop him. He has the power to make sure that you wouldn't be able to open another establishment or get another liquor license anywhere in the States. He'd ruin you without a second thought. Doesn't that make you mad? Because it infuriates me."

Roan shrugged a broad shoulder and turned to pour a beer from the draft tower behind him. He handed it off to one of his servers before turning back to me with a serious look on his face.

"I don't agree with the way Win bullied you. I think it's bullshit he hurt the people closest to you to get you to agree to his scheme. I can see the benefits now that he has you over a barrel and you have little choice in the matter. There's a lot you can do with that kind of money, and you've always wanted to be more involved in Winnie's life. Plus, you work yourself silly to keep your mom in that facility. I know that you're struggling to make ends meet now that you live on your own. If Win is offering to pay for her care indefinitely and all you have to do is survive in the Halliday mansion for a couple of years, it's a decent trade. Move into that big ass house and give Colette a taste of her own medicine. Make her life a living hell every single day. If you ever wanted payback for how she treated your sister, the opportunity is right in front of you." He gave me a small grin and added, "Win is asking you to play doubles with him against his mother, and he's willing to compensate you accordingly to be his teammate."

I snorted and finished drinking the glass of water. It made some of the fire in my heart cool down when I thought about Win's smug face as he handed me the contract.

"Are you trying to tell me he can't win against his mother on his own?" I couldn't imagine Win being anything other than victorious.

"Didn't you once say he wanted to be a violinist when he was younger, but Colette refused to even consider that as a possibility? She would never let him do anything other than take over Halliday Inc. He's in the same boat as you are. That's his mother. He's all she has left. Of course he can't win when it comes to her. Everything I've ever heard about her from anyone who lives in or around the Cove is the stuff of nightmares. No one wants to be on her radar."

My frown deepened. "How come I never realized I talked about the Hallidays so often?" I couldn't recall telling Roan half of what he mentioned to me tonight. I thought I had done a decent job of locking that family away in my mind for as long as I could remember.

His little grin turned into a soft smile. "Didn't you always say that your first husband was over-the-top jealous and felt like he was your second choice? I bet you thought he was talking about me when he gave you a hard time. He wasn't. He always meant Win. The difference between us is that I know you're loyal to a fault. You have more love in your heart than you know what to do with."

I looked at the man whom I thought understood me better than I understood myself in disbelief. "You are not telling me that you think I could ever *love* Win, are you? If so, you're as crazy as he is, Roan."

"What I think is that you've always had a lot of feelings for him since you were too young to recognize what they were. Over time, they got muddy and bled together as things went south between your families. Now, they're all in a big ball, and you can't separate your emotions where Win is concerned. If you ever take the time to untangle all those threads, you're going to be shocked to see where they start and end." He snapped the bar towel that had been hanging from his back pocket and asked me if I wanted to wait for him to close the bar so he could take me back to my apartment.

I waved off the offer and told him I would catch a cab. I couldn't sit in the bar and drown my sorrows if he wouldn't serve me anything else to drink. Plus, I was admittedly unnerved that he didn't seem to think the idea of marrying Win was absolutely absurd. I always told Roan that if I were meant to be married, he and I would have figured things out. We genuinely loved and respected one another. We shared the same values. He understood my history and helped me navigate the grief and subsequent breakdown of my family after my sister's death. I couldn't fathom that he honestly believed I felt anything other than absolute revulsion for the Hallidays aside from my niece.

I went outside to wave down a cab. It was drizzling again. I felt like the weather was an exact reflection of all the turmoil I was feeling lately: dark, gloomy, and miserable.

My phone beeped with an incoming message, and I scowled when I saw Win's information on the screen.

It was late enough he had no business bugging me. I thought the high and mighty went to bed at a reasonable hour so they were fresh to pillage their way through enemy territory bright and early.

~ My assistant sent the revised contract to your email. Did you look it over?

I shook the phone as if the action would transfer to the man on the other side. Of course I'd looked it over. Why else would I be drinking my life away at my ex-husband's bar in the middle of the week?

~ I looked it over.

~ Are you going to sign it?

It took all my self-control not to send him a big fat NO. I tried to envision signing the paperwork, but my hands shook so badly, I could hardly scroll through the draft. I had no clue how I was supposed to go through with this farce if I couldn't even handle the basic paperwork.

~ I'll read through and approve it — eventually.

Because he left me no choice.

~ Approve it before tomorrow. We'll take care of everything at once.

I wasn't sure if it was the alcohol or if I was too dumb to understand what he meant. I wanted to throw my phone against the ground and disappear.

~ What's happening tomorrow?

I wracked my brain to remember if I'd made an appointment with him that I'd forgotten. Every interaction with Win felt like it was seared into my brain, so I doubt I'd forgotten. Even more so, now that I realized I unknowingly talked about the man, in great detail, to others.

~ Tomorrow we're getting married. Meet me at the courthouse in the morning. I'll have my assistant send you the details and final draft of the contract to sign.

I stopped breathing. I felt my knees get weak, and I nearly melted to the ground in a hysterical heap.

~ I don't remember agreeing to that.

~ You didn't. I decided for you, because you keep delaying the inevitable. What's done is done, Harvey. Just get it over with so we can both move on with our lives.

~ How romantic. How could any woman resist the urge to fall at your feet with sweet words like that?

I hoped a slight fraction of my scorn and disgust would come across in my reply.

~ I don't need you at my feet. I need you by my side. If you don't show up when I tell you to, I'll come and get you. You know how things go when you do things the hard way.

My teeth clenched together so hard, my jaw hurt. He knew damn well I didn't want to do anything the difficult way ever again.

~ I'll sign the paperwork and meet you at the courthouse. I still think this is a terrible idea. Your mother is going to kill you — or me. Probably both of us.

I flagged down a cab. I practically fell into the back and I stumbled over my words when I gave the driver my address. I felt a rattling sensation throughout my entire body.

~ I won't let anything happen to you. See you in the morning, Harvey.

I didn't realize until I got home and fell into bed that he hadn't mentioned his own safety once his plan was in motion. Somehow, I was more alarmed by that knowledge than I cared to be.

Chapter Six
win

Channing was nearly an hour late.

I wasn't surprised she was dragging her feet since she'd made it abundantly clear that she wasn't a fan of her current circumstances. Then, her appearance took me off guard when she showed up. She emerged looking as if she rolled out of bed and headed directly to the courthouse. Her hair was a mess. Giant sunglasses covered most of her face. I was almost positive the black shirt she had on underneath an oversized blazer was a pajama top. She smelled like she'd rolled around on a bar floor and looked like she'd been rudely woken up after a bender.

"Nice of you to dress for the occasion." The sarcasm was thick in my voice, but Channing didn't even blink. Instead, she quickly put the giant sunglasses on top of her head, glancing between the notary, the lawyer, and my personal assistant Conrad, who were gathered around me. I never waited for anyone or anything, so the group naturally stared at the disheveled woman with a mixture of annoyance and curiosity.

Channing reached into her bag, pulled out the crumpled contract, and smacked the papers against my chest. She muttered loud enough for me to hear, "I should be dressed like I'm going to a funeral. Be happy I showed up at all."

I handed the contract over to my lawyer, who blinked in surprise. "You could've authorized it digitally and emailed it over."

Channing flushed in embarrassment and snapped, "This is my first time being blackmailed into marriage. You'll have to excuse me if I don't know the ins and outs."

The lawyer frowned, then moved to huddle together with the notary to make sure everything was in order. While they had their heads bent together, Channing grabbed my elbow and pulled me a few steps away, saying she wanted to talk to me before we finalized the nuptials.

I had to bend my head down to hear her because her voice was low and shaky with suppressed emotion.

"I don't care what you plan to tell your mother or the general public about this situation, Chester. But I care very much about how we explain things to Winnie. She's not dumb. And you know how sensitive she can be. How do you plan to make her understand that you went from forbidding me to see her to moving me into the room next to hers? She's only thirteen. She doesn't deserve to be disillusioned about love and marriage at such a young age. Both of us are setting a terrible example for her. You for bullying me into this, and me for being weak enough to agree."

Her bloodshot eyes had dark circles underneath them. It was easy to tell she was under a great deal of pressure and barely keeping herself together. Her dreary demeanor communicated that I was supposed to feel guilty and a touch remorseful for being the cause of her distress — but I didn't.

"The only two options are to tell her the truth or lie. If we explain that this is the best way to keep my mother from bringing strange women to the house all the time, Winnie is smart enough to understand the reasoning behind our decision. Once she knows you'll be in her life on a more permanent basis, I think she'll focus on that. The details won't matter."

"We have to sit down and have a discussion with her before I come to the Cove. We can't drop this on her with no warning." Channing heaved out a deep breath and lifted her hands to rub at her irritated eyes. "I won't tell her I'm doing this against my will. We come at it as a united front so she won't hate you or see how manipulative you can be." The light-blue in her eyes glowed like a solar flare. "You're still her guardian. You need to show her right from wrong." She waved her hands around wildly, indicating the courthouse and the men I brought with me. "All of this is so very wrong."

I lifted an eyebrow as we stared each other down. "You know that there is a high likelihood Winnie will take over Halliday Inc., don't you? I don't have children. Archie is gone. My mother would rather lose everything she has than let my father's bastard son take over. That leaves Winnie. She needs to know how things work when you're a Halliday. This could be a very important lesson for her." I was only partially serious. Winnie was the next in line to take over the family legacy, but I wanted more for her than to be chained to a familial obligation for the rest of her life. I was achingly aware of what it was like to live at the end of that criminally short leash.

Channing's hand tightened on my arm where she was holding me. She narrowed her eyes at me and practically growled, "She'll follow in your footsteps over my dead body. You don't have permission to ruin her like your family ruins everyone in their orbit. It's your job to protect her. That is so much more important than whatever else it is you do all day. Is it worth giving up everything that makes you human just so you can force Winnie into the same endless cycle you've been caught in since birth?"

"Sir, all the paperwork is in order. Since we're running late, we need to meet with the clerk and the judge now. If not, we'll have to reschedule." My assistant seemed to hesitate when he interrupted our intense conversation. He gave the redhead a thinly veiled look of disgust. Conrad never bothered to hide his annoyance with Channing. He often parroted my mother's many complaints when he spoke about my longtime nemesis. My feud with Channing was just for show, but the people closest to me had no clue. I had to clench my teeth to keep from letting my real feelings toward the woman show.

Channing cleared her throat and raked her fingers through her hair, removing the sunglasses that held the reddish-blond strands away from her face. "Let's get this over with." She squared her shoulders and moved to follow my lawyer, who took the lead through the courthouse. Her show of bravado was kind of cute and fitting for a woman who showed up to get pretend-married in her pajamas.

"Sir, I feel like I have to ask one last time. Are you sure you want to go through with this? I know you insist it's the best way to deal with your mother, but I can't help questioning how this benefits you. Ms. Harvey has always liked to make trouble for you."

My personal assistant was an old college friend. Conrad Beck had a similar family background. His family was new money, well-to-do, and had sky-high expectations of Conrad because he was their only boy. There were a fleet of sisters who were all expected to marry up, but Conrad was tasked with building and maintaining his family's generational wealth. He was a former swimmer. He'd aspired to be an Olympian when I first met him, but his parents wanted him to devote himself to his studies and find a white-collar career that would support the burgeoning dynasty. Why it was *his* responsibility to carry the financial burden for all his relatives was a mystery to both of us. However, just like I gave up the violin, he gave up the sport in which he excelled at the decree of his parents. Conrad and Rocco were the only people on my payroll who would dare to question my intent. I paid them both better than if they were CEOs of their own companies. I considered both friends outside of our business relationship.

I nodded as I watched Channing march down the hallway, her back straight and her head held high. "I want to do this. Marriage is the best solution." Channing was the *only* woman I could do this with.

"Aren't you worried about your mother's reaction? What if things end up like they did when your brother brought someone home she didn't approve of? Neither you nor Ms. Harvey are going to have a moment of peace once she finds out what you've done."

I gave Conrad a look out of the corner of my eye. I wasn't used to having anyone aside from my mother question my decisions. I was the shot caller, even if I didn't want to be. "I'm not Archie. I won't let her do to Channing what she did to Willow."

When my brother brought his family home, my mother was far from pleased. She made no secret that she wanted Archie and Winnie to stay, but never wanted to see Willow again. She was unrelenting in her mission to get my brother to divorce his childhood sweetheart. The problem my mother couldn't work around was that Archie and Willow married very young, so there was no prenuptial agreement. If they divorced, Willow would be entitled to not only an extraordinary sum of money, she would also get half of my brother's shares in the family company and subsidiaries. There were hundreds of smaller businesses under the Halliday Inc. umbrella. Willow would've had a stake in all of them. She was going to walk away a very wealthy woman if she and Archie split. And there was the possibility Willow would take Winnie away from my very fucked-up family if she left, as would be her right. My mother refused to let any Halliday live outside the family manor. I returned very reluctantly after winning a war over my personal autonomy, only after she threatened to harm herself. It was one of her many hypocrisies, since she wouldn't have anything to do with my much younger half-brother.

Archie was a good kid. He was easy-going and had a free spirit. Since he wasn't the first-born, he didn't have to bear the same weight of obligation as I did. I never thought he would run away from home in the name of love or be strong enough to defy our mother. I was honestly envious of his few years of freedom until the responsibility of providing for his family drove him back into the nest of vipers. It was a shame his defiance and stubbornness weren't strong enough to stand up to my mother's onslaught of shame and blame. He did his best to be there for his wife, but every day they lived under my mother's roof, Willow was under attack. Instead of letting her escape the torment, my brother held onto her tighter. He figured they could suffer together and that would be enough. My mother never stopped to consider that if she went too far, Willow might take Archie down with her when she went over the edge.

To this day, Colette Halliday took zero responsibility for her hand in the tragedy that crumbled two families. I didn't live at home then. I was in the city, being a good little heir. And I wouldn't have gone back if it weren't for Winnie's mental instability and my mother's suicidal ideation. I wanted to take Winnie out of the house and get her far away from her grandmother, but I was worried my mother would follow through on her threats to end her own life. There was a real concern that my mother might take me to court to seek custody of Winnie, not because she wanted to be a full-time guardian, but to punish me for daring to want more than she allowed.

Marrying Channing made the likelihood of losing to my mother much slimmer.

She really was the best solution to a whole host of problems I couldn't navigate on my own. It was rare that I couldn't manage any situation that came my way. When I needed help, it was easier and more efficient to demand assistance than ask for it. Channing should be able to see that she was special. I never tied myself to anyone willingly. And here I was, ready and willing to offer her two-and-a-half years of my life.

Conrad couldn't continue to protest because it was time to get the wedding license and go before a judge.

With everyone in suits, no family or close friends present, and my business associates standing in as witnesses, it felt more like we were conducting a business meeting than a wedding. The judge looked over at me and then Channing, his gaze lingering on her unkempt appearance. I was positive we weren't the oddest couple he'd ever seen, but he gave Channing a long time to answer when he asked, "Channing Harvey, do you know of any legal impediment which may prevent you from marrying Winchester Halliday?"

She shook her head, and the judge reminded her that she needed to verbally answer.

It took a second before she responded through gritted teeth. "I, Channing Harvey, do not know of any legal impediment which would prevent me from marrying Winchester Halliday." She looked like she wanted to bolt, but she stayed put as I repeated the same spiel back to the officiant.

There were no vows or anything extraneous aside from the mandatory legal bits and pieces. The whole thing was as romantic as a root canal and took less than ten minutes. The judge pronounced us husband and wife and was ready to dismiss us. I could tell he was deliberating about adding the kiss-the-bride portion at the end. It didn't seem fitting considering Channing had barely looked at me while she repeated her required script.

I lifted my eyebrows and watched the older man deliberate before his professionalism finally won out. "You may kiss the bride."

Channing turned to face me and rolled her eyes. She looked like she was about to tell me not to even think about touching her. She froze when I reached out and pinched her chin between my thumb and forefinger.

She gasped softly when I dropped my head and touched my lips to hers. It was far from a real kiss, but I felt her breath brush across my lips and her body stiffen. She tasted minty. I guess I should count myself lucky she took the time to brush her teeth before she showed up for this farce. I quickly snuck in a small lick across her plump bottom lip, and Channing jerked backward. One of her hands curled into a fist, and I could see she was contemplating taking a swing at me. I always considered her as a woman who was very average, other than the huge way she loved those most important to her. Channing's heart and unwavering loyalty had always been the most attractive things about her.

However, now that my lips landed briefly on hers, I thought she tasted superb. Like a breath of fresh air.

I was used to kisses feeling cold and clinical.

The women who passed through my life in a romantic way always had a bigger agenda than sex and satisfaction. Normally, kisses were the bait of someone desperate to get a wedding ring on their finger and half my money in their bank account.

With Channing, a kiss was nothing more than a kiss, because she had never desired anything from me. A shiver slithered down my spine as I let my mind wander to the thought of what it would be like to kiss her for real. That tiny brush of lips was a thousand times warmer and sexier than all of my recent sexual encounters. It was like walking in the rain after years in a drought.

I winked at her before straightening and turning to shake the judge's hand. It was a subtle reminder of where we were and why she couldn't lose control of her temper.

We walked out of the room, and I dismissed the lawyer and notary. I asked Conrad to go to the Cove and get Winnie after school and bring her to the city. He left with a last disapproving glance at my brand-spanking-new wife. I felt it was best to explain this to my niece away from my mother. That woman could turn the simplest thing into a major drama, so it was better to keep her out of it until I brought home my reluctant bride.

When we exited the courthouse, Channing shoved the massive sunglasses back on her face and spun on her heel like she was going to sprint in the opposite direction. I caught her arm, the way she had done to me earlier, and pulled her to a halt.

Even though her eyes were covered, I could still sense her glaring up at me. "Winnie won't be in the city until this afternoon. I don't have to be back at the office for a couple of hours. I'm pretty sure you didn't eat breakfast this morning. Let's grab a bite."

Channing was seething. "I don't want to sit down and have a meal with you." She lifted the back of her hand to exaggeratedly rub her lips. "I need to brush my teeth again."

I chuckled at her antics and shrugged. "Fine. I will follow you back to your place and help you pack. You're on the verge of being evicted anyway."

She snorted. "Thanks to you."

I smirked in response and told her, "When you find the place where you really belong, no one, regardless of their influence, can make you leave." I was speaking from my own experience. Once I left the Cove, I swore I would never go back. It was exhausting to live my life for everyone other than myself. My freedom was short-lived because my mother dragged me back. In the game of control, I always seemed to lose to her. I was forever searching for the place I just described to Channing.

Instead of arguing, Channing relented. "Fine. I'll let you feed me. I don't want your hands on anything else of mine today. I can pack and get down to the Cove on my own."

It was on the tip of my tongue to remind her that it was my lips that had touched her, not my hands. I smiled to myself when I thought of her reaction earlier.

I doubted she would appreciate the distinction.

Chapter Seven
channing

"Wait a minute."

Winnie's face twisted into a cute look of concentration. Her eyes skipped between me and Win. "You got married because you don't want to get married?" Her questioning gaze landed on Win. "And you asked Aunt Channing to go along with your plan because you didn't want to bring a stranger home to live with us?"

Win shifted his weight. If I didn't know the kind of man he was, I would think he was nervous about being grilled by his young niece.

"That's a big part of it. I am sick and tired of your grandmother bringing surprise dates home because I know my relationships will directly affect you. I will never agree to a long-term commitment with someone you didn't like and respect, Winnie. Making a deal with your aunt is the best option right now. It gets your grandma off my back and allows you and Channing to spend more time with each other. We agreed to be honest with you about the situation, so you didn't get the idea that this relationship between me and your aunt is the real deal."

The teenager's eyes switched to me. I wanted to squirm in my seat but managed to stay still. I reached out to hold her hand and forced a weak smile. "I know this must be a bit of a shock. It's okay to be confused and angry. But I want you to understand that your

Uncle Chester and I know what we're doing." I was lying through my teeth, but both my words and my smile were real when I told her, "As long as I get to spend more time with you and be an active part of your life, nothing else matters." I shifted my hand so I could tug on her earlobe playfully. "Everything will be okay. I promise."

Winnie gave her head a slight shake and muttered, "I thought you didn't get along. Whenever you're in the same room, all you do is argue. Aren't you going to make each other miserable for the next couple of years if you go through with this?"

Win cleared his throat and leaned a little closer to the young girl. "There is a lot your aunt and I don't see eye-to-eye on. However, we both love you and want what's best for you. You don't need to worry about anything other than that. We're the grownups. It's our responsibility to make sure you're happy and healthy. Not the other way around."

His voice was deep and steady. It was hard not to believe every word he said. No wonder he was so good at running Halliday Inc. All he had to do was use that soft, confident tone, and people would sign their life away to him the same way I had.

Winnie turned to stare at me. She lifted her hand and pulled on her bottom lip nervously. It was the same anxious tic my older sister used to have. My heart squeezed painfully as the image of the teenager and her mother overlapped in my mind.

"Aunt Channing," she paused like she was trying to put her thoughts in order. "Are you sure you can move to the Cove? What about Grandma? Didn't you tell me that you were never going back to the manor? You hate that house." She shivered slightly. "I do, too. No one believes me when I tell them that it's haunted and scary. I guess if you move in with us, you can help me prove that something supernatural is going on."

The topic shift between her grandmother and ghosts was hard to follow. I guess both those things could scare you to death. "I'll be fine. If your grandma has a problem with anything, your Uncle Chester will handle it. She pushed and pushed until he had to come up with this crazy idea to get her to back off." I wiggled my eyebrows at her playfully. "I can help you prove it if the house is really haunted. Two sets of eyes and ears are better than one."

Win grunted and motioned for the server to bring us the bill. The restaurant where we'd met was close to his office in the city and more upscale than one I would pick on my own. He flatly told me I needed to change out of my pajamas if I wanted to be allowed into the establishment. I had to fight the urge to find an even uglier, tackier set of pjs to throw on under my go-to blazer. However, I needed to be there to talk to Winnie. I didn't want Win to speak for me or leave out details that would give her false ideas about our fake union.

"Stop indulging her, Harvey. The manor isn't haunted. It's just old and drafty. The staff moves around in other parts of the house and the sound travels through the vents and ductwork. It can explain whatever Winnie thinks she's hearing." Of course, he would have a boring, pragmatic explanation for whatever spooked our niece.

I fought an eye roll and sat back in my seat. "That estate has been in your family since the pilgrims landed on the East Coast. It's ancient and full of history." Including the tragedy that befell Winnie's parents. "There can be more than one explanation for what Winnie is experiencing."

Win's eyebrows shot up, and the fingers of one of his hands tapped steadily on the table in front of him. The rhythm made the water in the glasses bounce. "You think ghosts are a more reasonable explanation than sounds simply carrying through a big, drafty house?" He sounded exasperated at the idea.

I shrugged. "It's not a reasonable explanation, but it is more interesting than yours. Sometimes it's fun to indulge in the unknown. Either way, Winnie is scared, and you haven't made an effort to ease those fears." I said the last part in a clearly accusatory tone. It baffled me that he was so insensitive to the fact that the little girl was living in the same home where both her parents had perished. It didn't seem like such a farfetched idea that Winnie was feeling spooked after everything she had lost within those walls.

I didn't want to tell either of them that I could imagine my sister's troubled soul staying behind to keep an eye on her daughter. I didn't really buy into the spooky and otherworldly. Though, while I worked at the curio shop handling antiques, there were times it felt like some of the really old, sentimental items came with the spirit of the previous owners attached.

I jerked my wandering thoughts back to the present and reassured Winnie, "I'm not afraid of your grandmother or ghosts."

Winnie sighed as she picked up her fork to poke at the expensive dinner in front of her. "Sometimes I think I'm losing my mind." She refused to meet my gaze as she practically whispered, "I know that Grandma Harvey and my mom were ill. Whenever I tell Grandma Colette that I'm creeped out by something in the house, she says it's probably nothing. She always asks me if I want to end up locked away from society like my other grandma. She constantly reminds me that something may be wrong with me."

I sucked in a harsh breath and whipped my head around to glare at Win. I couldn't believe he let his mom talk to an impressionable teenager in such a way. The memory of her parents should be something sweet and sacred. Not a threat as to what the girl might face if she didn't conform to Colette Halliday's plans for her. I was surprised to see that Win looked equally disgusted by Winnie's revelation.

He swore under his breath and told his niece, "There isn't anything wrong with you. Even if you inherited some of your mother's struggles, that's simply a part of what makes you unique and special. We all have some challenges. No one is perfect, and your grandmother is very much in the wrong for trying to make you think otherwise." He cocked his head in my direction. "Plus, there is no guarantee you will have to deal with mental illness in the future. Look at your Aunt Channing. She's difficult, but not ill. And even if she were, it wouldn't make you love her any less, would it?" Winnie emphatically shook her head.

I scowled at Win across the table but didn't refute his claims. I had never sought or received a clinical diagnosis like my mother and sister because I was responsible for holding our shattered family together after Willow's death. Even if I had an underlying problem, I masked it well, because there was no other choice. My role in my family didn't allow me to have mental struggles along with everyone else. I faced the same unreasonable expectations as Winnie.

I cleared my throat and gave Winnie a slight smile. "When you finish this semester, I'll take you to meet your other grandma. Maybe if you spend some time with her and see how much she loves you, your fears about the future won't be as scary."

That was one of the primary conditions I added into the marriage agreement. If Win wanted me to sign on the dotted line, he had to let Winnie meet my mom. Initially, he refused. It was a sticking point. He didn't want to scare Winnie or worry her more about things that were far beyond her control. I flatly refused to move forward until he relented. My mother never recovered from my sister's death. It felt like she was forever trapped in that moment. Although her mind was complicated and unpredictable, I secretly hoped that seeing Winnie and realizing what an amazing gift Willow left behind would help her move forward. I believed it would sincerely benefit Winnie to understand that there was an entirely different world outside of the Halliday estate. I wanted her to know that money couldn't solve all of life's problems, and that sometimes you just had to do the best with what you were handed. After an intense back and forth, Win conceded and agreed that I could introduce Winnie to my mother, as long as he was present.

Winnie smiled back at me with real delight shining out of her pretty eyes. "I would like that."

After we finished the five-star meal, Winnie asked to go somewhere less uptight for dessert. When Win recommended a small ice cream shop a few blocks away, I was surprised. He didn't strike me as the type who had a sweet tooth or would indulge in dessert. However, the staff behind the counter knew him by name and greeted him with a warm welcome. I waved off his offer to buy me something and avidly watched the tall man in his custom-made suit hover over the teenager as they eagerly picked out what they wanted to order. I had never really gotten the chance to witness how Win was with Winnie in their unguarded moments. I assumed he was as insufferable to her as he was with me. I was pleasantly surprised to see that he treated her with care. He wasn't nearly as heartless as I believed him to be.

When they came back to the table, Winnie appeared to be much more relaxed than she was at dinner. I reached out to dig my finger in the whipped cream on top of her sundae, but Win interrupted the move. He gave me a narrow-eyed look and handed over his spoon that was filled with the fluffy white confection.

"Don't use your hands." His gruff reprimand made me roll my eyes.

I took the spoon and shoved it in my mouth, mostly to see if he would stand and fetch a fresh one or continue to use the one covered with my germs.

"Aunt Channing, if you're moving back to the Cove, does that mean you have to quit your cool job?" Winnie looked in my direction, but I was watching Win use the spoon that had just been in my mouth. I couldn't believe he didn't get a clean one. I guess since he placed that brief kiss on me at the courthouse, he wasn't too concerned that I might pass along the plague.

When my niece asked again, I jerked my attention back to her with a bit of effort. "Yes. I'll have to find a new job. Don't worry. I'll look for something that has hours during the day while you're in school. I want to spend as much time with you as I can." That was another agreement that I'd worked into the marriage contract. I demanded that Win let me find employment outside of Halliday Inc. I couldn't stand the idea of being stuck in the house with Colette all day, and I didn't want to deal with him at both home and work. If I didn't find something to do while Winnie was in class, I was going to climb the walls and feel even more trapped. He didn't argue, but he added a clause that dictated the job be within certain hours and be something he deemed appropriate. I couldn't go work in Roan's bar — my first choice — or suddenly decide I wanted to be a stripper.

"The company has a lot of contacts with auction houses. I can have Conrad send you a list. If I get you in the door, I'm sure you'd get hired on the spot."

I blinked at Win like he was speaking a foreign language. I couldn't hold back a sarcastic laugh. "I'm not qualified to work in those places you're talking about. I handle tchotchkes, not gold recovered from the *Titanic* and Banksy paintings. I'm used to selling to tourists and quirky home decorators. Not serious collectors, and definitely not experts." Some items that moved through the high-end auctions were archaeological treasures. I couldn't fathom putting a price tag on something with such historical significance. "I don't know what I'm going to do, but I'll find something." I had a mishmash of unique skills I'd acquired by working multiple jobs since I'd been old enough to be employable. I married my jerk of a first husband when I was eighteen instead of going to college. I was on my own after Willow ran off with Archie, and even more so after she passed away. I'd never been afraid of hard, dirty work. Often, it was a pleasant distraction from everything else going on in my life.

"The bakery where your mom used to work is still in the same location. It's changed owners a few times, but it's still a local favorite. You practically grew up there. Maybe you should see if they're hiring." Win offered the information in an offhand manner, but I could hear the deep nostalgia in his tone.

His fondness when speaking of the bakery shocked me. Especially since it was where Willow and Archie met and fell in love.

Winnie glanced at me. I laughed at her and reached out to wipe a bit of chocolate sauce off her face. "Do you know how to bake, Aunt Channing?"

"A little. Your grandma taught me. Your mom was awesome at it. Way better than me. Everything she made turned out amazing, even though she never followed a recipe exactly. She was very talented."

When Archie and Willow ran away to get married and escape Colette's reach, my sister's baking kept the two of them afloat. It didn't take Archie long to realize that living paycheck-to-paycheck was not the lifestyle he wanted for his family, even though the two never went hungry or had to worry about having a place to live.

Winnie made a sad sound and got a distant look in her eye. "I wish I could remember more about my parents. I have a vague sense of being very loved. I guess that's more than some kids get."

Win told her very seriously, "That's everything, Winnie. There are kids with both parents in their lives who won't ever know that feeling. If your dad had the choice to leave anything with you, it would be the knowledge that he loved you deeply. He made a lot of mistakes along the way, but he truly wanted to do right by you and your mom."

I felt a pang in my chest at Win's words. As long as I'd known him, I'd never heard him speak with sentimentality or vulnerability. I always viewed him as a robotic CEO who only had the endless pursuit of profit in mind. It shocked me that he could show such an unguarded side of himself with Winnie.

My niece finished her ice cream and settled back in her seat. After spending the evening together, she appeared less resistant to the idea of Win and me joining forces through the fake marriage. It was a lot for a young girl to take in. Luckily, Winnie was wise beyond her years, and it helped that she came from a world where the people didn't follow rules; they made them.

"I'm happy that you'll be around more, Aunt Channing. And I'm glad you're able to help Uncle Win. As long as the two of you try to have a civil relationship, I won't interfere with your business. But if you're making each other feel bad all the time, I won't stand by and stay quiet. When you fight, it really stresses me out."

Win and I exchanged a knowing glance. We were both achingly aware just how challenging her request would be. He and I were simply too different. There was always friction when we were together, even if neither one of us was looking to start a fire.

"I'm sure we can all get along and make this work with a bit of effort." I said the words, though it wasn't hard to tell I didn't believe them.

Even if Win and I managed to play nice for the duration of the contract, Colette was going to make my life a living hell as soon as I stepped into her domain.

Chapter Eight
win

"You want me to die, don't you? You want me six feet underground with your father and little brother. I can't believe you would be so cruel as to bring a member of *that* family into my home again. I always wondered if you hated me. Today I have no doubt, Winchester."

I ducked my head and pulled Channing behind me to avoid the extremely expensive teacup my mother threw at my head. I anticipated an extreme reaction, but I wasn't prepared for her to throw a tantrum like a child. It didn't suit her cool, aloof personality.

"I don't hate you. And I don't want anything bad to happen to you, Mother. You've been demanding that I get married, regardless of my protests. You're furious when I don't do what you want. Now, you want me to feel guilty for listening to you." Channing grabbed a handful of my shirt as she leaned around my body to peek at the hysterical woman. I felt she was quietly enjoying being able to witness Colette Halliday so flustered.

"I want you to get married, but not just to anyone who wandered in off the street. You need to marry someone appropriate. Someone with status. There are an endless number of women who can benefit our family and make you a happy home. I will never agree if you tie yourself to someone unworthy of the Halliday name." She would never miss an opportunity to put someone in their place. It was unreal that she was more than willing to put me in the same position as she had been with my father. They never hid the fact that their marriage was based on business, not love. My father was practically a big game trophy my mother worked night and day to bring down. She sniffed and coldly continued, "I won't share my home with some stray you dragged through my door. You should know how it ends when people from different walks of life try to combine their lives. Nothing but tragedy awaits if you continue to be stubborn about this." My mother sniffed and crossed her arms over her chest.

She was fairly tall and carried herself with a sense of entitlement that was unmistakable. People often referred to the Hallidays as American royalty. Colette fully embraced that illusion. She truly believed she was a queen, and everyone outside of the Hallidays were her subjects to rule.

I grunted as Channing pinched the skin on my side and whispered, "I told you so."

"I'm not letting you handpick a bride for me. I'm not marrying someone with the sole purpose of helping Halliday Inc. I've let you design my entire future without complaint up to this point. I have to draw the line somewhere. I've known Channing longer, and I trust her more than any of the random women you've coerced me into meeting for these last couple of months. Winnie loves her, which is the most important reason I asked her to marry me."

"I forbid it." My mother narrowed her eyes, and it felt like she was trying to burn holes through my body so she could glare at Channing. "No Harvey will ever be welcome in my home."

I was getting really annoyed at the repetition and the way she was treating anything I said as irrelevant. Arguing with my mother was always like this. She firmly believed that only her ideas held value and weight.

"Fine. If you forbid it, I'm taking Winnie and Channing back to the city. You can stay in this huge house all alone. Just you and the ghosts Winnie swears are in the walls. I don't need your permission to make choices about my private life, Mother."

"How dare you threaten to take my granddaughter away from me!" Her voice rose to a shriek. I shook my head and lifted a hand to rub my ringing ear.

"It isn't a threat. Channing and I are married. If she's not welcome here, then I'll take her somewhere she is. Where I go, Winnie goes. Don't forget, I'm her guardian, not you." I sighed and gave my mother a pointed look. "You're making this much harder than it has to be. You had to know I would never passively let you arrange a business marriage for me. I told you that if I agreed to follow in Dad's footsteps the way you wanted, I was done sacrificing my own wants and needs for the good of this family. You have no one to blame for this current situation besides yourself. You should've listened to me when I told you to stop bringing women home for me. When it affected Winnie and you still ignored me, you left me no choice but to find a work-around."

My mom huffed and puffed in outrage like an angry exotic bird. "What good can come from this selfish trick? Don't you remember what it was like when we lost your brother? Her sister killed him, Winchester. The only plausible reason you could have for marrying her is to torture me. You've always hated me for wanting more for you than a life as a struggling musician. You resent me for pushing you to be something better." I couldn't refute her claims. I had a boatload of harbored resentment that she forced me to walk a path I had no interest in traveling. Who wouldn't hate having all their choices and freedom stripped away under the guise of family duty? I despised this woman for snatching happiness in any form away from her children. It often seemed that my only role was to suffer alongside her. "Are you certain *she* isn't here to finish the job her sister started? What if she wants to murder all of us in our sleep? You're so worried about Winnie. What will you do if she harms her?"

I opened my mouth to tell the older woman she was being ridiculous, but Channing stepped around me and met my mother glare for glare.

"If you hadn't pushed my sister to the breaking point, no one would've been hurt to begin with. She was fine until she moved into this house and had to deal with you every single day. You're a wicked woman, Colette Halliday." She pointed a finger in my mother's direction and snapped, "The only reason I agreed to help Chester is because I knew it would make you miserable. I can't wait for you to feel a fraction of the torture you inflicted on my sister. I don't care about money, or your company, or this fucking cursed manor. I'm here to enjoy watching you suffer every single time you see my face."

"You..." My mother took a step forward, and so did Channing. I caught the redhead's collar and hauled her back to my side.

She flashed me a fiery look but stilled when I gave the back of her neck a small squeeze.

"We're going around in circles. I am married to Channing. I can't marry another woman, nor do I want to. If you force Channing out of my life for the duration of our marriage, she gets half my shares in Halliday Inc. That applies to anything that happens to you while we're married, as well. If you hurt yourself, as you constantly threaten to do, I inherit all your shares.. I'll make sure Winnie and Channing split them equally." I had to maneuver so she couldn't use self-harm to influence my decisions or hold my emotions hostage. "We can stay here, and you can continue to watch Winnie grow up and appreciate the great gift Archie left us, or I can take the girls and you can rot in this house on your own. I'm sick and tired of the manipulation. I shouldn't have to worry about protecting myself from my own mother." I dragged a hand down my tired face. "I wish you would stop and look at how we ended up here. If we had just behaved like some version of a normal family, we could've avoided this nonsense." I had let go of that dream a long time ago. There was no *normalcy* when a family was bonded by ambition and greed.

There was a long, tense moment where my mother tried to figure out what to say that would get me to yield. I'd reached a point where I refused to surrender to her control when it came to my personal life. I was sick of feeling like her puppet. I should've cut the strings much sooner.

"Fine. Do what you want. It's obvious you don't care about how I feel." My mother sniffed and tilted her chin defiantly. "I will not make that woman feel like she belongs here. I'm not lifting a finger for her. I'll instruct *my* staff to do the same. She's on her own." I nodded as Channing scoffed in amusement. If she'd come from the same means my mother was used to, her threats might've felt intimidating and insulting. Channing had been on her own for so long, she had no concept of what it was like to be waited on hand and foot. It was impossible for her to miss something she'd never had. My mother suddenly smirked and gave me a look that sent a chill down my back. "If you are so determined to have a Harvey in my home, you can share your space with her. I don't want her wandering around where she isn't welcome. Since you were so willing to marry her, you won't mind having her in your wing of the house exclusively, will you, Winchester?"

Channing and I exchanged a look. My space in the manor was more like a separate apartment than a typical bedroom. It was the remodeled quarters of the former staff. There was plenty of room for two people, but we shouldn't have to live on top of one another when we lived in a house that was closer to a castle than a single-family home.

It was on the tip of my tongue to tell my mother she was going too far. But Channing was faster than me and far more eager to push my mom's buttons.

She turned to face me, her hand reaching for the loosened knot of my tie. The look in her eyes was vicious and taunting. I'd never seen an expression like that before. The more I was around her, the more it became strikingly obvious that my impression of her as someone who was bland and ordinary was totally off base. Channing did a solid job of hiding that she was extraordinary.

Our height difference was enough that Channing had to pull me down to her level and lift on her toes to reach her goal. I shouldn't have been surprised when her lips met mine. Regardless, my breath caught when the softness of her mouth brushed across mine.

This time, she tasted like candy. The kiss was sweet, and I was a man who appreciated dessert. Indulging in something simply because it tasted good and made me happy was one of the few guilty pleasures I allowed myself. I was startled that kissing Channing Harvey gave me the same rush.

She was braver and more thorough than I'd been when she kissed me. There was no hesitation or fear in her movements. She was a great kisser. Or, maybe I didn't have enough data to compare, because I'd spent most of my life handling the Halliday's affairs and not experiencing all that life had to offer. Either way, kissing Channing had moved toward the top of my list of small gratifications that had nothing to do with business accomplishments.

I let out an involuntary gasp, and as soon as my lips parted, I felt the tip of her tongue sneak into the opening. It flicked across my own, and her teeth nipped at my bottom lip. My breath caught in my lungs as my hands unconsciously moved to hold her waist and pull her closer. My mind wandered to silk sheets and entwined bodies. I could picture Channing's pale skin underneath my hands while she writhed in pleasure. I would never consider myself a man with an overtly carnal side, but the longer the kiss went on, I wondered if I knew myself as well as I thought I did. I was uncomfortably warm, and my heart was pounding in an erratic rhythm I'd never experienced before. I forgot I was kissing a woman my mother hated right in front of her. It slipped my mind that Channing considered us enemies. All I could focus on was the fact that I suddenly felt more human than I had in a long while.

It wasn't until the teeth she was using to tease me bit down hard enough on my lip that I came to my senses. I looked over the top of Channing's head in my mother's direction and noticed that she was absolutely seething.

Channing turned to face her with a victorious smirk. "I'm happy to share a room with Chester. It'll give us plenty of time alone. Who knows how close we'll get when we live in a small space together?"

"You are a worthless piece of trash. All Harveys are." My mother hurled another piece of antique dishware in my direction. I managed to catch this one before it smashed into Channing or the wall. "Take your hands off my son. I'll never let you corrupt him the way your filthy sister ruined my youngest."

This was probably the most unhinged I'd seen my mother since Archie's death. Before I could interject, Channing marched directly in front of her and told her in an icy voice, "Your opinion of me is irrelevant, because you aren't a woman I respect. I couldn't care less what you have to say about me or my sister, but if I hear you whisper one derogatory word about either of us to Winnie, I won't let it go. You have no right to poison that child's mind with your hatred. I won't stand by and let you taint the few fond memories from her childhood with your disgusting prejudice." She took a shuddering breath and glared at the distinguished older woman. "I have nothing to lose the way Willow did. I'm not afraid of you, Colette."

My mother lifted her hand as if she were going to smack Channing across the face. I moved to intercept the action, but Channing didn't need me to protect her.

She simply caught my mother's hand and twisted her wrist at a very sharp angle. My mom let out an undignified howl of distress and turned her panicked eyes in my direction. I shrugged carelessly. She brought this upon herself.

"I'm a single woman who lives in a big city. I don't have a security staff to watch my back. That falls on me and me alone. Don't try me, Lady Halliday. You won't like the outcome." Channing threw my mother's hand away and spun back around to face me. "Show me where your room is, Chester. You can help me move all my crappy, secondhand stuff into your mother's pristine home. It'll be fun." She cut my mom a dirty look. "I didn't bother to check for bedbugs or other creepy crawly things that might've hitched a ride from the city. Won't it be fun if I cause an infestation my first week back to the Cove?"

My mother looked stunned. She blinked and her hands clenched into fists at her sides. I grabbed one of the staff and asked them to monitor her and make her some tea or a strong cocktail to help calm her down. As I guided Channing away from the formal living room, my mother called, "I hope you're happy. Since you were a little boy, you've always pushed back against me, even though all I wanted was what was best for you. It's thanks to me that you're the man you are, Winchester. You've always tried to punish me. I hope you can live with yourself if something bad happens. I don't know how you'll be able to sleep at night when there's someone by your side who has nothing but ill will toward you and your family."

I sighed because I was finished with the whole charade. There were only so many times I could hear the same threat before the sentiment lost all meaning.

"I'll sleep just fine." Those were my final words as I grabbed Channing's elbow and walked to the large foyer in the front of the house. It featured two giant staircases: the left side of the house was the main living area and my mother's domain. The right side was where Winnie and I stayed. There was another small staircase that led to the wing of the house that was mostly abandoned. That was the area that burned and took the life of Winnie's parents. The flames had died, but there was no repair for the resentment and regret that remained long after the physical damage was fixed. The estate staff that routinely cleaned the area were the only ones who ventured to that part of the manor.

"There is plenty of room in this house. You can ignore my mother's efforts to make you uncomfortable. I'll have someone clean whichever area where you're most comfortable." I rubbed my temple where I felt a headache starting to take shape. "If things get too difficult to handle, you can use my apartment in the city when you need some breathing room."

Channing snorted in response and gave me a cold look. "Oh no. I'm moving into your room and staying. Not only will it drive your mother bananas, but it's bound to be inconvenient for you. When have you ever had to share your space or be considerate of another person's needs?" A grin that showed a hint of malice tugged at her mouth. "I wasn't joking about the bed bugs. Nothing would make me happier than making you grossly uncomfortable. It serves you right for forcing me into this stupid marriage."

I grunted to acknowledge her valid anger toward me. I would never admit to her that what made me most uncertain were the recent kisses we'd shared.

Chapter Nine
channing

I didn't bring much from my apartment. Since most of my belongings were thrifted and well-loved, it made little sense for me to put them in storage. I'd end up paying more in fees than anything was worth. All I brought with me were my personal effects, a couple of plants I worked hard to keep alive, a handful of beloved books, and a box of sentimental items from my childhood I couldn't bring myself to part with. I was experienced in moving and starting over, so it took less than a couple of hours to settle into Win's bachelor suite and claim my place.

The huge room resembled a high-end hotel more than someone's home, but the black and gray décor didn't feel overly sterile. I was surprised to see pictures of him and Winnie at various ages and functions scattered around the room. And there were pictures of his younger brother and even a family photo with my sister in it. There were signs of our niece all over the masculine rooms. Her pink hoodie was hanging on the back of a barstool. A couple of her schoolbooks and loose papers were on the expensive coffee table near a tablet covered in glittery stickers. Someone had tucked a cute stuffed animal into the corner of the black leather couch, and the gourmet kitchen was stocked with the kinds of snacks and drinks the average teenager would crave after school. My views of Win shifted slightly askew the more I learned about his relationship with our niece.

I always thought he'd handed the young girl off to his mother and her staff while he was busy making millions. I never pictured Win as someone who was actively parenting the teenager. The two of them were closer than I imagined, and Win's talk about wanting to do what was best for Winnie, no matter the cost, felt authentic. I wanted to believe this fake marriage was a way to punish his mother and manipulate me, but it was looking like Win's motives were more cut and dry. He really wanted to give Winnie a stable, regular life. He was willing to sacrifice his time, money, and freedom to ensure she got it.

It annoyed me that a hint of respect for him crept under my skin.

"There's a guest room. Right now, it's full of Winnie's stuff, but I can have it cleaned up for you." I jumped when Win appeared silently at my elbow.

I shook my head. "I'll share her closet for now. That's all I need. I don't want to kick her out. I think it's nice you gave her a space of her own that's close to you. Figuratively and literally. I'm not planning on staying in your room indefinitely, just long enough so that it firmly gets underneath your mother's skin." I waved at the fancy sofa. "I can crash there. It's nicer than the recent bed I've been sleeping in. All I need is a blanket and a pillow. I can sleep anywhere. It's kind of my superpower."

Win grunted. "That's ridiculous. There are no less than twenty beds on this property. There is no reason for you to sleep in the living room."

I laughed and nudged his side. "You can always be a gentleman and offer me your bed. You can take one for the team and sleep on the couch since we're in this mess because of you."

He gave me a considering look. His eyes were always intense because of their chilly color and his general demeanor. I didn't notice hints of blue hidden within the gray until recently. His gaze looked like a storm demolishing a bright, beautiful day.

Win didn't comment further on our sleeping situation. He walked over to one of the massive windows that overlooked the back garden and the steep cliff that dropped to the coastline. He poked at the plant I'd set on the windowsill and quietly muttered, "I'm not a man who apologizes for much, but I feel like I owe you one on behalf of my mother. This is only the beginning. She's going to get worse."

I let out a dry bark of laughter. "Didn't you concoct this scheme because you have faith that I can hold my own against Colette? Don't apologize for her actions. You should be apologizing for being such a pushover where she's concerned." I lifted my eyebrows at him mockingly. "I never thought I would see the day when someone successfully bullied a Halliday."

Win's voice was soft when he replied, "Every living being has a natural predator they fear. The only thing I have to fear in life is my mother. Do you know what it's like to love and hate someone with equal intensity?" He shook his head, and for the first time since I'd known him, a look of defeat crossed his face. "I've never had an actual mother. She's always been more like a handler or the executive director of my entire life."

I didn't want to acknowledge that his words resonated within me. It caught me off guard when Win allowed himself to be vulnerable and show the cracks in his golden armor. Between finding out he had a sweet tooth, a soft spot for Winnie, and learning he wasn't as immune to Colette's cruelty as I previously believed, it was hard to ignore just how human he actually was. If anyone asked me a month ago, I would've classified Win as someone who was born to be extraordinary. How could he be anything else? However, the glimpses of him being completely ordinary were doing funny things to the reservations and resentments I'd built between us like a wall.

"I don't know what it feels like to be caught between love and hate. I do understand the need to go to extreme lengths to save someone from themselves, though." I glared at him. "The only reason I have to help you manage your mother is because you threatened mine. Let's not forget how all this came about." I ruthlessly squashed the tingle of sympathy I had for him.

"I won't forget; you remind me every five minutes." He shoved a hand through his hair. The silvery strands in the front stood on end, giving him an endearing appearance. "I leave for the office around six in the morning. Earlier, if I'm going to the main office in the city. I've delegated most of our international work as Winnie has gotten older, but there are times when I'll be away for several days, maybe even weeks, at a time. Winnie's driver takes her to school around seven. She has extracurriculars after class most days. When she gets home, she usually comes here and does her homework. I try to be back in time for dinner. My mother was making a big deal about eating as a family the last couple of months. What she actually cared about was finding me a wife. I told Winnie she didn't have to sit down for a formal dinner anymore if she didn't want to. I have a personal housekeeper who monitors her when I'm unavailable. There's always someone around to make sure she eats and gets her schoolwork done. She used to have her own suite on this floor. But ever since she started claiming that the house was haunted, she's been sleeping in her room here. You're familiar with the contract terms. I won't dictate how or where you spend your time, as long as it doesn't negatively affect our niece."

"I've lived in a lot of places. I'll figure out a schedule and how to best benefit Winnie while I'm here. You don't have to change anything to accommodate me. Save that consideration for when you have a *real* wife."

He looked like he wanted to reply, but Winnie interrupted us by bounding into the room. She dropped her designer backpack on the floor and rushed to me. She threw herself into my arms for a tight hug. Her small body was practically vibrating with excitement. Her eyes were bright, and her face was flushed.

I squeezed her back as she told me, "I'm so glad you're here, Aunt Channing."

I smoothed my hand over her reddish-brown hair and soaked in the moment. I never thought there would be a day when I would be able to welcome Winnie home from school. I'd missed out on so much of her childhood because of a pointless feud.

"I'm happy to be here with you, Winnie." I truly was. Joining forces with my archenemy was worth it if I could stockpile warm memories like this.

Winnie zipped around the elegant suite as if she owned the place. Win directed her to change clothes and clean up after herself, then forced her to sit down and work on her homework, even though she was too excited to sit still. While the two of them bent their heads over math problems, I quietly slipped away to finish putting my things in Winnie's massive walk-in closet. I couldn't help but laugh when I saw all my no-name clothes hanging next to her designer wardrobe. I couldn't fathom a situation in which Winnie would need an authentic Chanel tweed blazer. It was ridiculous that the thirteen-year-old had two of them.

I made a mental note to take her thrifting when I got an opportunity to take her to the city with me. Someone needed to show Winnie how to make ends meet and survive on a realistic budget. It was unlikely that she would ever financially struggle, but the girl needed to cultivate some average life skills.

Winnie begged Win to order pizza for dinner, and he relented, but of course, it wasn't a greasy to-go pie. It was a homemade pizza, straight from a brick oven somewhere on the property. The ingredients were fresh, and the smell was divine. I couldn't argue that it was a good pizza, but it wasn't better than the giant messy slices you could pick up at any pizzeria in the city. I added taking Winnie for an authentic slice to the list of experiences I wanted her to have before my deal with Win ended.

Win and Winnie kept up a steady flow of conversation throughout the evening. They were noticeably comfortable in each other's company, and I was jealous of the connection they shared. I was glad Win wasn't as uptight and authoritarian as I imagined. It put the way he dealt with me in sharp contrast. He treated me more like a wayward child than the actual child he cared for.

After we ate, Winnie went off to her room to talk to a friend and get ready for bed. Win disappeared into what I assumed was his office, leaving me to my own devices.

I walked to the big Oriel window and looked at the ocean that seemed endless in the dark. People would kill for a view like this. There were only a handful of homes on the highest point of the cliff. Builders constructed these homes a hundred years ago when houses were made of stone and had ornate stained glass in the windows. They looked more like castles than family estates. They were the legacy that was handed down from generation to generation. The only way to own one was to be born with the proper last name.

When I was younger and I begged Willow to bring me along when she delivered to this house, it felt like a fairytale whenever I stepped on the immaculate grounds. It was easy to picture a princess running through the flowers in the gardens or a prince strolling down the majestic staircase. It was fun to pretend that the estate was a magical place. As an adult, it felt cold and empty. The house was stunning, but it was hollow. Aside from this little hideaway where Win and Winnie lived, there was no life or love anywhere within the stone walls. It was more like a prison than a fantastic wonderland. I began to understand why Win was so detached from everyone and everything. How could anyone who grew up in a place that felt so barren know what it was like to be surrounded by warmth? Weren't we all a byproduct of the foundation we'd been given? Win's was rigid and unforgiving.

As the night wore on and it seemed like Win wasn't going to reappear from his office, I gathered what I would need for a shower and poked around the extensive suite until I found the main bathroom. I tossed everything haphazardly onto a marble countertop and reached out to fiddle with the brass knobs in the shower. I giggled a little when I noticed the levers looked like little swan heads. Rich people's aesthetic was both atrocious and adorable.

I hummed under my breath and stepped into the shower. The water rattled in the pipes but heated fast. I closed my eyes and tried to wash away the earlier encounter with Colette. There was little doubt that I needed to brace myself because the battle had just begun. Now that it was the end of the day, my reservations were piling up.

I was tired. It was exhaustion that made your soul ache and had you questioning every step you took that led you to this point. There was no going back but going forward felt overwhelming.

I let the water rush over me and tried to loosen some of the tension in my neck and shoulders. I lost track of the tune I was humming and let my mind drift away, making a mental note of potential job opportunities in the Cove and the surrounding areas. I wasn't sure I could emotionally handle stepping back into the bakery where I'd grown up. Though it would be nice to see what had changed since my mother left her career behind. The last time I remembered her smiling was in that bakery. While she was highly emotional and unpredictable, she always seemed to keep it together and mask her more debilitating traits when she was elbow deep in dough.

The pipes squeaked and rattled again when I turned off the water. As I pushed open the glass door and stepped out of the steamy enclosure, I paused and tilted my head. A faint sound seemed to whisper underneath my feet. I looked down at the custom tile and shivered as I wrapped a large towel around myself. I couldn't tell whether Winnie's ghost stories were getting to me, but I swore the song I was tunelessly humming minutes ago was whistling back at me through the floor. I screwed up my face and pressed my ear against the wall. It was warm from the steam of the shower, and my skin slipped against the surface. As soon as I touched the cool marble, the sound disappeared. I chalked it up to my being mentally drained and overstimulated.

I did my skincare routine and brushed my teeth. By the time I was done, I was fighting to keep my eyes open.

The lights in the suite were dimmed, and a blanket and pillow were on the couch. I popped my head into Winnie's room. She was curled in a ball, clutching the pink stuffed animal that was in the living room earlier. I was taken aback by the sudden burn of tears in my eyes and the tangle of emotions at the back of my throat.

My sister was robbed of the opportunity to experience simple and quiet moments like these, it didn't feel fair.

I whispered, "Sweet dreams," and went to set up camp on the couch. I had no idea if Win found me a blanket and pillow. If he did, I had no intention of thanking him. The light was still on in the room where he'd locked himself away earlier. He probably had a pile of stuff to catch up on since he'd been juggling our marriage arrangements and dealing with his mother the last couple of weeks. He worked tirelessly at a job he detested, making him a better man than most.

I thought I heard the faint tune trickling through the ancient walls, but I fell asleep as soon as my head hit the pillow. I was so out of it; I didn't even move a muscle when I was forcibly picked up and moved into the primary bedroom hours later.

When I woke up the next morning, fully refreshed by myself in Win's massive antique bed, I felt like I'd sleepwalked into an alternate reality. Like a romance novel where the average, relatable girl suddenly caught the eye of a handsome billionaire.

I should've known that regardless of how prepared I was for the upcoming challenges, this house and the secrets hidden inside the walls still had the ability to surprise me.

Chapter Ten

win

I learned a lot about Channing Harvey in the few short weeks she'd been at the estate.

She really could sleep anywhere. The couch. The big recliner in the corner. Winnie's room. On the floor. Propped up against the big, sea-facing windows. If she found a place to rest her head and closed her eyes, she was out like a light. It'd become a nightly habit to move her from whatever awkward location where she'd zonked out into a bed. More often than not, I surrendered my own and slept on the chaise lounge in my office. Occasionally, she stayed with Winnie in her room because my niece was prone to nightmares and fitful bouts of night terrors. I wasn't certain Channing was assuaging Winnie's fear that there was something hiding within the walls. I frequently found her pressing her ear against the barrier and knocking on old structures throughout the house like she was trying to find a hollow spot or secret entrance.

I discovered she was impervious to insults from those she considered unimportant. My mother had gone above and beyond to make sure Channing knew she was not wanted in her home. None of the staff acknowledged the redhead. They treated her as if she were air, and the frigid cold shoulder extended beyond the walls of the estate. When Channing started looking for work, every business that operated in the Cove refused to even let her apply. My mother spread the word that anyone who had interactions with Channing would no longer be considered for business or service opportunities for the Hallidays and their acquaintances. Not to mention, there were various companies and services my mother funded that I had nothing to do with. She had too much pull on the local economy for me to interfere. I think my father gave her control of whatever opportunity caught her eye to keep her out of his hair. Or maybe they were bribes to keep her silent about the affair. There was no way in hell that my mother didn't know what the old man was up to behind her back.

My mother made it nearly impossible for Channing to take part in school functions with Winnie.

One of the first things she did when she moved in was teach Winnie that while privilege was nice and came with a slew of advantages, there was no guarantee in life that a person would always have whatever they needed. When she found out Winnie's school was only a five-minute drive away, she bought a couple of old-fashioned beachcomber bicycles. The girls spent the weekend sanding them down and painting them bright colors. Channing wanted Winnie to ride her bike to and from school when the weather permitted. I agreed, as long as a member of my security team tagged along to make sure nothing happened on the way. Initially, I was worried the other kids who attended the elite private school would taunt my niece. Channing told me it was okay if they did, because Winnie needed to learn how to differentiate between real and manufactured criticism. She insisted it was a perfect way for our niece to weed out who her real friends were, and who only hung around because of her last name.

It turned out that a handful of her classmates thought riding a bike to school was cool in a retro way. There was even some envy that she had a bit of freedom most of the children from extremely well-to-do families rarely had.

The problems arose when Winnie wanted to bring Channing onto the school grounds so she could introduce her to her friends and her favorite teachers. The school's security team refused to let Channing beyond the gilded gates. They told her if she tried to enter the property, with or without Winnie, they would have her arrested for trespassing. My niece felt outraged and insulted on Channing's behalf. She called me and yelled in my ear for nearly twenty minutes. I promised I would call the school and add Channing to the visitor's list. Unfortunately, it was a promise I couldn't fulfill. My mother wasted no time in making moves to keep Channing from the places she deemed her unworthy of entering. The director of the school did not hesitate to brag about the obscene monetary donation my mother had made in Archie's name to the school. Unless I wanted to build them a new building, or double my mother's fake charitable act, Channing was stuck close enough to see how the influential and powerful were educated but far enough away that she wouldn't learn their secrets.

However, my mother miscalculated Channing's skills and motivation. She was self-sufficient and didn't need the staff at home. My personal housekeeper was required less and less because Channing could cook. And while a job close to the estate would be convenient, Channing never intended to spend her time toiling in Colette Halliday's backyard. When I asked her what she intended to do since she was adamant to go back to work, she smiled at me in a way that made the back of my neck itch and told me I would just have to wait and see. Her tone indicated she had a plan, and it was nowhere near as harmless as going back to the bakery.

As for the situation with the school, she couldn't care less. As long as she got to drop off Winnie at the gates and pick her up so they could ride home together, she was content with the status quo. In fact, most of Winnie's friends attempted to breach the invisible barrier so they could meet Channing. Winnie had always sung her praises and told anyone who would listen how cool and fun her aunt was. The kids from the upper-class treated Channing like she was an animal on display in the zoo. It was almost like they'd never witnessed a woman who wore torn jeans and old sweatpants before.

When she dropped off Winnie while wearing her pajamas, they gawked at her and asked her ridiculous questions about living a pedestrian lifestyle. Twice, she was mistaken for a staff member. She laughed it off and joked that if she worked for one of the families in the Cove, she would be far better off financially. From the secondhand information I received, Channing took the innocent curiosity in stride. Her unbothered attitude just made my mother angrier.

The older woman tried to use my same tricks to get Channing to leave the marriage and the estate. She went after her parents and her friends and tried to dismantle her life. Unfortunately for my mother, I'd learned how to play dirty directly from her. I blocked every move she tried to make and warned her again that if she kept trying to push Channing out of our lives, she was going to lose more than she bargained for. She never listened. Thus far, Channing remained unfazed, but no matter how strong she was, there was bound to come a time when she couldn't handle the abuse. I did my best to be a buffer, so I was spending more time at home and less at the office. It was the first time in my life I experienced a reasonable work/life balance. Not even when I took over as Winnie's guardian did I dedicate an equal amount of time and focus on what was happening at home. I was programmed to prioritize Halliday Inc. over anyone and everything. It wasn't until Channing Harvey disrupted the ebb and flow of my very existence that I realized I should want more for myself. No. That I *needed* more than a company and an unwanted inheritance to be successful and feel fulfilled.

Today when I got back to the sprawling estate after having been away for several days, the large manor was eerily hushed. None of my mother's staff was bustling about, and there was no sign of the older woman. Winnie's room was empty, and there wasn't a hint of a single living person in my private wing.

The silence made me frown as I took off my suit jacket and pulled at my tie. I secretly looked forward to being greeted by Channing and Winnie. I'd never had the kind of family that was excited to see one another at the end of each day. It often felt like we were work colleagues rather than relatives. Sharing a space with Channing changed all of that. There was always a sense of warmth when I returned. If my days spent grinding and scheming for the company were an unchanging black and white, Channing painted the time we spent together with every color of the rainbow. It was a stark contrast that was altering the way I'd viewed a bleak future.

I called Winnie's name and looked in all the different rooms for Channing. I sent Rocco a text and inquired if he had knew the whereabouts of my niece, since one of his guys was supposed to watch her when she was away from the estate. He reported back that Winnie was still at school for a special presentation. He'd arranged for one of his men to bring her back when the event was over in advance. Rocco paused when I asked where Channing was. He didn't have anyone assigned to watch over the rebellious woman, but he knew me well enough to know that he should be able to answer when asked about her general whereabouts.

"She took a train into the city after she dropped off Winnie at school. I'm not sure what she did there, but she caught another train back to the Cove a couple hours ago. She should be at the estate. Colette's made it impossible for her to go anywhere else in town."

My frown deepened as I stepped into the hallway that led to the rest of the house. I called Channing's name, but there was only silence in response. The estate was so big and empty, sometimes a voice would echo, but not today. There was nothing. An uneasy chill creeped up my spine.

I told Rocco to find out what Channing was doing in the city today and ordered him to let me know if he found her before I did. He grunted in agreement, alluding to the fact that he found supervising Channing below his considerable paygrade.

I wandered up and down the long stretch between various rooms. I cracked doors I'd never opened before and continued to shout for the missing redhead. She had to be somewhere in this house, but I couldn't imagine her wandering in the places that were off limits unless she was intentionally trying to irritate my mother.

Eventually, I arrived at the stairway that split the house into different parts. I cast a glance toward the main house and knew without a doubt there was nothing in that direction that would interest Channing. I scowled as I took the first few steps toward the wing where my brother died. I'd refrained from stepping foot in those rooms since the remodel was finished. I treated that area as a tomb. The air always felt heavy and ominous when I crossed the threshold. There was nothing more than tragic memories and regret there. I imagined what I wanted to avoid was exactly what Channing was searching for if she'd entered the forbidden zone. If she'd asked before exploring on her own, I would've told her there was nothing left from the time her sister lived on the property. The fire ate every single trace that there had ever been a Harvey here. It decimated all proof that a happy, healthy family had ever existed inside these unyielding walls.

"Harvey! Are you up there? You shouldn't be wandering around this part of the house." My voice was gruff, and the concern I tried to hide was clear as my words carried down the hall. "I've been looking for you for over twenty minutes."

I called her name again, and this time there was finally a response. Channing yelled from Winnie's former nursery, "Give me one second. I'll be right out."

I breathed a sigh of relief and started walking in that direction. I was grumbling under my breath about her being impulsive and irresponsible when a door suddenly slammed shut. I jerked my gaze toward the sound, but the door to the nursery was wide open. Channing's head poked out as she looked around for the source of the loud noise. Her eyes drifted to mine and her brows furrowed.

"Was that you?"

I gave her an impatient look in response. "I don't slam doors. It was probably the staff. Or maybe a strong draft of wind. I told you a house this old has life to it."

She stepped out of the room and tossed her messy ponytail over her shoulder. "These antique doors weigh a ton. It would need to be a hurricane-grade wind to blow a door shut with that much force."

Channing craned her neck and looked up and down the hallway in confusion. "I walked this way because I heard another door open and close when I was at the base of the stairs. I swear on my mother there was something tapping inside the walls guiding me to this room. In a normal house, my guess would be mice. But I doubt Lady Halliday would allow something so undignified in her presence. No wonder Winnie thinks this house is haunted. Weird stuff keeps happening. It's not in her head."

I crossed my arms over my chest and gave her a pointed look. "Why don't I hear anything strange?"

She rolled her eyes and followed me as I led her away from the wing that I was starting to believe might really be cursed.

"You heard the door slam just now. That wasn't my imagination." She huffed a bit, and I found her extremely cute when she was frustrated. I froze for a second because I could not remember the last time I considered anything 'cute.' Maybe when Winnie was a newborn? There wasn't much use for soft sentiments in my day-to-day. It was another unconscious change that happened because I was spending more time with Channing.

"There's a rational explanation. There always is. You're as bad as Winnie. You should set a better example for her."

She gave me a dirty look and stomped back to the safety of my domain.

"Whatever. I know I heard something, and I know it wasn't a breeze that slammed those doors." She pouted and kicked the edge of the big recliner in the living room. "Maybe your mom is having the staff play tricks on me. She knows my mother has mental health issues, and I'm sure she could tell Willow struggled with similar symptoms. There is no question that the illness is hereditary. It's entirely possible she wants me — and you — to doubt my sanity."

I pulled off my tie and rolled my head to loosen the tension that had my neck muscles in a chokehold. "If you have suspicions that my mother is playing games with you, then you shouldn't let her win. Don't feed into whatever narrative she's trying to get you to follow."

I yawned because I hadn't slept well the last few days. I'd worried about whatever was happening back at the estate. For good reason, it seemed.

Channing swore loudly and gave me a dirty look. This was far from the warm welcome I'd secretly imagined when I was headed back from London.

"Winnie won't be home until later. Do you want me to arrange something for dinner, or did you eat?"

"I've eaten. I met up with a friend in the city this afternoon." She turned and gave me a haughty look. "And I found a job."

I blinked in surprise. "What sort of job? You're going to work in the city? Isn't that inconvenient?" I did the commute several times a week. Granted, I used the time in the car to work, but I still preferred not to spend hours on the road.

Channing shrugged, and the corner of her mouth quirked upward in a mocking grin. "I'm going to be a personal assistant. Just like that annoying guy who was following you around at the courthouse. I'm only working a couple days a week, so the commute shouldn't be terrible. I made sure the job fits within the confines of the contract and Winnie's school hours."

"A personal assistant for whom?" I started silently planning to have Rocco run a background check and do a deep dive into her new employer.

She opened her mouth to respond, but suddenly her expression changed, and she frantically darted over to the massive window that faced the seascape. Along the windowsill sat the potted plants she had carefully brought from her apartment. When I left a few days ago, they were thriving. Now, they looked brown, crunchy, and very dried up. They appeared as if someone had drop-kicked them across the living room when no one was looking. They were most certainly dead.

"Did you do something to these?" Channing whipped around and glared at me. "Why are they suddenly like this? I've had these plants for years. They've never even wilted before."

I grunted and lifted a hand to rub the back of my neck. "Did you forget that I've been gone? How could I do something to them?"

She scoffed and gave me a narrow-eyed look. "What about your housekeeper? Maybe your mother paid her off to mess with me." She picked up one of the pots and gave it a sad look. "This is so unnecessary. What did this poor plant ever do to anyone?"

"I'll ask, but I think it's unlikely. Everyone who works for me directly knows it is grounds for immediate termination if they are swayed by my mother. Maybe it's too hot by the window. Are you sure you didn't forget to take care of them while you were busy running back and forth to the city?"

Channing's whole body stiffened, and she whipped around to give me a look that would've had a weaker man quivering on the spot. I immediately regretted questioning her thoughtfulness. If I weren't exhausted and stressed over the war waging between her and my mother, I wouldn't have made such a careless faux pas. We were just now settling into a nice sort of truce, and I instantly destroyed the peace with my carelessness.

"I would never let anything happen to my babies. I've kept these plants alive for years because Willow gave them to me for my birthday the last year she was still here. They were her final gift to me. She could never keep anything green alive. Whatever she touched withered away. She told me it was my job to take care of all the delicate things she couldn't." Channing barked out a bitter laugh and narrowed her eyes at me. "Did you ask me who I'm going to work for?" She flashed a smile that was all teeth and malice. "It's someone you should be familiar with since he's family. They say the enemy of my enemy is the best friend you can have in a fight. Your half-brother fits the bill perfectly. If your mom doesn't want me working for anyone in her precious town, it makes perfect sense that I go and work for the only person who openly dislikes her as much as I do."

My heart twisted and a cold sweat broke out all over my body. "You're going to work for Alistair DeVere?" I'd only encountered my half-brother a handful of times. Other than looking nearly identical to me, there wasn't anything that stood out about the young man. If I was being honest, it was the fact that Channing and the bastard had more in common than she and I did that made me want to keep her away from him. She always had a history of falling for the underdog. Alistair DeVere wasn't an exact match for that description, but he definitely came up short when stacked up against me. The idea of her being allured by my face on a completely common man rubbed me the wrong way on so many levels. "I forbid it."

Channing laughed, but it was a harsh and bitter sound. "You don't get a say in the matter, Chester."

She picked up the dead plants and disappeared out the door that led to the small, private garden.

I swore under my breath and dragged myself to the bathroom so I could take a shower. I didn't mean to start a fight with her as soon as I returned home. Being at odds with her gave me a headache and made my heart feel like someone was squeezing it in a vise. And I definitely didn't want her to join forces with my not-so-innocent half-brother.

There was a laundry list of things I *didn't* want when it came to Channing. If I were to sit down and make a list of what I *did* want, I was scared to admit there was only one thing I could think of.

I wanted her to want me the same way I wanted her.

Chapter Eleven
channing

"Are you still mad about the plants?" Win's voice taunted me. I'd refused to say a word to him after he sprung the unwelcome task of being his plus-one for the evening on me. I had no desire to rub elbows with the rich and famous. The idea of spending hundreds of thousands of dollars to attend a charity event, instead of just donating directly to a worthy cause, was wasteful and grandiose. I didn't consider it a good time to dress up to see and be seen for nothing more than a tax write-off.

Sitting stiffly in the back of a limousine, I kept my face turned to look out the darkened window, remaining silent as the luxury car carefully navigated through the tangled city traffic.

"Among other things." I was still angry about my dead plants, but there were plenty of other incidents recently that added to the list of why I was pissed off.

First and foremost, I was annoyed that he sprung this event on me at the last minute.

It was absurd that he thought I was a woman who would wear an outrageously expensive designer gown and accompany him without warning. If living in the city had taught me anything, it was that I was far from a sample size. Couture designers did not create their designs for women with average height and figures. When I refused to allow him to have something custom made in a rush, it spawned another argument over our different life experiences and status. He didn't understand why I wouldn't want an expensive dress tailored to fit me perfectly. I didn't understand how he couldn't see that a dress like that, which could only be worn once and then disappeared into the back of a closet, was wasteful and unnecessary.

I told Win if he required me to go with him to an event I had no interest in, he had to let me wear whatever I wanted. It took him a little while to agree. And he only did so after I promised not to show up in my pajamas. I owned nothing that would fit in with the other women attending the gala, but I could find something that wouldn't embarrass Win too badly.

Other things on the growing list of things getting under my skin were the escalating occurrences of unexplained weirdness within Halliday Manor. I was convinced that Colette had her staff slipping in and out of Win's wing to mess with me.

My cell phone charger went missing, as did other insignificant things I left lying around. My favorite t-shirt was gone. I couldn't find a pair of earrings I wore regularly. A pair of sneakers I left by the door disappeared. A photo album from my childhood that I brought every time I moved vanished. I left a bottle of wine on the kitchen counter one night, and the next morning it was empty. Typically, I would've blamed Win, but he was away for work when it happened. The worst was when my hairbrush disappeared while I was in the shower when I knew I left it on the counter. I hadn't heard anyone walk into the bathroom or felt my internal warning system ring at all. It was unnerving to know that while I was naked and vulnerable, someone was close by without alerting me. And the whistling and humming from the walls never stopped. Some days, the sound was louder and clearer than others. But it was always there. I felt like I was being watched and I was never actually alone. I felt more unsafe living in the million-dollar estate than I ever had living in a shitty apartment in the city.

No wonder Winnie was convinced the house was haunted.

The whole inexplicable situation heightened the tension between me and Win. I wanted to put nanny cams all over the apartment to catch whomever was messing with me. Win had an entire security team at his disposal. It enraged me that he wasn't taking the circumstances more seriously.

He kept insisting his mother wasn't behind the abnormalities. He assured me that he'd spoken with her and the staff on the estate. He told them that if anyone attempted to mess with me, he would promptly fire them. Colette was indifferent, but the people who kept the home running were acutely aware of who paid the bills. Win seemed to take offense to the fact I constantly questioned his control when he wasn't at home.

I included Win's endless interference with my new job on the list of things that routinely made me angry.

Once I made an alliance with his half-brother, things between the two of us wouldn't be as easy. Playing house with him for a couple of weeks was fine and dandy while I found my bearings. However, I wasn't about to let Win forget that I was sleeping under his roof unwillingly. As uncomfortable as he was with Alistair being in my life, it paled in comparison to my unease under the vengeful eye of his mother. It made sense that if I had to suffer, so did he.

It was fortunate that Alistair DeVere was so much easier to deal with than the Hallidays. He was significantly younger than Win and far less uptight. He'd grown up in a fairly average, middle-class household. He had two loving parents and three younger sisters who treated him like he was a superhero. It wasn't until Win's father passed away, leaving Alistair a huge chunk of money and access to a portion of Halliday Inc., that the secret of his mother's affair with the affluent man was revealed. The news caused a lot of friction in his parents' marriage. The father who raised him wanted him to turn down the inheritance and stay clear of anything to do with the Hallidays. His mother felt like Alistair was owed everything bequeathed to him since his father had never offered a cent of support over his lifetime. Alistair told me he was torn between the two, especially since his parents separated after the news came to light. Unfortunately, his youngest sister became very ill not long after his birthright became front page news. The only way the family could pay for her round-the-clock medical care and pricey treatments was for Alistair to accept his portion of the inheritance.

True to form, Colette kept the kid tied up in litigation for years after the death of her husband. She didn't want him to see a penny of the Halliday fortune.

His sister almost died while Colette tried to use the law as a weapon. Alistair was barely an adult at the time and in way over his head.

The scorned widow didn't want to give him anything. But Win still had a tiny sliver of his heart left. He offered to pay the medical bills for the ill sister if Alistair agreed to relinquish his shares in the company. He could fight Colette for the money, but Win knew his mother like the back of his hand. As soon as the claim to Halliday Inc. was off the table, Colette would back off. It sounded messy. It was no wonder my new boss hated the Hallidays as much as I did.

Now, Alistair was running his own interior design business and doing well for himself. He didn't hesitate to hire me when I finally landed a meeting with him. I wasn't sure if he actually needed a part-time personal assistant or if he just wanted me on the payroll to irk the Hallidays. Either way, I liked his attitude and enjoyed getting away from the Cove every few days. I was starting to view him as a mischievous younger brother the more time we spent together. It was a perfect set up, aside from Win hounding me endlessly about every aspect of my job and relationship with his half-brother.

Win sighed as the limo pulled in front of one of the most luxurious hotels in the city. There were paparazzi behind barricades on either side of the road. Uniformed police officers patrolled the area with cautious eyes. It looked more like an award show than a charity event.

The driver moved to open the door. Win caught my hand as I tried to exit the car. Our eyes met, and he gave me a look that conveyed his complicated feelings. "I know you're mad for a lot of reasons, but I'm asking you to help me put forward a united front for the evening. We're supposed to be a team, Channing."

"I think we're each playing a different game, Chester." I slipped out of the car and stood next to the sidewalk, blinking against the bright lights from the flashing cameras. Win unfolded his tall frame to stand next to me. I heard someone shout his name and felt him stiffen. I glanced at him out of the corner of my eye and noticed that he appeared to be very uncomfortable with the attention focused directly on him. He was a real estate developer after all, not a celebrity.

He put his palm low on my back and guided me toward the entrance while offering a slight wave and smile to the waiting press. He refused to answer the questions that were lobbed at him, including the identity of his date. The back of my plain black dress was low enough that the heat from his hand touched bare skin. When I shivered, I blamed it on the chilly evening air, not my unwitting response to Win.

I tried to tune out the voices asking who I was and what my connection to the Hallidays might be. All it would take is one Google search to figure out my sister was once married to Archie Halliday and that the family blamed her for his death. It was enough to make society gossips froth at the mouth. I was acutely aware of what it was like to be weighed against the name Halliday and be found lacking. I would never have put myself in that situation again if Win hadn't forced me.

We made it through the press gauntlet and stepped inside the elegant hotel. The place was filled from top to bottom with wealthy people who could donate millions of dollars to whatever cause was on the agenda. Everyone wore quietly luxurious designer clothes. Their jewels looked like they should be in a museum, and the conversations could make or break the stock market. This was as close to a modern-day royal gathering as one could get.

I had no business being here.

I felt like everyone was watching me walk next to Win and cataloging my faults. I heard someone ask in a comically loud whisper, "Who is she?" Which set off a ripple of unfavorable speculation throughout the crowd.

Win must've sensed my apprehension because his hand slid along my spine like he was trying to soothe a spooked horse.

"We aren't staying long. Just hang in there until dinner starts. We can slip away after I give my obligatory speech." The only reason Win agreed to appear tonight was that Halliday Inc. was the major sponsor of this event. His mother was the host, but Win's name was on the invitation. People came to a gala like this hoping to exchange a few words with him. This event was more about making connections and making deals than about helping a cause.

Win shook a hundred hands and introduced me to a parade of well-dressed people as he tried to maneuver to the ballroom. I kept a blank expression on my face and returned the same level of interest back to the people who couldn't care less about who I was. There was a voice in the back of my head telling me to make sure Winnie knew how to have fun in a group like this, because I couldn't recall a gathering ever being *less* enjoyable. And I'd been divorced twice and forced into an unwanted marriage.

Once we were inside the lavish ballroom, Win offered to get me something to drink. He waved down one of the white-gloved servers and asked what I wanted. Before I could respond, an overweight gentleman who acted like he deserved Win's undivided attention pulled him into a conversation that had no place for me. I wasn't sure I could pick out Dubai on a map, let alone know about the difficulties of their real estate market. I could tell Win wasn't happy about being trapped in the discussion. However, while the enthusiastic gentleman occupied him, I slipped away from Win's side and found a bar on my own.

It was fairly easy to slip through the crowd once I ditched Win. No one was searching for me to talk business, and I didn't look like someone whom the hosts would hold in high regard. Win's face —

and his wealth — were too eye-catching. Our marriage wasn't necessarily a dirty secret, but it wasn't something either of us advertised. It was almost as if we never uttered a word about it, we wouldn't have to face what we'd done. Who signed up for a contract marriage in this day and age? While the curious might wonder why he brought someone with him to this gala when he usually came alone or accompanied his mother, not a soul directly inquired how I was affiliated with Win. It weirdly felt like they didn't ask because they were afraid to hear the answer. Win was a notorious bachelor. It was common knowledge that he never brought a date anywhere publicly. He avoided being tied to anyone to prevent rumors. I was an anomaly in this world in more ways than one.

Once I reached the bar, I ordered a shot of whiskey, stole a toothpick loaded with olives because I doubted whatever was on the menu was something I could stomach, and searched for a vacant corner to wait out the drudgery of the evening.

There was a beautiful piano on a stage at the front of the room. A stunning young woman was singing a song in a foreign language. I didn't know much about opera, but whatever she was performing for the affluent crowd sounded magical and sophisticated. I was a bit entranced as I continued to watch her while I sipped the whiskey that tasted smoother and went down easier than any alcohol should.

"Your outfit is interesting. Is it vintage?"

Breaking free from the reverie of the music, I looked at the young woman standing in front of me who'd asked the snarky question. She was probably a decade younger than me, close to Alistair's age. She was taller and thinner than I was. Her makeup was flawless, and so was the diamond and pearl choker on her neck. She had dark hair that looked like she could shoot shampoo commercials, and her sharp features made her almost aggressively attractive. She looked like a modern-day Audrey Hepburn, but she lacked the grace that made her so memorable.

I looked down at my plain silk dress. It was the most expensive item I owned, but I bet it didn't cost as much as anything the other woman was wearing, including the bejeweled hair pin holding her hair in a French twist. I bought the dress after Roan and I got divorced. I attempted to use retail therapy to make myself feel better when my heart was hurting. All I was left with was regret and a dress I couldn't afford. I didn't need a fancy little black dress; I needed to pay rent and keep the lights on. I was angry at myself for being reckless with my money and angrier when I tried to return the garment and was told it was on sale, so there would be no exchanges or credit.

"Sure. Since I've had this for over six years, I guess you could call it vintage." I bit back a laugh when I saw the young woman's expression sour at my disinterested tone.

"Who's the designer? I don't recognize it. I work in fashion, so I'm familiar with most houses' collections. Even from as far back as five or six years ago."

I lifted my shoulder and let it fall carelessly. "There is no designer. I'm sure it was assembled in a factory somewhere. I bought it off the rack at a department store. I'm sure hundreds were sold around the same time. It was a very popular style back when I purchased it."

The woman's retort seemed to be stuck in her throat as she blinked at me. After she coughed to clear the way, she looked me over and frowned. "Why would Win Halliday let you out of the house dressed in a department store dress if you're his plus one? Is he attempting to humiliate you? Is he trying to make a point about sustainable fashion? I don't understand."

The first question was supposed to be a dig at my expense, but she sounded genuinely baffled. I chuckled and took another sip of my drink. "Maybe I'm trying to embarrass him."

The brunette opened her mouth, then snapped it closed again like she couldn't figure out what to say. I silently laughed as I turned to walk away from her. A flawlessly manicured hand latched onto my arm. Her fingernails dug into my skin and made me wince.

"You do know that Colette Halliday wants Win to get married, right? She plans to handpick her daughter-in-law. I don't know who you are to Win, or why he brought you here tonight. But I know that you don't belong with him. His mother will never allow it. You should set your sights a little lower. I'm sure there are plenty of men who don't mind being with a woman who wears off-the-rack clothes to a black-tie event." Her tone indicated there were exactly *zero* men in this circle who wouldn't care about being seen with someone as basic as I was. She seemed particularly offended by my presence, which made her a perfect fit for what Colette wanted for Win.

I tried to walk away from both the woman and the pointless conversation, but a cultured voice interrupted the showdown and stopped me.

"Whether it's a designer dress or not, all men care about is how easy it is to get off. And how it looks on the bedroom floor. If he cares more about a label on the garment than the woman wearing it, he's not worth an ounce of her time." I hadn't noticed the opera singer had finished her set and was taking a breather when she stumbled onto this ridiculous conversation. Her eyes were bright and sharp. She looked as disgusted by the brunette's entitlement and outdated sentiments as I felt.

If I were somewhere else, I would've offered the short-haired woman a high five. Instead, I could only smile at her and nod in agreement at her blunt statement.

The brunette took off in a huff after the singer firmly shut down her classism. I offered to get the singer a drink, but she turned down the offer since she wasn't done performing for the evening. I thought she might mingle with the rest of the crowd, but she seemed content to hide in the unobtrusive corner. I introduced myself and learned her name was Beverly Taylor, and that she was a graduate student at Juilliard. She was studying to be a professional opera singer at one of the major opera houses abroad. Her level of education and sophistication was evident in every word she spoke.

"You have a beautiful voice. You're very talented." She really was a startlingly impressive young woman. When I was her age, my life was an absolute mess. I couldn't imagine having such a clear career plan with a singular goal the way she did. I thought she was very impressive and less irritating than the other wealthy guests milling about. Beverly was beautiful. Her spirit shined through her big eyes, and her compassion and warmth were clear in the way she came to the rescue and stuck by my side as the vultures circled. She was noticeably fit and took care of herself. Everything about her screamed youthfulness and self-discipline. She reminded me a lot of Salome. I immediately categorized her into the "good person" box in my mind. I thought the singer was the most interesting person in the room and was glad she didn't seem to mind lying low in the corner with me while I waited to make my escape.

It was one of those encounters where I felt like I made an instant friend, which I never imagined happening in Win's world.

We chatted happily for several minutes. I mentioned that my niece was interested in a bunch of different things and asked if she had recommendations for voice lessons near the Cove. I figured Winnie would try singing, eventually. It was a pleasant surprise when Beverly informed me that her family had moved to the Cove from Texas after she'd gained admission to Juilliard. She mentioned that she often went home to visit on the weekends. We exchanged numbers, and she told me she would be happy to help Winnie out if her interests turned to singing and performing.

A familiar, haughty voice interrupted our conversation.

"Beverly. I can't thank you enough for taking time away from your schedule to perform for us tonight. I've been looking for you. I want to introduce you to my son. I promised your mother I would make this event worthy of the time you had to take away from school. I apologize for not being able to set up a private meeting sooner. Win is incredibly busy, as I'm sure you know."

Colette appeared like a specter. Her snow-white hair was wrapped into a flawless twist, and she wore a glittery gold ensemble that sparkled from head to toe. She was doing a damn fine job of passing herself off as a false god. She didn't bother to look in my direction. She treated me like I was invisible, which was fine by me.

It saved me from forcing my expression away from the automatic scowl that took over my features the second I saw her.

My new friend didn't seem to appreciate Colette's cold shoulder on my behalf. "I'm very busy, as well. I told my mother I was happy to help because this event is for charity. I had no other motive." She leaned closer to me and whispered, "I'm only twenty-three. Who wants to date, let alone marry, an old, stuffy man like Win Halliday?"

I nearly choked on the sip of whiskey I'd just slugged back to avoid saying anything biting to Colette. The age difference between Win and the singer was enough to raise a few eyebrows, but the age gap was undeniably common in these circles. Rich men liked to have a young, beautiful woman on their arm. Of course, Beverly was a better match for Win in Colette's eyes. Any woman here would be.

The older woman wanted to drag the singer away, but a new rumble worked through the crowd that had nothing to do with the questions and contempt from my arrival with Win.

"Isn't that the Halliday bastard?"

"Who invited him?"

"He looks so much like Win."

"Does Colette know he's here?"

"Did the Hallidays decide to recognize him as a rightful heir?"

"He's so handsome."

"The press should follow him around since Win doesn't ever speak to them. I bet he has so much dirt to spill on the Hallidays."

I cocked my head to the side as I caught a slight glimpse of a tall, dark-haired man moving through the crowd like he owned the place. Alistair had a totally different vibe than Win. His was no less intimidating, but it didn't feel so oppressive. Win would hate it, but Alistair viewed him as a role model. I didn't tell the younger man that Win was secretly envious of his normal childhood with a loving family. In my heart, I guessed that Win would trade all the money he made for Halliday Inc. for a fraction of the love Alistair experienced.

Colette gritted her teeth and maneuvered in the intruder's direction. A dignified matriarch would never bulldoze through a crowd.

Even if she obviously wanted to. I caught Alistair's eye and gave him a slight finger wave in greeting. I liked his fearlessness. Then, Win appeared out of nowhere, grabbed my hand with his much bigger one, and forcefully pulled me out of the nearest exit.

"Hey, Chester. Let go of me. That hurts." I tugged on my hand and tried to break free as Win shoved me into the nearest bathroom and moved a 'Closed for Repairs' sign from a stall to the entrance. He shut the door and prowled toward me. I rubbed my wrist and watched with a guarded gaze.

Win whipped back around and stalked toward me like a predator. I backed into the sink and lifted my hands to his chest when he pinned me against the edge of the marble countertop. A stray puddle of water seeped into the fabric of my dress, but that wasn't what made me shiver.

The look in Win's storm-colored eyes pricked my skin and made all my senses go on high alert. It was unnerving to be on the receiving end of such intensity.

"Did you ask Alistair to meet you here?" His tone was icy.

I scoffed. "No. First of all, if you recall, I didn't know about this event until you sprung it on me last minute. Second, why would I want to subject anyone else to such a boring and purposeless evening? Alistair never mentioned that he was attending, and I didn't see it on his schedule. Even if I did, he's got just as much right to be here as the next rich son of a bitch. You should be thrilled to have another big fat bank account in attendance if this charade is really about helping people."

"I don't like him, Harvey." He practically growled the words next to my ear.

"I know you don't. But I *do* like him. He's not scared of your mother, and I need an ally like him if I'm going to make it through the next two years. I can't rely on you to have my back when it comes to her." The way he decided to ignore the strange happenings in the manor was proof that his allegiance was questionable.

Win blinked, and I noticed his eyelashes were unfairly long and thick. His eyebrows dipped and his voice deepened.

"Let me be clear, Channing. I. Don't. Like. Him."

I inhaled sharply and tried to push him away so I could breathe. His broad chest was unyielding, and his big body put off an immense amount of heat.

"And I don't like being dragged to this event and treated like an animal in the zoo. I never wanted any part of your life, Chester. You forced this on me, in case you forgot."

His eyes narrowed, and he seemed to freeze. "Not even me?"

I was confused and tilted my head to the side. "Not even you, what?"

"You don't want any part of my life, including me?"

"I..." I felt bewildered by the question because I was blindsided by the hint of longing in his voice. And then an all-consuming kiss suddenly slammed down onto my lips.

It was the first kiss we shared that didn't involve putting on a show.

It was the first kiss that didn't feel poisonous.

It was the first kiss that made me question whether I *wanted* him kissing me.

This kiss made me wonder if I was losing my damn mind.

Chapter Twelve

win

Channing wasn't the only one with a growing list of grievances. I was sick of unexplained things happening at the estate when I wasn't around. It was one thing to blame a teenager's overactive imagination. It was another that Channing had a detailed list of odd occurrences. I understood why she wanted cameras inside our wing, but my home was the single place I wasn't being watched. It made my skin crawl to think about adding surveillance to my private space. I didn't want to worry about Winnie. No security system was one hundred percent secure. If I installed one at home and it got hacked, I couldn't imagine the damage it would do or how big of a bargaining chip the footage would be in the wrong hands.

Channing firmly believed that the missing items would resurface in a sinister manner. She questioned if my mother might frame her with an evidence trail that led from a crime that would lead to Channing's arrest. It sounded diabolical, but my mother was indeed conniving and clever enough to frame someone. Which meant I had to be on high alert.

I was at my wit's end because my mother swore she wasn't behind the supposed haunting, and for once I believed her. I wasn't as convinced she didn't have someone messing with Channing on her behalf, but so far Rocco hadn't been able to find any evidence of that.. The more I pushed, the more ammunition it gave my mother to question Channing and Winnie's sanity. She accused me of enabling the redhead and warned that the growing paranoia would adversely affect my niece. Without concrete proof that she was involved, we were at a stalemate. It grated on my last nerve that my hard-won sanctuary was anything but peaceful.

I was furious whenever Channing left for the city to work for my half-brother. I understood it was a strategic move on her part, and that she only took the job to taunt my mother. I hated the mere thought of her breathing the same air as that bastard. I didn't want her to become too familiar with him. I didn't want her to be sympathetic to him. I didn't want her to get close to him or speak of him fondly. If she was going to hate a rich man, namely me, then I wanted her to hate *all* men who were well-to-do. However, if I made a move to have her fired, or forced Alistair to let her go, it would be an unforgivable offense in her eyes. I'd taken so much from her; it might break her if I demanded more. We had two years to be tied to one another. I didn't want Channing to be an empty shell when we parted ways. I spent so many years feigning disinterest to keep her safe. I wouldn't ruin all that hard work just because I was admittedly jealous.

The final thing that made my temper flare was the obvious mistake I made by dragging Channing to this event.

I knew she wouldn't want to go if I asked, so I forced her to come. Just like I coerced her into marrying me.

It was clear to me that she wouldn't attempt to blend in or create a favorable impression, but I had no idea how angry it would make me to witness her being blatantly ignored and silently judged. It was impossible for me to be blasé over how poorly she was treated. Everyone turned their heads when we walked in and instantly decided Channing didn't belong. My reaction was different. Amid a vast array of high-fashion clothing and precious gems, Channing left the biggest impression. Her imperfection in a sea of immaculate perfection took my breath away. Her hair was messy. Professionals did not do her makeup. She wasn't dressed to the nines. She didn't wear diamonds, but in contrast, the antique locket she wore around her neck had a hidden picture of Winnie on one side and her sister on the other. The value was immeasurable. But none of these social elites would understand that. The only time she smiled was when the singer engaged her in conversation. She didn't belong, and she made it clear she didn't want to. While everyone else found her worthy of ridicule, I was unable to take my eyes off her. Channing was like a spot of sunshine moving through a room full of storm clouds. I realized how wrong I'd been to think she was a bad influence on Winnie.

It was much better for my niece to take after her aunt than any of these women full of false pretenses.

When I saw my half-brother enter the room, all my functioning brain cells stopped working. All I could feel was jealousy. I refused to share her with him. I'd given so much to my father's mistake. I wouldn't let that bastard take my *wife* away from me. It didn't matter that our marriage wasn't real; the feelings that were percolating deep within my darkest places were.

Since I didn't want to make any more demands on Channing, I decided it was best to ask for forgiveness for kissing her instead of permission.

I trapped her between my body and the bathroom counter. I was past worrying about being interrupted or whether this was proper behavior in public. All I could think was that I wanted to kiss her. I wanted those bothersome people outside to know I was fortunate to have her on my arm for the evening. Not the other way around. There was so little in my life I'd ever wanted to claim. It unnerved me that the first thing I was ready to disrupt my stagnant but successful life was this woman. She'd been a nuisance in my life for so long. How did I miss that being near her made me feel like I deserved to have something that was just for me? I had everything, but none of it could fill the gaping void where my heart was supposed to be.

Channing put her hands on my chest to keep a slight space between our bodies. She gasped when I kissed her, but she didn't pull away. Since her mouth was open in surprise, I slipped my tongue between her teeth so I could taste her fully. There was an intoxicating flavor of expensive whiskey and what I assumed was pure sunshine lingering on her tongue. Her hand curled into a fist where it rested against my collarbone, and I could feel a tremor shake her body. I couldn't tell if she was trembling with fear or enjoyment. I was fine with either response. As long as it wasn't revulsion, I would take it.

Her lips were soft. Her hair was silky. Her skin was smooth. She made sweet sounds while I kissed her with everything I was worth.

I could count on one hand the times I'd lost my head, and I would still have fingers left over. Ever since I decided that joining forces with Channing was a ticket to freedom, I forgot every hardwired rule my mother had drilled into me. I willfully ignored who I was and what I was supposed to be, because when I was with her, I felt like I was someone better than I had ever been allowed to be.

I fisted a hand in her hair and pulled her head back to deepen the kiss. Her lips moved underneath mine, and her tongue started to twist and turn as mine flicked across hers. My skin heated and my breath caught. I used my free hand to catch the hem of her dress and pull it up along the soft line of her thigh. The material wasn't anything to get excited about, but the flesh hidden under it felt like velvet. She had never been a woman who was waif thin, so there were more than a handful of curves to fill my palms.

I planned to stop the caress when my hand landed by her knee. However, my control wasn't as steady as it normally was. The next instant, my hand held her bare hip and her dress pooled in dark folds over my forearm. My thumb played with the edge of her barely there underwear. Channing stilled and pulled away. I bent my head so that I could kiss down the side of her arched neck. Her pulse was fluttering rapidly, and her breath was raspy. Her hands on my chest flattened as she pressed back, silently asking me to give her some space.

"What are you doing, Chester? We are not friends. And we are most certainly not lovers. This is outside the realm of whatever we are."

I licked a lengthy line from the base of her throat until my lips landed next to her ear. I whispered, "We are married, Harvey." It seemed like the most obvious answer to her question. Didn't married people touch each other? Didn't they kiss like their lives depended on it? Didn't they want each other beyond reason?

I caught her earlobe between my teeth and moved my hand across the quivering surface of her thigh. I wanted to sink into her warmth. I wanted to get lost in her body within her embrace.

"We aren't married for real. We're enemies at best, Win."

I froze. It was the first time she called me Win. It was always *Chester* because she liked how much it bugged me.

I liked the way my name sounded when she said it.

It sounded like victory.

"We can be enemies — enemies with benefits." I thought she would walk away from our arrangement with enough to make it worth her while. And yet, I kept finding. things I wanted from her. I was racking up a debt that might not be payable. "We should be on the same side of this one thing, Harvey." It would make the next two years far easier to bear.

I regained my momentum and licked the shell of her ear. I shifted my hand between her legs and touched her through the thin material of her panties. She didn't close her thighs or pull back in protest. One of her hands curled around my neck as I kissed her temple. I shifted my hold from her hair to her back so I could pull her closer. Her other hand grasped a handful of my hair. Her skin was damp and fragrant. I really wanted to strip her naked and explore her from head to toe. She felt so much more alive than the partners I typically took to bed.

Nothing was practiced or planned about her response to me.

She couldn't hide the fact that she liked the way I touched her and enjoyed the way my kisses made her feel. She couldn't cover her hesitation. The way she responded was almost shy. The hesitation was endearing. I wasn't sure I'd ever been with a woman who didn't want anything from me and was unsure of taking what I offered.

The way her hands were holding on to different parts of me for dear life made my blood pump furiously and sent my head spinning. It was the first time she'd touched me in a way that betrayed her typical frosty attitude. She was clutching me like she never wanted to let go. That feeling overrode the slight sting from the frantic way she pulled my hair.

I continued to stroke her through the thin barrier and watched as her chest and neck flushed a bright pink. She gulped and her eyes widened. Her head tilted back with no help from me, and her grip went from pushing me away to pulling me closer. My shirt was going to be a wrinkled mess and there would be no hiding what we'd been doing in this bathroom.

That's what I wanted.

I wanted my half-brother to know. I wanted my mother to be aware of the uncontrollable desire she was up against. I wanted all those people with more money than compassion to understand that *I* was lucky enough to have a real gem in my hands. A jewel that shone brighter than any they brought out for special occasions.

My lips skimmed across her jaw as I let my fingers dip beneath the garment that was keeping me from touching bare skin and delicate folds. She was wet, making my touch glide easily to her most sensitive spots and right to her fluttering opening.

I wanted to imprint the sound she made on my brain. I memorized the way she moved, how her eyes dilated, and what made her body writhe. Those would be recollections I planned to lock away and hold close forever.

She was silky and hot.

I wanted more than my fingers deep inside of her. The thought made my head spin.

I kissed her again. This time, she kissed me back. Our tongues tangled. Our lips collided. Our teeth bit and nipped hungrily. I caught her chin with my free hand and held her in place, preventing her from pulling away until the last of her breath ran out.

Her body clamped down on my fingers moving inside of her. Every quake and quiver made my mind spin and had my sanity slip further away. I was not a man who indulged in much. I had every vice beaten out of me when I was young. It was a novel experience to covet something. I squeezed her jaw and forced her to look at me while my fingers moved deeper, and I flicked my thumb against her clit. Her gigantic eyes popped larger, and the pink blush crept onto her cheeks. It wasn't just her hair that made her look like a strawberry ripe for the picking.

I very much wanted to devour her.

Channing whimpered, and her fingernails dug into the back of my neck. The slight sting sent tingles of pleasure shooting through my nerves. I was literally hot under the collar. I wanted to strip off my custom suit so we could be skin-to-kin.

"Win..." The way she breathed my name made my dick hard.

"Channing..." The way I whispered hers made her come on my fingers and her entire body trembled.

"Did you just call me by my name?" She sounded dazed. Her head dropped to my shoulder and her shoulders shook as she worked to catch her breath and pull herself together. The words were thin and bewildered.

"Didn't you use mine?" I pulled my hand free but kept her caged against the counter. "Don't you think we should be on a first-name basis, all things considered?"

She sniffed and pushed me backward with a hand. She tried to smooth her hair, but her hands were still shaking. She turned to face the mirror and gave our rumpled appearance a startled look. I handed her one of the monogrammed towels so she could clean herself up. There wasn't much that could be done about her soaked under garments. A fact that made me strangely proud. She wiggled out of them and tossed the minuscule garment into the trash can. Now that she was fully naked under her dress, I was going to have a tough time focusing on anything else.

"I don't think we should be *anything* given the circumstances. This feels like the start of trouble I can't afford to get myself into. We both know what happens when someone from my family plays with fire near someone from your family. Neither of us have recovered from the flames, Chester."

I lifted a hand to the top of her head and let it drift down the length of her hair. Since she was always slightly ruffled, her appearance seemed less illicit than mine. My clothes were wrinkled, her lipstick was smeared across my mouth, and my hair was sticking up from her fingers clutching at it.

I wanted to tell her I was exceptionally good at putting out fires. I'd been doing it for the Hallidays for years.

I didn't get the chance to say anything because someone pushed the door open, and the last person I wanted to see, aside from my mother, stuck their head inside the bathroom from the antechamber.

"Channing, are you in here? I've been looking for you everywhere. You've been gone a concerning amount of time. They served dinner and are moving onto the silent auction. Win is missing, too. Lady Halliday is about to have a heart attack." I gritted my teeth when I heard my half-brother use Channing's nickname for my mother.

Alistair DeVere looked like he belonged in my family. While Archie took after our mother, both DeVere and I favored our father. He was a younger, slicker, happier, better adjusted version of me. I thought I couldn't resent him more if I tried. Then Channing took him under her wing, and all my negative feelings toward him multiplied.

Channing shoved her elbow into my stomach and stepped away from me. She reached up to smooth her hair and belatedly tried to repair her messy makeup.

"I'll be right out." Her voice was steady, as if our tryst did not affect her in the slightest. "I didn't think anyone would miss me for a few minutes."

Alistair snorted. "Most of those people wouldn't notice if a bomb went off in that room. But Win is missing, and you were the last person seen with him. Did you put the sign outside the bathroom so you could hide?"

Channing stepped forward and gave me a sharp look indicating she wanted me to remain mute.

But I had no intention of letting her leave with Alistair or lose the opportunity to make my position in Channing's life — and soon, her bed — clear.

I stepped next to her and met the surprised gaze from the brother I refused to acknowledge. "I put the sign outside the door. I didn't want to be interrupted. Harvey and I had some important business to discuss."

The kid's achingly familiar gaze skimmed over us, and a smirk broke out on his stupidly attractive face. "Looks like it was a pretty intense conversation, but you better get back to the gala. Your mother is ready to send in the National Guard to find you. I overheard someone complain that they paid over a hundred grand to get their single daughter seated at your table for dinner. I think your mother plans to have a bachelor auction with exactly one candidate on the block."

I grabbed Channing's hand before she could slip away. I squeezed her fingers and met my brother's curious gaze with a pointed one of my own.

"That's impossible. My mother knows that Channing and I are married. She can't auction me off, regardless of what she promised."

I wanted him to know Channing was off limits. To my surprise, Alistair barely reacted to the news.

"I know that you've got a shady contract marriage going on. That was one of the first things Channing told me when I hired her. Your mother conveniently seems to have forgotten that you're spoken for.

Which doesn't surprise me. She's treated you like a pet since you were young." He wiggled his dark eyebrows at Channing. "Do you want to get out of here? I wasn't officially invited. They were about to kick me out when I decided to find you. This party isn't any fun. I can show you a wild time since you're in the city for the night."

Before Channing could agree, I pushed Alistair out the bathroom door and stepped back into the busy hotel. Several pairs of curious eyes found the three of us.

"Channing's my plus one. We're not staying much longer. She's coming back to my apartment with me, and I'll take her home tomorrow." It was a direct declaration of ownership.

Alistair lifted his eyebrows and hummed softly. "Shouldn't Channing get to decide if she wants to leave with me or wait for you?"

I clenched my teeth. She should have had a choice, but I was worried it would be him. I couldn't handle that, so it was best to snatch the decision from her.

"Come on. If my mother is determined to sell me off to the highest bidder, we need to ensure that person is you." I pulled Channing toward the banquet room. I heard her tell Alistair she would contact him later. I was pleased that she didn't seem upset that I dragged her away from my half-brother. I gave her a hard look and saw her smile fade. I cleared my throat as the frost surrounded us once we stepped back into the high-end circus.

It didn't feel like we were playing with fire the way Channing warned. We were toying with something that could be harder to control than a firestorm.

Feelings were far scarier than flames.

Chapter Thirteen
channing

I was shell-shocked from what Win and I had done in the bathroom. There wasn't enough whiskey in the world to excuse the way I lost my mind the second his hands touched my most intimate places. I could chalk it up to my year of self-care and celibacy. It'd been a while since I'd felt a man's touch and even longer since I let my wants and needs override my common sense. If someone told me a couple of weeks ago that Winchester Halliday would be the reason I let my resolution to spend a year alone fall by the wayside, I would've laughed in their face. The man historically made me want to fight — not fuck. There was no denying that I felt incredibly turned on as soon as he caressed me. I was supposed to be past the messy, rushed fingering stage in my romantic life. I thought I was beyond attraction to a man I could never be with.

Leave it to Win to send all my convictions tumbling to the ground. It seemed like he wouldn't rest until he had dismantled every certainty I'd had about him. He even turned the idea of being enemies into something sexier and more compelling. Who said only friends could have benefits? Was it necessary to like each other to sleep together? They said the only emotion that could rival the intensity of love was hate, and I had plenty of that where Win was concerned. It was possible that I could want him without having any affection for him. People had relationships all the time based on lust and mutual need rather than love. I was the weirdo who fell head-over-heels at the drop of a hat and started planning a future as soon as someone showed an interest in me because I didn't want to spend the rest of my life alone.

I wanted to ruin Win just as much as I wanted to fuck him.

He was right. We were married. We were stuck together for two years, no matter what. When I vowed to be alone and focus on myself, I did so with the idea that I would come out of the sexual drought a better version of myself. There was no way to anticipate that Win would turn my social life into a wasteland. Either I feast on him or suffer through a carnal famine until the contract was up. With only those two options, of course I was going to eat. If Win was willing to be a warm body and willing cock to meet my needs while the contracted years dragged on, who was I to say no? Plus, when would someone like me get another chance to fuck a billionaire? An extremely handsome billionaire, at that. A billionaire I spoke of often, according to my second ex-husband. Maybe I'd always been a bit curious what it would be like with Win. I would never give those troublesome thoughts room to grow. I didn't have to like Win for him to get me off. He easily proved that.

It was far too easy to talk myself into thinking that enemies with benefits might not be such a bad idea. And it would make Colette apoplectic if her precious heir lowered himself to roll around in the sheets with a commoner like me. Anything that would raise her blood pressure was a win in my book.

After we went back to the banquet, his anxious assistant and his mother immediately whisked Win away. He didn't look happy that he had to leave me behind. Alistair graciously decided to stay to keep me company. He even offered to get me another drink. I declined, since I'd gotten myself in trouble after the first one.

I could feel Win glaring at me from the stage where he was giving a stilted speech, thanking everyone for coming and for their generous donations. He made a stale joke about the food barely being worth the price of admission. It was obvious he was trying to hurry through the formalities, but his mother refused to let him. Colette clutched his arm and kept him rooted to the spot as she took over the microphone, playing the generous and humble host. I looked around the room for my new friend, Beverly. I wanted to introduce her to Alistair. They were close to the same age, and both were talented and driven. I thought they would have a lot in common. I wasn't a matchmaker given my horrible track record, but I wanted to try my hand with the two of them. Before I could locate her, Win's head of security stopped in front of me and Alistair. The large, muscular man looked fierce enough to make anyone take a step back.

I was used to him lurking in the shadows since I'd been at the Halliday estate. Alistair wasn't as familiar with Win's team, though, and made an audible noise as he shifted his weight nervously away from me.

"The boss said you weren't invited, kid. He wants you to leave." The man's gravelly voice was no nonsense and flat as day-old soda. "I'm happy to escort you out."

Alistair gave a low chuckle and lifted his eyebrows. "I came as a plus one. I paid the entrance fee and bid in the auction. I have as much right to be here as anyone else."

Rocco's expression didn't fluctuate in the slightest. He continued to stare at the younger man to the point that I couldn't handle the awkwardness any longer.

"I wasn't invited, either. And I didn't pay a dime to get in. If Chester is kicking people out based on those requirements, then you should ask me to leave, as well." I could feel Win's eyes on me from across the room as I confronted his go-to person. "Let's go, Alistair."

I turned toward Alistair to push him in the direction of the exit. He protested, but Rocco quickly held out a hand to stop me from leaving.

"Mr. Halliday made it clear that you're supposed to wait for him to finish his speech, Ms. Harvey. Please don't make me make you stay."

Alistair frowned and opened his mouth to argue about the thinly veiled threat. I was used to Win and his people threatening me into getting their way. I'd learned that to circumvent the pressure, it was best to pretend that you weren't afraid of your opponent.

"If I 'make you' cause a scene to keep me here, Lady Halliday will have your boss's head. And then he'll have yours. If you make the 'kid' leave, I'm going with him. Tell Chester I said he can suck it up. Family is family. He should know that better than anyone else."

Rocco and I had a tense staring contest. I could see him weigh the pros and cons of hauling Alistair away. He must've decided I wasn't worried about embarrassing myself or Win and beat a hasty retreat. I shook my head at his broad back and faced a timid Alistair.

"I don't know why you're so determined to have a relationship with Win. He's more trouble than he's worth. And he comes with his very own Wicked Witch." I poked him in the arm playfully and noticed the wistful look in his eyes. The gray gaze was lighter and brighter than Win's. Unlike his older brother, he couldn't weaponize his stare. It made the difference in their upbringing obvious. "Your family loves you. I don't understand why you're beating your head against a brick wall to get something from a Halliday. They can barely tolerate each other. I'm not sure they know what love is."

Alistair gave me a lopsided smile and shoved his hands into the pockets of his pinstriped pants. He was dressed in a custom suit that was more stylish than a lot of the others in the room. It only took a glance to know this kid didn't come from old money. He was new money through and through. He stood out in an entirely different way than I did.

"I don't know why I want to be acknowledged by him so badly, either. I owe him a lot for stepping up when my sister was sick. I admire his business acumen and the way he handles himself. When I went into design, I did so because it was the best way to stay adjacent to the Halliday's business. Win buys and develops properties. I make those assets beautiful. In my heart, I've always wanted to partner with him on a major project. I won't ever get the opportunity to know my real father. I guess in my mind, Win is the closest I'll get to understanding what I may have missed." He poked me back and forced a smile to dispel the gloomy mood. "And it's fun to get him worked up. The sound an iceberg makes when it cracks isn't something everyone gets to hear."

It was an interesting comparison. I was all too familiar with that particular sound when it came to Win.

"Don't hold your breath waiting for Win to come around. He's stubborn. And more importantly, he's still grieving the loss of his other brother. He never talks about it, but he adored Archie. I'm not sure he has room in his itty-bitty heart for another brother just yet."

He was furious when Archie had come back home with his tail between his legs. I always got the sense that Win wanted his brother to keep his wife and daughter as far away from the Cove as possible. Even though he missed him and was alone to carry out Colette's bidding, he didn't want Archie to succumb to the pressure of being a Halliday. He wouldn't wish that fate on his half-brother even if he didn't acknowledge him or their relationship. "You're a decent man, Alistair. Take the money and run."

He gave me a look out of the corner of his eye. "Is that what you're going to do?"

I blinked because I rarely remembered that I would be a wealthy woman once my marriage with Win was dead and buried. "I'm not exactly the running type. I'll slowly stroll away. Or ride away on the cool bike I just bought." My situation was different because I'd never managed to get the Hallidays fully out of my life. I had a lingering fear I would still be involved with Win even after our deal was done. Until Winnie was old enough to make major life decisions on her own, I was stuck with him. "And I don't know if I'll take the money. I don't want Win to have anything he can hold over me for the rest of my life. You should give me a raise and a promotion when the time is right."

I was only kidding, but Alistair nodded and told me, "I plan on it. I didn't know you had a background in antiques and collectibles.

We're always looking for authentic, one-of-a-kind pieces for our clients. You can work for my sourcing and acquisitions department when you have the availability."

"I'm not qualified for a salaried position like that." I repeated what I told Win when he thought he could get me through the back door at one of the exclusive auction houses. "I don't have the education or contacts that a career like that would require."

"You have real-life experience in handling customers and evaluating objects. Plus, you're likable, and you seamlessly fit into any situation. You make people feel comfortable. You seem trustworthy at first glance. You're disarmingly honest. You possess a lot of qualities that cannot be taught. They have to be earned through experience, Channing. That's why I hired you."

I couldn't believe this kid was nearly a decade younger than me. He sounded like he'd lived a thousand lives. He sounded very different than Win. One was arrogant and told me he would make a place for me if it was what I wanted. The other was encouraging and assured me I could find a place that was mine, because I'd earned it.

I gave him a stunned look. I disclosed none of my previous employment when I went to work for him. All I shared was that we had a common enemy, and if he hired me, it would benefit both of us and infuriate Colette. I had no intention of using Alistair to secure a legitimate job in the future.

There was thunderous applause as Win and his mother stepped off the stage. People immediately surrounded them. Colette was holding onto her son's sleeve to keep him by her side, but it was a futile effort. It only took a moment for Rocco to help Win navigate the crowd until he was standing in front of me and his half-brother.

He glared at Alistair and reached for my hand. I wanted to avoid his hold because I was still emotionally unsteady over what happened in the bathroom, but he didn't give me a choice. He tugged me to his side and muttered, "Let's go."

His tone left no room for argument.

Part of me wanted to be contrary and make his exit difficult. Only, I was done with the dog and pony show. And I was acutely aware that my underwear was still in the bathroom trash can, just waiting for someone a tad too curious to stumble across.

"Stay clear of Colette. Don't tangle with her without backup." I gave Alistair a wave goodbye and let Win drag me out of the fancy hotel. When we got outside, my skin prickled against the chill and the breeze tossed my hair around my face. I was fairly sure I'd never been in more of a state of disarray than I was tonight. I wondered if it was obvious to everyone who looked at me that I'd had Win's hands all up under my basic black dress. It felt like I was wearing my lapse in judgment loud and clear.

"Why are you so nice to DeVere? I thought you had a predisposition to dislike anyone who came from money." Win pulled open the door to the limo before the driver could and stuffed me inside. I nearly knocked my head on the doorjamb and growled at him in protest as he followed.

"Alistair didn't come from money. He inherited it. He grew up in a very sitcom-like family. He didn't face any tumultuous waves of judgment until he got tangled up with the Hallidays. I understand how that feels. We get along so well because we're just trying to ride out the same storm." I shoved my tangled hair out of my face and glared at him. "You sound jealous."

The words were mocking because I couldn't fathom that scenario.

I stopped breathing when he responded, "I am."

I wasn't sure how to process his honesty. Did I dare believe him?

I leaned my forehead against the window and let the cool glass combat the heat rising in my cheeks.

"There isn't a reason to be jealous, Chester. Alistair feels like my little brother. Which is exactly how he wants you to see him. If you think we're too close, or that I'm too kind, you only have yourself to blame. He sees me as a substitute for you."

"We're back to Chester? What do I have to do to get you to call me Win again?" He sounded like he was at the end of his rope. It was rare to see him so exasperated.

I laughed, and it fogged the window. "Since the only time we don't argue is when our mouths are busy doing something else, I'll call you Win when you make me forget you've always been Chester."

He caught my hair in his hands, which startled me. Win directed me across the leather seat until I was pressed against his side. His eyes locked on mine. There were chaotic emotions in the unreadable depths of his gaze that made me feel like I was the lone survivor of an unrelenting gale.

"Are you saying yes to being enemies with benefits?" I shivered from head to toe as he dragged the tip of his nose across my cheek and down the side of my neck, then nuzzled into the hollow of my throat.

I fought myself from surrendering to this touch. I wanted to keep some of my dignity by the end of the night. "I'm not having sex with you in this limo." The poor, street-smart girl caught up with the obscenely wealthy CEO was so fucking cliché it made my teeth ache. After what happened to Willow, I wasn't interested in living out a real-life version of *My Fair Lady*. Being extraordinary wasn't on my bucket list.

Figuring out how to be happy was.

Win's low laugh brought goosebumps out on my skin and my thoughts scattered in different directions. "Tonight? Or ever?"

I found it a lot harder to answer his question than it should have been. Especially after he bent his head and kissed me breathless for the second time that night.

Chapter Fourteen

win

My city apartment was in a high-rise building that had an amazing view. At night, the lights from the city reflected off the water and gave the whole place a dreamy, otherworldly feel. It was decorated similarly to my suite at the manor, with top-of-the-line furnishings and fixtures. It was very bland. My surroundings were uninteresting and lifeless until I dragged Channing kicking and screaming into my staid environment. When I allowed myself to look at things through her bright and curious gaze, the whole lot seemed lacking. I included myself when I ran down a mental list of everything she'd openly disdained since I forced her back to the Cove. I could not envision any other woman so obviously disgusted by the grandiose display of wealth she encountered every single second she spent with me.

The fact that my life was too loud, too much, too cold, too superficial, too extraordinary for Channing is what kept me circling back to her. Even when what she craved most was something ordinary and simple. I found myself toying with her commonplace wants and needs. I could hand out money, jewelry, business opportunities, and make profitable connections. I did not have the first idea what it would take to offer even the smallest part of my heart to someone. I was starting to see all the less obvious risks Archie had taken when he fell for Willow.

I thought he was weak for crawling back home and cruel for forcing Willow to endure my mother's wrath. I was bitter because I always believed he would still be alive if he had stayed away. Now, I could understand his desire to make sure his family had the best of everything, even if those benefits and advantages weren't wanted. Similar to Channing, my brother's wife never wanted much. A man who was a supportive father and a loving husband was more than enough for her. She asked for things no Halliday knew how to give, but my younger brother came the closest.

It was a shame close didn't count when it came to being enough for another person. Either you were or you weren't. The minute Archie brought his family back to the wolves' den that was our childhood home, he stopped being the man Willow fell in love with. He immediately reverted to a Halliday. Not a soul had a better idea of how hard a Halliday was to love than I did.

I would never make the mistake of thinking I could buy or manipulate my way into Channing's good graces. However, I was callous and confident enough to believe I had the skills required to negotiate and seduce a path between her legs and into her bed.

She wordlessly followed me into the bedroom like she was resigned to our shared fate.

I could not resist the opportunity to get as close as possible to the only person in my life who didn't pretend with me. It was refreshing and painfully attractive. For years, I set myself up as her combatant because I could never be her equal.

I functioned as a shield. I didn't want our niece caught in the crossfire between basic and billions. I kept Winnie isolated from her aunt's regular life because it was the only thing I could never give her. As a Halliday heir, she faced a life full of everything except the little things that mattered. I grew up barely knowing either of my parents. Making a happy home was never a priority. There was no heart and soul in my life, only drive and ambition. Even now, I couldn't tell you my mother's favorite color or to whom my father looked up. Winnie was fortunate that she had Channing, because the teenager never had to question what it felt like to be loved unconditionally. She was gifted more than any Halliday who came before her.

"What are you thinking about?" Channing's sharp question broke through my wandering thoughts. "If the answer is anything other than what you're going to do with me when you have me naked and willing, you can forget about taking this evening any further."

She sat up on the edge of the king-size bed. It was easy to get her nude since her underwear was long gone and she hadn't worn a bra since the back of her dress was cut so low. I tossed the cheap black garment somewhere on the floor next to her well-worn heels. She was right. My focus should be on her pale skin dotted with small freckles and her wild hair, which looked exceptionally sexy, tousled and messy from my hands. She was like a Renaissance painting, lush and curved. Everything about her appeared soft and seductive, as if she were begging to be touched and revered.

"I'm thinking that my bed looks much better with you in it. The entire apartment feels brighter with you here." My tone was gruff. I kept my hands gentle as I reached out to tuck some of her strawberry hair behind her ears so I could see her expression clearly while she gazed up at me. "I never realized that I was surrounded by so much gray before. I paid a fortune for an interior designer. How did it still end up so dull?"

Channing's eyebrows lifted as she reached out to unfasten the closure of my dress slacks. My jacket, shirt, and tie were somewhere on the floor with her clothes. Typically, I tried to treat my things with more care. However, as soon as Channing's dress came off, all I cared about was getting my hands and mouth on as much of her bare skin as possible.

"The gray matches your eyes — and your personality." The corner of her mouth lifted in a lopsided grin as she tugged down the fabric. "It's not bad. You just need an accent color to liven everything up a little. Just like a bright yellow umbrella in the rain."

An accent color. Something that could break up the monotony. When I was younger, playing the violin was the accent color that allowed me to see past my austere surroundings. After giving up the instrument to follow in my father's footsteps, I stopped looking for anything that might not fit into the sterile, strict life where I was stuck. Unwittingly, I'd built myself another high-class jail cell and tossed away the key. Channing's presence opened my eyes and reminded me there was a world of colors beyond the gray. She was my current accent color. I was smart enough to know that quitting her would be much more difficult than walking away from my previous passion.

Once my pants were down far enough for my cock to spring free, Channing pushed me back a step with a hand on my stomach. She used her thumb to trace along one of the lines that delineated my ab muscles and gave a low whistle of appreciation.

"When do you have time to work on a six-pack? I thought all billionaires were pasty and doughy from sitting in meetings with other rich people all day. You don't have even a hint of a dad-bod. With your sweet tooth, you shouldn't look this good without your clothes on."

I grunted when she used her fingernails to scratch a trail through the coarse hair that arrowed down to the base of my throbbing dick. I wanted to persuade her to change her mind when she nixed the idea of fucking in the limo, but I figured I'd pushed her far enough after getting her off in the bathroom. Every inch of my being was achingly aware of how lucky I was to have this woman falling to her knees in front of me.

"I work out a couple times a week and play tennis regularly. Winnie likes to swim. I try to hit the pool or the ocean with her as often as possible. My mother would never tolerate a pasty, doughy Halliday heir. She thinks I'm a direct reflection of her. I can't tell you how many times she's tried to get me to dye the silver in my hair." I gave a dry chuckle. "She's forgotten that she's the reason I went gray so early."

Channing wrapped her hand around my cock and lowered the leaking tip toward her mouth. "You actually know how to defy her? I never would've guessed."

I shoved my hands into her hair and pulled her closer to my painfully hard erection. I nearly forgot my name when her lips touched the tip. Her breath was hot and moist as it drifted over the sensitive surface of my skin.

"Can we not mention my mother when we are about to fuck?" Talk about a mood killer. "Or ever." I'd had enough of the subject, frankly.

Channing hummed her agreement. The next second, her tongue darted out to lick along the leaking slit pressed against her soft lips. I sucked in a breath and forced myself not to yank her head forward to swallow my whole cock down. I was used to civilized, choreographed sex. I didn't know what to do with the primal urges this woman brought out in me.

My breath caught as she swirled her tongue around the tapered head she drew into her mouth. Her grasp tightened on the base of my cock; the pressure made my hips push forward unconsciously. A tingle shot up my spine, and I lost the ability to form a coherent thought. The deeper she took me in, the further away my sanity slipped. The last time I let myself surrender to sensation and get lost in indescribable feelings was when I created beautiful music that came from my soul. Eons passed between that moment and this one. If anyone ever asked, I would gladly leave my foolish childhood dreams behind if I could have more of this — more of her.

Her tongue swirled and slicked along every inch she could take into her mouth. Her fist slid along the damp skin, creating a new sensation that made my nerve endings tingle. When the head of my erection hit her soft palate and she swallowed, I forgot I was trying to maintain control and keep a fragment of decorum. I used my grip on her hair to pull her closer and force farther into the heated cavern surrounding me. Channing gave a slight whimper. It was hard to tell if the sound was protest or pleasure.

Her eyes glimmered, and the way her face flushed, it seemed like she liked it. The hand wrapped around the base of my cock tightened, and I hissed when I felt the point of her fingernail trail along the thick vein that pulsed on the underside of my erection. The tip pressed at the back of her throat dripped uncontrollably in response. I was like a toy she was playing with. Channing knew exactly where to touch, how to stroke, when to swallow. I reacted to whatever she did effortlessly.

For the first time in a long time, I was able to shut out everything else and focus on one single thing.

Channing Harvey.

My entire world narrowed to her and how she made me feel.

At this moment, I didn't feel like the CEO of Halliday Inc. I didn't feel as though I was Colette Halliday's son.

I felt like a man. A man who desperately needed to lose himself inside of the woman in front of him. There were no checks and balances between me and Channing at the moment. If there were, I would be lacking.

I let out a faint sound as Channing's free hand skimmed across her full breasts. Her pebbled nipples were a perfect princess pink that darkened when her fingers toyed with them. The freckles I'd never noticed before looked like a tiny galaxy spread across her creamy skin. I wanted to kiss all of them and get her puckered nipples between my teeth. When I felt the edge of her teeth against my straining cock, I abruptly pulled away from her mouth. Her lips were wet and puffy. Her eyes were wide and glassy.

She was the sexiest thing I'd ever seen.

I hoisted her up and pushed her back toward the bed. She watched me kick off my pants and lean over to fetch a condom from the bedside table. While I slid the latex down the length of my dick, Channing continued to move her hands over her body. One hand caressed her breasts while the other disappeared between her legs. She moaned loudly, and I could see that her fingers were glistening and wet. If there was anything hotter than knowing that a woman got hot while sucking off her partner, I didn't have a clue what it was.

I stepped between her legs and bent to lick the peak of the nipple trapped between her playful fingers. I put one hand next to her head to brace my weight and used the other to wrap one of her legs around my waist. When her heel dug into my ass, I pressed my hips forward and felt the back of her fingers and her heat as I aligned my cock with her entrance.

I switched my attention to her other breast and pulled a full nipple into my mouth. I used my tongue and teeth to tease the tiny bud into a rigid peak and brushed my erection against her moving fingers. When Channing gasped for breath, I lifted my head to kiss her.

Her lips were a touch swollen and tender from my relentless onslaught of kisses in the back of the limo. Channing was the only woman I'd ever sloppily made out with. The only woman I'd kissed in a hungry, desperate way. I should be ashamed of how needy I was becoming around her. Instead, I reveled in it.

I wasn't a man who knew what it was like to *need* something. It was novel. And it was enlightening.

I dropped a barely there kiss on her parted lips and asked, "Are you going to let me in?"

I could shove myself inside of her with no tact, the way I invaded the rest of her life. But here, I needed her explicit agreement. I had no qualms about taking anything else, but it was necessary for us to share this defining moment. It was explicitly different from all the ways I'd ever felt.

Rather than giving me an answer, Channing grasped my waiting cock. She guided the tip into her wet entrance. All it took was a slight thrust, and I was buried deep inside of her. We both moaned and her back arched off the bed.

"Win."

"Channing."

The names burst out simultaneously. Our eyes locked. She shuddered while I stiffened.

What was in a name?

Turns out, a lot.

We couldn't hide from one another behind throwaway nicknames. We were just two people trying to get as close as possible, searching for something that would fill in a few of the missing pieces they shared.

At first, I took things easy, moving within her nice and slow. Every clench of her body, every shaky breath, went straight to my head. The wetter she became and the noisier she got, the faster I moved. The kisses we shared were enough to bruise our lips, but the pain made the pleasure clearer. When she moved her fingers back to her body to stroke and fondle her clit, I couldn't hold back anymore. I released the breast that was cupped in my palm and shifted my grasp to the back of her thigh. Her muscles tensed when I stood and pulled her close to the edge of the bed so I could move more freely. She made a little sound each time I pulled back and thrust forward. Channing tossed her head from side to side and closed her eyes as her body started to flutter and pulse around mine.

I liked the way her fingers felt when they rode along the top of my dick as she continued to touch herself while I hammered into her like I'd turned into a feral beast. Her chest heaved and her entire body turned a rosy pink. When she moaned my name and I felt her release rush around my body, I lost the last remnants of my control. It was honestly a miracle I'd lasted this long considering I'd been semi-hard since our tryst in the bathroom. My fingers dug into her flesh, and her name tripped off my tongue as if it were the only word I knew how to speak.

Pure pleasure spread from the lowest part of my spine and blazed throughout my body. My vision blurred for a heated moment, and my lungs ceased working. I felt her everywhere. Even in places I was certain were long, cold and numb — like my heart. I fully let myself go and surrendered to every fiery, foreign sensation. I'd never felt less like a Halliday in my life; I would never give up this feeling of freedom and release.

I was deeply relieved that I'd tied her to me for the next two years.

I had plenty of time to figure my feelings out and make hers change.

After all, I was trained by the best to be one persuasive son of a bitch.

Chapter Fifteen

channing

I woke up groggily when my phone rang. I groped around on the unfamiliar nightstand, knocking over a glass of water and sending more than one condom wrapper to the floor. My hair was hanging in a tangled mess in front of my face. I could barely see Salome's name on the screen. I felt worse than the day of my courthouse nuptials when I had the hangover from hell. Right now, my whole body throbbed, and muscles I didn't even know could be strained from overuse were screaming in protest. I groaned as I answered the call. I squinted at the time and was surprised to see it was well into the afternoon. I could hardly move, but the other side of the bed was icy cold, indicating Win was long gone. I didn't hear him get up or sense him place the glass of water next to me on the nightstand. The small act of consideration tickled the edges of my heart. I solemnly and silently ordered the stupid thing not to read too much into the events of the past night because he was still enemy number one for threatening my mom and friends. No amount of mind-blowing sex could erase his evil deeds. I forcibly turned my attention to the phone call with my best friend.

"What's up?" I coughed to clear my throat. My voice sounded even rougher than normal after an evening screaming Win's name.

I heard Salome laugh. I sat up in the massive bed and tugged the wrinkled sheet to cover my bare body. I was sure I looked as utterly debauched as I felt.

"I waited for you to call and tell me how the party went last night. It was your first date with your fake husband. I know the tea from the gala must be piping hot. I saw some pictures from the event that are trending." Salome's tone was playful, but I could hear a hint of concern underneath the merriment. She was worried when I told her I refused to play dress-up. I had thick skin, but it was hard for anyone to constantly be found unworthy. Salome let it be known she was concerned that my feelings might be hurt, and my self-confidence could take a hit after I spent the evening with a bunch of judgmental socialites.

I looked at the mess I'd made on the floor, thinking I could really use that glass of water.

"It wasn't too bad. Not everyone was as awful as I imagined. Although, I met a lovely young opera singer, and my new boss showed up unannounced."

I cleared my throat again and bent over the side of the bed to pick up the evidence from the long night spent under and on top of the last man I ever pictured having sex with. Not just sex, but really, really good sex. Never in a million years would I have imagined Win being an attentive, slightly unhinged lover. There wasn't anything he said no to. There wasn't a position or location he was unwilling to try. He was hands on and laser focused when it came to running his empire. I was wholly unprepared for that intensity when it was directed toward bringing me pleasure.

I forced myself to focus on the conversation at hand. "Colette used the event to parade a legion of single socialites in front of Win. Including the singer who is barely in her twenties. I don't know why Win thought faking a marriage for a few years would be enough to stop her. That woman has always been relentless."

"I didn't see any pictures of the two of you together. There weren't any pictures of Win at all, which I thought was odd. He's fine as fuck. There's usually a whole spread of him after a big night out like that."

I snorted. "He was busy getting me off in the bathroom and then dragging me off to his penthouse apartment so he could fuck me senseless all night. He definitely didn't have his mind on his public image."

I climbed off the bed and went in search of something to wear. I doubted I'd ever be able to put on the black dress again without being immediately bombarded with heated memories from the previous night. Plus, it was a wrinkled mess. The cheap fabric looked like it'd been through as much as my body had.

Salome paused, then a shriek rang through the phone loud enough that I moved the device away from my head. "You slept with Win? You got dicked down by a billionaire? Unbelievable."

I groaned as her questions stabbed into my aching head like nails. "There was very little sleep involved. I just woke up when you called." I sighed and walked to Win's closet. I could commandeer a shirt until I figured something else out. "I had no intention of having sex with Win — ever. But he pointed out that we're legally married and stuck with each other for the next two years. I already gave up sex until my birthday. If I waited until our contract was up, my vagina might shrivel up from disuse."

"You let him negotiate his way between your legs?"

I dropped a bitter laugh. "I sure did." After I was covered up, I stumbled to the bathroom to clean up. "Hey. I'm in the city. Can I get you to bring me a change of clothes?" My gaze drifted across the spotlessly clean marble counter and the crystal sink. "And a toothbrush." Of course, a man like Win didn't have an overnight emergency stash. I was probably the first woman he slept with on the spur of the moment.

"Sure. I can reschedule the client I have after lunch and bring you what you need. I'm dying to see what a Halliday property looks like on the inside. And you can tell me how you ended up doing the nasty with your nemesis."

My gaze scanned the mostly white bathroom. It was beautifully decorated, but there was no soul in the space at all. The entire apartment felt that way. If Winnie hadn't left her mark all over Win's wing of the manor, it would be the same. They were places for Win to live, but neither of them felt like a home.

"I honestly have no clue how I got here." Salome knew me well enough to understand I wasn't only talking about the intimate change in my relationship with Win. "I don't belong here. That's for sure."

A soft hum came out of the phone. "I was about to remind you, that man still thinks your sister killed his brother. And his mother is a lunatic. Getting laid is one thing, but you need to protect that tender heart of yours. I don't want you to read more into things with Win the way you always do with the other losers you date. You aren't dealing with those street dogs anymore. You're facing off against a wolf, Channing."

"I know." I tried to comb my hair with my fingers and got nowhere. I dug through Win's drawers until I found something I could use to untangle the mess. I glanced toward the walk-in shower and blushed when pictures of being pressed against the glass wall as Win moved behind me flashed through my mind. I really let go of all my inhibitions last night. "I'm sure Win sees sleeping with me as a means to an end and nothing more. He has a public image to maintain. Eventually, someone is going to dig up our marriage license, and the fact that we're legally married will be news. He won't risk being caught running around on his wife. Bad press is bad for business. If the shareholders think he's going to lose part of the company in a divorce, they'll make life incredibly difficult for him. I'm his only option for a lot of things at the moment." I could never forget the way his family blamed mine for their greatest loss.

My best friend was silent for a drawn-out moment. When she spoke again, her tone was serious with a hint of warning. "Men who can make the world move at their whim always have options. And nothing you've told me about Win Halliday leads me to believe he's simple. I'm all for you getting railed by a billionaire, but you are famous for always giving more than you receive. You need to let that man spend his money on you while you're married to him. Get you some of those expensive purses and exotic vacations. Stock up on designer shoes and fancy jewelry. None of your other men were able to spoil you. You've always tried to buy your way into someone's heart. But if you catch feelings for him, I see nothing but heartache for you in the future."

I didn't tell Salome there was no need to worry about catching anything from Win. Whatever I felt toward him had been simmering under my skin for a long time. Those emotions weren't strong enough to bust through the veil of hatred that covered the Hallidays. So far, that veneer remained impenetrable. However, after last night, I couldn't deny that cracks were forming on the surface.

I opted to change the subject rather than talk about my penchant for terrible decisions when it came to my sex life. I rattled off the address of the high-rise and asked, "When do you think you'll be able to get here? If you have time, I'll take you to lunch once I don't look like I went on a bender in Vegas."

"I've got a client processing and another coming in for a cut. It'll be like an hour or an hour and a half. If you can't wait that long, call Roan to rescue you. He's off today."

I paused for a bit and gave myself a curious look in the mirror. "Why do you know Roan's schedule?" Salome and I had spent several happy hours at my ex-husband's bar. The two of them were always cordial. But I didn't think they were close enough to know each other's comings and goings.

"Uh... I saw him earlier this week, and he mentioned his days off in passing. I gotta go. I need to finish up here so I can save you. I'll text you when I get to the building. I know the door attendant won't let me up without a secret password or ancient talisman."

She hung up before I could question her further. I stared at my reflection, trying to gauge how I felt about my best friend and my favorite ex-husband having a relationship that didn't involve me.

Roan and Salome were both amazing people. Each of them loved me in different ways when I was at my worst. They were both strong and independent. And there was zero question that they were two of the most gorgeous individuals on the planet. I'd never noticed any sparks or obvious chemistry between them. Considering they were my closest friends and chosen family, if they had developed something beyond friendship, it wouldn't be surprising if they hid it from me. I made a mental note to bug Roan about it when I hadn't been railed within an inch of my life. He wouldn't lie to spare my feelings the way Salome would, even if I were reading too much into things.

I found a bottle of mouthwash and swished some around. I was going to text him about his poor morning-after protocol when my phone rang again. I figured it would be Win checking in but, to my surprise, it was Winnie. The teenager was supposed to be in class since it was the middle of the day. Her school had a strict no-phone-during-class policy, and since she'd only recently gotten her privileges back after being grounded, I doubted she would risk calling me over nothing.

I hurriedly swiped to accept the call and immediately asked, "Are you all right?"

"No!" Winnie was sobbing hysterically. "I saw a monster, Aunt Channing!"

Winnie was screaming into the phone. She sounded like she was about to hyperventilate. "Take a deep breath, Winnie. I can barely understand you. What do you mean you saw a monster? At school? Is someone giving you a hard time? Are you getting picked on?"

She was such a reactive young woman. When she said 'monster,' it could mean a million different things.

"I stayed home from school today. I don't feel good. Grandma wanted to call the doctor, but it's just a stomach bug. I told her I would feel better if I got some sleep." She took a giant, sucking breath and sniffed loudly into my ear. "I slept most of the morning. I think I have a fever. I woke up and was all sweaty and gross." Her voice was shaky, and I could clearly picture her pale face, even though I couldn't see her. "There was a monster in my room. Something was standing over me when I woke up."

Winnie continued to sob as I frowned. "What do you mean, something was in your room? Like one of the staff? You were surprised to see them, so they scared you?" I was having a hard time putting her rushed words in context.

"It wasn't the staff. It wasn't Grandma. It was a scary monster. I know what I saw!" She sobbed so loudly I was worried she might pass out.

"Maybe your fever is too high, and it's making your mind play tricks on you. If you're sick to your stomach, you probably haven't eaten enough and are dehydrated. I'll head back to the Cove as soon as I can to take care of you. Okay?"

"It's not that. Grandma said the same thing. Only now she says she wants to have me committed. She told me I have tainted blood, and that I was always going to go crazy. Just like my mother. She didn't believe me."

"Fuck that." I couldn't hold back the harsh words. I leaned against the bathroom counter and tried to get Winnie to calm down. "Let's just say you really saw a monster. What did it look like? Let's think about what else it could be. Don't worry about your grandmother. Your uncle won't let her do anything to you without his permission."

Winnie sucked in a breath through her teeth. "It looked like a man. A man with a melted face."

"Melted?" I couldn't picture what she was describing.

"I'm being serious. It looked like a normal man, but his face was... melted. I can't think of how else to explain it."

"What was this monster doing?" I didn't want to feed into her overly active imagination, but her breathing evened out and she seemed to calm down the more questions I asked her.

"Nothing. It was just standing in my room. Watching me. I screamed my head off once I realized I wasn't alone. The monster ran away when it noticed I was awake. Uncle Win's security guys came running right away, but they said they didn't see anyone in the hallway. Grandma made them check the security cameras from the other parts of the house that have surveillance. There was nothing. She really thinks there's something wrong with me. Am I going to end up hurting my family like my mom did?"

Now I wanted to cry. "No. Absolutely not. You have me and your uncle. We won't let anything happen to you or your loved ones. We both regret that we couldn't do more to help your parents. We can't let them down. We'll always do our best to protect you. Win and I can take care of ourselves." I added another thing to the list of things I was mad at Win about. Leaving Winnie alone with his mother. She was the least effective caregiver I'd ever come across. "I don't care what Chester says, I'm getting cameras. If we catch your monster on tape, no one will question either of us anymore."

"I'm still scared."

I had no clue what the teenager saw, but her fear was palpable. "I'll call your uncle's housekeeper and have her come sit with you. Go sleep in your uncle's room. I'm heading your way as soon as possible. It'll take a couple hours because I'm in the city."

I was going to call Win and tell him to have his security team go over the manor with a fine-toothed comb. I didn't believe in imaginary monsters; but there was no denying the human variety were all too real. Colette Halliday was a prime example. I had no clue what Winnie saw, but I didn't doubt there was *something* lurking in her room while she was asleep. Just like I never questioned that Colette did her damnedest to drive Willow to the point of madness.

Winnie stopped crying. She sounded exhausted when she offhandedly asked, "Can't you just take the helicopter and come home?"

I blinked at my reflection and tried to put her outlandish question together in a way that made sense. "Helicopter? You want me to fly to the Cove instead of taking the train?" It was a short train ride. Why would anyone need to fly such a short distance?

My niece sounded genuinely puzzled when she responded, "Yeah. Uncle Win has a helicopter he uses for work. Sometimes he has to get to and from the city in a hurry for business. I bet he would lend it to you so you can come home faster."

I rubbed my forehead and pushed down the instant irritation that arose at her indifference to the obvious excess. "I'm not taking a helicopter home. Or anywhere. You need to stop thinking that the things that apply to your Uncle Win's life apply to anyone else. He's always had the opportunity to jump on a helicopter when it's convenient. That's not true for most people you'll come across in your lifetime." I refused to get used to privileges that would vanish once Win and I were no longer fake married. I looked at my crumpled dress, resigned to putting it back on and making the trip to the Cove looking a mess. I needed to catch Salome before she left, so I didn't send her running to save me for no reason. Getting to Winnie was my top priority. "Go rest. By the time you wake up, I'll be home. I'll make you some soup and crackers. You'll feel much better after some old-fashioned TLC." Nothing could replace the classics.

Chicken noodle soup would do more for her in her lifetime than a private helicopter. I sent up a wordless prayer that Winnie would realize the difference before my time playing Win's wife was up.

Chapter Sixteen

win

"Stop trying to alienate Winnie by threatening to send her away." I watched my mother from across the antique desk in her expansive library. I felt like I was having a meeting with a business competitor, not sitting down for a heart-to-heart chat with my only remaining parent. "I'm serious about taking her to the city with me if you can't figure out how to be kind to her. You need to start treating her like she's your granddaughter, not like she's a replacement for me once I step down as CEO. If the only thing you can concern yourself with is making sure Winnie is a proper heir to Halliday Inc., I have no problem intervening on her behalf."

I refused to let Winnie experience the same neglect and harsh training I barely survived. The teen had been ill for several days and my mother couldn't be bothered to show a hint of concern. She was too intent on pushing the agenda that Channing's presence was pushing Winnie toward another mental episode.

My mother gave me an icy look. "Sending Winnie away is undoubtedly the right call. Anything that removes her from questionable influences and excessive coddling will be an improvement. I'm trying to save her, not hurt her. I know what's best, Winchester. You never used to question that."

I felt my frustration rise to a dangerous level. I was used to her speaking to me as if I were one of her subordinates. I was immune to it. Hearing her speak about Winnie in the same detached and unfeeling way pushed me beyond the rigid control I kept when dealing with her.

"Is it your opinion that it's best to isolate a girl who lost her parents from her only remaining family? You don't think it will be detrimental to send a child who is terrified there might be something wrong with her to a place full of individuals who are actually dealing with severe mental illness? Do you honestly believe telling Winnie that she's crazy, just like her mother, is helping her?" I shook my head. I deeply regretted letting her coerce me to bring Winnie to live at the manor.

I should have been smart enough to see that my mother wasn't honestly considering suicide. She wanted to use guilt to trap me into staying by her side. She used the fact that I felt immense remorse for not being there when both Archie and my dad died. Even if I was absent because I was running the company just like she wanted. I found it hard to find an excuse for letting my mother bear the brunt of the fall of our family all alone. The woman was a better manipulator than anyone I'd come across.

"She's claiming to see monsters, Win. That woman's mother is institutionalized because she has schizophrenia. You must acknowledge that Winnie is hallucinating and getting progressively more unstable. She needs more help than you can provide. Being kind to her isn't going to fix whatever's going on in that messed-up mind she inherited from that other family." My mother sniffed in indignation. "Things have just gotten worse since you dragged that despicable woman back to the Cove. I wouldn't be surprised if she's the reason Winnie's behavior has regressed to what it was like when she was a child. She should toughen up. She's a Halliday, after all."

My hands curled into fists. Talking to her was like banging my head against a brick wall. She was so rigid and unforgiving. She couldn't even admit that Channing played an enormous role in helping the little girl heal after she'd lost everything. There was nothing I could say that would change her mind. It felt like I'd been traveling along this barren and lonely stretch of road for a very long time. I was tired of the journey. There were some roads you shouldn't go down.

"I've told you repeatedly that what you think where Winnie is concerned is irrelevant. I make the decisions related to her health and wellbeing. While I don't believe she saw a monster in her room, I do think something spooked her. She's been timid and afraid long before Channing came to the manor. Even if what she saw is a by-product of inherited mental illness, the solution isn't to send her away for repair like she's a broken piece of equipment. If Winnie is struggling, then so am I. I won't let her face her challenges alone." I narrowed my eyes at my mother and forced myself to release my fists. "And neither will Channing. That is why Winnie has been so insistent on keeping her aunt in her life for all these years."

I sighed heavily and shoved a hand through my hair. I was ready to pull out the strands in aggravation. There was no getting around the fact that I could no longer trust my mother not to harm Winnie. Be it intentional or accidental.

This was the perfect time to leave the manor and the Cove behind. This place was toxic on numerous levels, and Winnie was scared out of her ever-loving mind. There had to be a reasonable explanation for what was happening in this house, but no matter how much manpower I threw at the problem, nothing was discovered. Now my suite had more cameras and surveillance than an airport. I felt like I was living in a fishbowl. The added level of security was the only reason Channing hadn't snatched up our niece and made a run for the hills. The redhead was as worried about Winnie's mental state just as much as the teenager. She kept reminding me about her things that had gone missing since she came to the manor. And she wouldn't let go of the thought that someone came into the suite and killed her plants on purpose. While Channing never came out and said she believed Winnie might've seen a monster, she was more open-minded about the whole situation than I was.

"I don't understand why you're defending a Harvey. You've always agreed Winnie was better off not emulating anything from that side of her family. If I didn't know any better, I might think that woman has you under a magic spell. Are you sure she's not manipulating you? She would take Winnie away from you in a heartbeat."

"I never agreed with anything you've said about the Harveys. Especially Channing." But I never opposed her when she spoke harshly about them. "If I ever mentioned the benefits of having Channing around, you'd stubbornly refuse to acknowledge it. I tried to stay indifferent to her because I was terrified that you'd try to destroy her if you realized I felt otherwise. I don't agree with every decision Channing has made, but I know she genuinely loves Winnie." I paused and exhaled a harsh breath. "I can't say the same about you, Mother."

I pushed to my feet and gave my mother a hard look. A lot of decisions I'd been avoiding had reached a tipping point. What sense did it make that I single-handedly controlled the financial future of thousands of Halliday Inc. employees and investors, but I couldn't make a single selfish choice for myself? If I had to choose who I wanted to live with, Channing won over my mother, hands down.

"If you think I will allow anyone to turn my granddaughter against me, you're delusional, Winchester." My mother's tone dripped with warning.

I turned my back on her and headed toward the door. "You said the same thing to Willow about Archie. Look how that ended up. One of these days, hopefully, you'll realize your focus should be on the people inside these castle walls, and not the ancestors who built them. This manor is nothing more than a haunted house." Where ghosts were treated better than the living.

I stopped in the hallway when she snapped at my retreating back, "Just remember, I taught you how to fight, Win. If you want to be my opponent instead of my son, don't come crawling back when you regret that choice."

"You're so certain you'll win?" I didn't bother to close the door, and I heard more expensive tableware shatter following the thinly veiled taunt.

When I started back to my wing of the house, I ran into Channing. She was sitting at the base of the massive staircase and her gaze was directed toward the library I'd just exited. I put a hand on the railing near her head and leaned on the carved wooden banister.

"Did you enjoy the show?" I tried to keep my tone flippant, but I could hear the disgust in my voice. The conversation with my mother was loud enough to carry through the large house. I was glad Winnie was at school. Otherwise, she couldn't help but overhear all the horrible things her grandmother said about her.

Channing looked up at me with a frown. "All these years, I thought you hated me and genuinely believed that I was a bad influence on Winnie. Why didn't you ever explain that you were being an asshole to keep your mother off your back? A simple conversation could've saved us so much strife."

I rolled my head to crack my neck and release the tension that had me in a chokehold. "I'm not used to explaining myself. And there were times when I didn't approve of what, and who, you were doing. As single-minded as my mother can be, she can sniff out bullshit from a hundred miles away. If I told you I was only pretending, she would've figured it out. Once she did, she would've come after you twice as hard to prove a point. You may think I fucked up your life to get you where I wanted you. My mother makes me look like an amateur when it comes to dismantling all that one might hold dear." My mom's bullshit detector was the reason I never considered trying to pass off our marriage as the real deal. She would've seen through the farce instantly. "Do you know that her parents passed away in a horrific car accident shortly before she married my father? She refused to move the wedding date. The funeral and nuptials were back-to-back. Imagine being raised by someone who couldn't even fake grief over such a huge loss."

Channing swore softly and shook her head. "All this time, I thought we were enemies when we were co-conspirators instead." She sounded like she was in disbelief over the revelation. "You're full of surprises, aren't you, Chester?"

I rubbed the back of my neck. "In business, you never want the opposition to know your next move." I met her curious gaze with a serious one of my own. "We're going to have to figure out a plan for Winnie. I can take both of you to the city, but that won't stop my mother from interfering. Winnie's current mental state complicates things. One thing my mother said that I do agree with is that Winnie needs professional help."

Channing propped her hand on her chin as she watched me with bright, clear eyes. "I don't think it hurts to find someone safe for her to talk to. It's hard for her to reconcile the conflicting feelings of having everything except the one thing she really wants. She's never been allowed to grieve the loss of her parents freely." She pointed at me with her free hand. "None of that takes away from the fact that there is something strange happening in this house. I don't believe Winnie is hallucinating or that she's delusional. She's scared."

"A strange man never came into this house. You've seen all the camera footage from that day. Unless someone climbed up the cliff and came in through my wing, there was never an intruder." We'd had this same conversation backward and forward since the day she rushed home from the city to take care of Winnie.

Channing poked my leg with her finger. "I've said it over and over again — this is coming from inside the house. What would an intruder want with my stuff when they could take one of your watches? They could snag a single pair of your cufflinks and pay for their life of crime for years to come. It doesn't make any sense that only Winnie and I are targeted."

I put my hand on the top of her head and messed up her hair. I liked how soft it felt when it brushed against my palm.

"I've vetted and re-vetted anyone who's had access to this house for the last six months. I haven't found a single red flag." Everyone who worked for my mom was squeaky clean.

"Did you have your mother investigated? She benefits the most if my sanity is questioned. She's been pushing to send Winnie away. It's obvious she doesn't like that you have the final say in what happens in our niece's life. I've never met more of a control freak than her." Her eyebrows arched upward. "Including you."

"You really think my mother is skulking around in the dark, sneaking in and out of rooms, just to mess with your head?" The image I conjured was ridiculous. There wasn't a chance in hell my mother would ever do anything so improper.

Channing shrugged. I moved my hand and bent to cup her face. I ran my thumb over her plump bottom lip and watched her multi-colored eyes darken.

"I don't think she's physically doing anything, but I think she has someone doing it on her behalf. Nothing happens under this roof without her knowledge. Something changed not too long ago when Winnie started telling you the house was haunted. You wrote it off as her imagination, but there's more to it. If I had the connections at my disposal that you do, I'd investigate what Colette was up to around the time Winnie started hearing things. And I'd dig into the background of this house. It's been around since the days people were allowed to own other people." She made a disgusted face at the thought and frowned. "Didn't they make buildings with secret tunnels and passageways between rooms to keep the staff separate from the homeowners? The sounds are coming from the walls, Win. You keep insisting that there's a logical explanation for everything, but you refuse to believe the simplest explanation is the answer."

I matched her scowl as a vague recollection from my childhood tickled the back of my brain. Archie and I liked to play hide and seek when we were younger. In a house this big, the hiding places were too numerous to count. During one particular game, I couldn't locate my younger brother anywhere. I looked high and low. Eventually, I had to ask the staff to help me figure out where he was hiding. To my utter shock, behind an armoire rumored to have first come over on the *Mayflower*, was a hidden entryway. Archie appeared to be very familiar with the secret space, but he was punished by my mother when she found out he was playing around with such a valuable piece of furniture. Anyone who admitted they knew what Archie was up to was fired on the spot. She had the door bolted shut, and the incident faded to make room for far more traumatic memories.

People might question Channing's intellect since she didn't have an advanced degree, but anyone who did was an idiot. There was a lot to be said for strong common sense and keen critical-thinking skills. If you dropped Channing into any situation, there was a solid chance she would figure out how to manage it before everyone else. Our marriage was a perfect example.

I shifted my hold on her face so I could stroke my thumb along her jawline. "You're right. I need to dig deeper. I've been going about things in a rational way. The person who thinks it's fun to terrorize a vulnerable teenager clearly isn't behaving in a logical way." My mother accused me of wanting to be her enemy. It might be time I started to treat her that way. I dropped a kiss on top of Channing's head. "I was serious about taking you and Winnie out of this house. I need some time to arrange things. Can you be patient with me, Harvey?"

She gave me a smirk. I wanted to kiss it off her face when she taunted, "Is that the first time you've ever asked for something instead of demanding it?"

My heart pounded. "The third time."

The first occurrence was when I asked my mother if I truly had to give up the violin. The second was when I asked Channing if she was going to let me in so I could fuck her. This was the third. There may have been another question scattered somewhere here or there throughout the years, but it certainly didn't happen often.

I was about to touch our lips together when my cell phone rang. The sound broke whatever pleasant lull we'd fallen into.

I wasn't surprised to see Conrad's name on the screen. My assistant and Rocco were two of the only people who would call me when I had personal business to attend to. Channing climbed to her feet and disappeared up the stairs. I let out a string of swear words as I watched her go. It always felt like the peaceful moments between us were fleeting.

"This better be important." I impatiently tapped my fingers on the railing.

"It is. There's an issue with the zoning permissions on the project we just signed the contracts for. Nothing can move forward until it gets straightened out." I could hear the urgency in Conrad's voice. "You need to fly back to England and meet with the lawyers. This is a high-priority project."

"Why can't the legal department handle this?" Normally, I'd drop everything and fly halfway across the world. Right now, my top priority had to be my niece. I paid millions of dollars in legal fees to delegate tasks of this sort down the chain of command.

"If the project is delayed, we need to find an entirely different company to contract the construction. The team we're working with now has back-to-back jobs for another developer. You need to smooth things over with the zoning commission or sign off on a new contractor. This can only be handled by *you*, Win." Conrad's tone was succinct. "I never had to explain things like this before you got married." I could hear the frustration in his tone.

I weighed the profits and losses in my head, even though there was no getting around making the trip.

"Figure out travel arrangements. I'll be back in the city in a couple of hours." I swore under my breath and grumbled, "The timing of this could not be any worse."

Conrad sighed like he was just as displeased as I was. "Have Rocco stay behind to keep watch over the girls if you're that worried about them."

I grunted as I started up the steps toward my wing of the manor.

It was a good idea. But I couldn't shake the irritation that someone else would be responsible for the safety of the people I cared the most about.

I wanted that to be my job. Not salvaging a billion-dollar deal.

Chapter Seventeen
channing

After Win departed for his emergency business trip, Winnie was a wreck. It didn't matter if I spent all day stuck to her side like glue; she was still overwhelmingly afraid. I thought that having Rocco shadow her might give her some comfort. It didn't. She was even more tense around the large man, as if she was worried that he might report her concerning behavior back to Win. She didn't want to be a burden, but it was impossible not to worry about her. She wasn't sleeping very well. She didn't have much of an appetite. Her focus was all over the place, and she was having a hard time with her classes. She was struggling to keep her emotions in check even though there hadn't been another monster sighting and the sounds from the walls completely disappeared. I felt like I was watching the way my sister slowly faded away all over again.

If Winnie wasn't in the middle of a school year, I would've taken her to the city and camped out at Salome's until she stopped jumping out of her skin at every single sound. I couldn't care less what Colette had to say. I settled for a rushed backup plan to keep Winnie's attention diverted to help with her anxiety. I called Beverly, the opera singer from the gala, and told her I wanted to take her up on her offer for singing lessons. My niece needed to get out of the house. Beverly immediately agreed and gave me her schedule.

I sent Winnie off with Rocco when the time came, and Beverly was available. While she was away at her lesson, I spent the morning poking around the manor. Win promised to track down the original building plans, but he had his hands full with whatever was going on overseas. I'd barely spoken to him since he left. When we managed to connect, we only had time for a quick update about Winnie.

I was determined to locate any secret doors or hidden passageways. I went through Win's suite and came up empty-handed. Nothing was out of place or noticeably covered. The walls appeared to be solid, even hidden behind the furniture. Winnie's room showed no signs of alterations. I went as far as to climb around in the closets looking for attic access, but I came up with nothing more than frustration and a hacking cough from the dust.

I attempted to pick through the empty wing of the manor where my sister had lived. I was surprised to find every door in that area of the house sealed shut. I rattled all the doorknobs and even tried to kick in the door of Winnie's old nursery. It didn't take long for one of Colette's staff to appear out of nowhere and inform me I was not allowed in that section of the house. When I asked why everything was locked, there was no response. I found the situation suspicious. However, I did my best not to push my luck when Win wasn't around. A full-blown confrontation between me and his mother with no referee was more than likely going to end with one of us doing something drastic. Regardless of who was at fault if things blew up between me and her, there was zero question who would be facing any consequences.

Since Winnie was gone for the day and I couldn't move freely around the Halliday estate, I decided to visit the mausoleum where my sister's ashes were laid to rest. I always thought Willow would have hated to be confined in such a small, dull space. I'd wanted to take her somewhere beautiful and vibrant to give her a beautiful send off. My older sister would definitely prefer to spend her ever-after carried across the world by the whim of the wind. Unfortunately, my mom was so hysterical, and in such denial after Willow's death, she refused to accept that her eldest daughter was dead. It took locking Willow away in this dreadful place for my mom to snap out of her fugue state and comprehend that Willow was gone. She kept my sister in a static, lifeless location so she could visit her anytime she wanted. Little did either of us know that she was going to have an irreparable break from reality and wouldn't be able to visit Willow at all. I often toyed around with the idea of setting my sister free and leaving her urn empty. No one in my family would ever know the difference. The only thing that stopped me was paying for an empty spot in the mausoleum. I couldn't throw my money away on something just to make a point. But now that Win was in the picture, I might liberate her ashes.

I always brought flowers when I visited my sister. It annoyed me to no end that she was trapped in a wall with strangers. Archie was buried somewhere on the Halliday property with his father and generations of Hallidays that came before them. Of course, Colette wouldn't let the spouses spend an eternity together. Different burial sites meant that Winnie rarely got to visit her mother, even though Colette forced her to spend time at her father's grave once a week. It was grossly unfair.

I spoke out loud to the picture of Willow on the marble slab. I told her how Winnie was doing and shared my concerns about her daughter. I unloaded all my pent-up feelings regarding Win and our fake marriage. I told her how desperately I missed hearing her advice. I vented about the ongoing war with her mother-in-law, and I told her that I still hated the Cove with every fiber of my being. I rambled on about meeting Alistair and how there was finally a member of the Halliday brood, aside from her daughter, who wasn't completely awful.

When I ran out of words, I cried. It happened every visit. I lost the hold over my grief. Whenever I looked at that smiling picture of a vibrant young woman who was gone too soon, I fell apart. Willow had loved me unconditionally. She never made me feel like I was too much or not enough. Since our mom was often difficult to deal with, and our father was a certified scumbag, Willow more or less raised me. I felt alone even though my parents were still around. Without Willow, I had no one to depend on. I had to face all of life's ups and downs by myself. I carried everything alone. My best qualities were directly attributed to her, and she always forgave my worst. She would have been the most amazing mom to Winnie because she'd had tons of practice with me.

Once I was out of tears, I wiped off my face with my sleeve and pulled myself together, just like I always did. I told Willow I would be back soon and promised to bring Winnie on my next trip.

I hopped on my restored bicycle and rode into the tiny downtown of the Cove. Since it was off-season, the main street was mostly empty. I didn't have to fight any sunburned, flip-flop-wearing crowds when I stopped to grab a smoothie. I sat outside and marveled at the empty streets and muted atmosphere. It was nothing like people watching in the city. I'd left this idyllic, coastal town the moment I was able. With my extensive dating history, I would never survive in a town where everyone knew everyone else. As soon as I dumped or got dumped, the entire population of Halliday Cove would know all the gory details. I would never have come back if Win hadn't blackmailed me.

By the time I finished my drink, Winnie texted that she was ready to be picked up from Beverly's place.

I rode to the house that was still on the seaside but not up a cliff. It was a modern mansion. Colette would turn her nose up at it, even if it cost several million dollars and she saw Beverly as an appropriate match for Win. The young woman met me at the gates and walked with me to the impressive entryway. The landscaping was lovely but not in the same league as the Queen of Hearts' gardens that sprawled around the Halliday estate. I planned to grab Winnie and head back to the manor, but Beverly's family insisted we both stay for dinner. Her parents and younger brother were incredibly welcoming. Beverly's mother was a stunning Hispanic woman, and her father was a distinguished African American. It was no wonder

Beverly was so beautiful. She got her distinct looks from both sides of the family. Winnie and Beverly's brother actually attended the same school but were in different grades. They were familiar with one another in passing. My niece seemed more relaxed surrounded by Beverly's family than she had been all week.

I felt like I could finally breathe once Winnie started smiling and laughing again. It was an immense relief that she finally ate a full meal and didn't pick at the food on her plate. We stayed through dessert. When it was time to head home, Rocco insisted on driving us back to the estate. Because the big man was only following orders to keep Winnie safe, I decided it wasn't worth a fight.

After saying an obligatory good night to her grandmother, Winnie took a quick shower and almost immediately zonked out. It was the first night she slept in her bed. I stayed with her until I was positive she wasn't going to wake up as soon as I left. She'd been having nightmares. It was likely that she would jolt awake later, which meant I only had a couple of hours to myself.

I took a shower, making sure I locked all the doors, and kept an eye on the bathroom entry while I washed my hair and scrubbed my body. I'd been on high alert for disturbances ever since my hairbrush vanished. Fortunately, nothing weird happened, and the walls remained silent.

When I fell into Win's bed, I was hit by a sudden bout of drowsiness. I contemplated getting up and grabbing a glass of wine, since I didn't plan to sleep for at least a couple of hours. I was combing through my wet hair with my fingers when my phone rang. I was surprised to see Win's name on the display. It was later than the middle of the night in London.

I answered the call and asked, "Are you still working this late?" I wasn't supposed to care about his wellbeing, but I couldn't help but have some sympathy for him. He was diligent for someone who openly hated his career.

"I'm getting ready to come home. I finally straightened out the issues with the project. I should be back sometime tomorrow afternoon. How's Winnie?" His voice was raspy with exhaustion. It did something to my heart when he let himself show me his human weaknesses.

"She's doing better. We spent some time away from the manor today. She's sleeping in her own room tonight. I'm keeping my fingers crossed that she makes it through the night. The poor thing is as haggard as I was when I went through my first divorce. She really wants you to come home. She feels safe with you."

He sighed heavily. "At least someone misses me."

I snuggled down into the luxurious bedding and rubbed my fingers along the top of my thigh under the hem of my silk robe. My skin was warm and soft from the shower. The touch made my skin tingle, but it wasn't nearly as exciting as having Win's hands on me.

"Oh, I think it's safe to say I miss parts of you, Chester." We didn't have much time to explore our enemies-with-benefits deal before all hell broke loose and he was called away.

I tilted my head back and let my fingers drift farther up my leg. I shivered when Win's deep voice rumbled in my ear, "What parts in particular do you miss, Harvey?"

My robe parted and I let my eyes drift closed as fingers reached the suddenly aching point between my legs. I let my thigh fall to the side and let out a shaky breath.

"It's your hands at the moment." I pictured the hungry expression stamped on his features whenever he got his hands on me. "And your face." It was unfair that he was blessed with a damn near perfect one.

"I would've done a video call if you let me know that you wanted to see my face so badly." His voice dropped lower, and I felt the vibration throughout my entire body.

"I wouldn't be able to do what I'm about to do if you were watching me." Not because I was shy. I didn't know that I could concentrate on giving myself satisfaction without wanting to return the favor. One of the few times I ever felt equal to Win Halliday was when we had sex. I finally had something I could provide to him that no one else could. And he finally had something I wanted to accept when he offered. We were equally greedy when giving and taking carnal pleasure.

I stroked my fingers over my soft center and felt my entire body heat. My chest lifted with a rapid breath and my nipples tightened. I needed another hand to touch all the places Win usually did when we were in bed together. Since I only had one free hand, fondling myself to completion would have to suffice. It felt better when he did it, but horny beggars couldn't be choosers.

I slid my fingers through my slippery folds and skimmed them across the surface of my clit. I gasped into the phone and dug my heels into the mattress. Win swore into my ear and growled my name like a warning.

"I feel like you owe me a play-by-play, Channing."

I wanted to laugh, but my breath felt like it was caught in my lungs as I stroked my fingers inside my wet opening. My body felt feverish and tense. My legs quivered and my nipples tightened, aching for stimulation.

"I've got my fingers inside of my pussy and I'm touching myself. I'm not doing nearly as good of a job as you did in the hotel bathroom."

He hummed a satisfied sound. "That's because you know what it feels like to touch you. Since it was something I'd only dreamed about, I had to give it my all so I could be certain you'd let me do it again."

I gasped as I moved my fingers deeper and rubbed my thumb against my clit. "You dreamed about touching me?" I must be hallucinating. Someone in his tax bracket had to have far more interesting things to fantasize about than my vagina.

I moaned softly when my body fluttered excitedly against my practiced manipulation. Win sighed. The sound sent shivers along my arms and legs.

"I have more dreams about you than I have money, Channing." He made another wistful sound. "I don't think two years will be long enough to bring them all to life. I'm willing to try, though."

I didn't know he could talk like that. The man didn't seem to have a romantic bone in his body. I guess when he put his mind to something, he would always be the best at it. There was no other option for a Halliday.

I kept my eyes shut and whispered, "My fingers can't reach as deep as your cock. That's the part of you I'm missing the most right now." The silken flesh surrounding my fingers got wetter. My body throbbed along with my racing heartbeat. I put more pressure against my clit and bit down on my bottom lip. My head thrashed against the fluffy pillows as Win's voice enticed me over the edge of the orgasm.

"It's crude to say that my cock misses you, but it does. I've been too busy to do anything but work and sleep. You should brace yourself for my return. I have a week's worth of pent-up frustration and desire you're directly responsible for." Each word was strained and tense. "I'm not sure I've ever been so distracted during a crisis before. You're taking up a lot of real estate in my head, Harvey. You should know just how pricey that property is."

"I'm going to come." I gasped the words as I interrupted him, not sure if it was my fingers or his words that broke open the floodgates. Whatever it was, my toes curled against the sheets and my entire body quaked with satisfaction in the aftermath. I panted my approval in Win's ear. He cursed quietly and told me he would hurry home.

Winnie was still asleep when I went to the bathroom to clean up. Once I was back in bed, I closed my eyes and fell asleep in a second. I was sleepy before the phone call, and the bone-rattling orgasm made it impossible to stay alert.

I regretted sleeping so deeply the following day. I didn't wake up until Win returned home, well past the time Winnie left for school. I rubbed my eyes and squinted at the handsome owner of the bed where I was currently sprawled. I was going to welcome Win home with a sexy suggestion, but his expression was horrible.

"What's wrong?" The question faded when I caught sight of the red and blond strands of hair scattered across my pillow. I gasped and lifted a hand to my head. I screamed when I felt huge chunks of hair missing on one side of my head. My gaze locked with Win's. He looked furious and lowkey afraid.

"What is going on in this house when I'm not here?" He sounded like he was on the brink of erupting like a long dormant volcano.

I wasn't going to cry that my hair had been chopped off while I slept. I'd experienced far worse things. However, I was once again beyond freaked out that someone was clearly in the room with me while I was in my most vulnerable state. I didn't like feeling preyed on while unable to fight back.

"I wish I knew." The words fell flat as Win reached out to gently smooth my butchered hair.

Someone was waging war on us, and they were winning. For the first time since we met, I was glad Win refused to lose at anything. His need to be victorious might be the only thing that would save our niece's sanity and my peace of mind.

Chapter Eighteen

win

I stared at the screen in front of me. Rage and the feeling of failure tied my entire body up in knots.

The cameras Rocco had installed in my personal space didn't record continuously. I couldn't stand the thought of being watched every minute. And I refused to have prying eyes on my private life, especially since Channing was at the center of it. There was a motion sensor at the doorway and the windows that triggered the camera to capture any movement. I had plenty of images of Channing and Winnie coming and going. There were a handful of pictures of my housekeeper doing her daily duties, and a snap of my arrival when I got back from overseas. However, a picture of whomever came into my home and into my room to cut Channing's hair was glaringly missing. It seemed like the perpetrator could walk through walls and appear out of thin air.

"Did you find the plans for the manor I asked you to locate?" I glanced at Conrad out of the corner of my eye. My long-suffering assistant knew I was furious at being called away on business while things at home were escalating. The truth was, I could've sent Conrad and my CFO or COO to handle the zoning mishap. The only reason I'd been roped into the negotiations was because one of the business partners wanted to set me up with his daughter. She was in charge of the negotiations for the other side. After I informed everyone involved in the crisis that I had recently gotten married, the back and forth dragged on as a highly unprofessional form of punishment. Because of our history and his attention to the littlest detail, there was little question that Conrad was aware of the ulterior motives before he sent me to the UK. He chose to ignore them for a reason.

Conrad cleared his throat and nervously shifted his weight in the antique leather chair. "I emailed you everything I could find. The manor is so old, finding the original design from the seventeen-hundreds is impossible. There have been several renovation projects over the different generations of owners. Including when you redesigned your wing and when the damage from the fire was repaired. I don't know if it'll be possible to locate any of the historic plans." He sighed. "I even checked with the historical society. They have old sketches of the outside and the plans for the gardens, but nothing for the inside. If there are trapdoors and hidden passageways, they're not on any paperwork I managed to dig up."

I scowled at him and tapped my fingers on the edge of the armrest. "Dig deeper, Conrad. I need to know how someone is moving around my house undetected."

My tone made it clear: his job was on the line. I couldn't stomach the fact that Winnie and Channing weren't safe under my watch. Every fiber of my being rebelled against sending them away to keep them safe, but it was the right decision. I could no longer write off Winnie's fear as an overactive imagination. Not after Channing had been sheared like a sheep. Her pretty strawberries-and-cream hair was now chopped into an edgy pixie cut. It was cute and gave the normally sunny redhead a more serious vibe. Channing said she wouldn't have minded the short style if she'd chosen it for herself, rather than end up with it out of necessity.

My mother accused her of cutting it herself to feed Winnie's paranoia. I stopped that nonsense conjecture in an instant. I saw Channing's shock and disbelief when she'd woken up and saw her hair on the pillow. Even if she was an Oscar-winning actress, there was no way to feign that depth of confusion and fear.

Out of spite and an abundance of caution, Channing refused to tell anyone where she was stashing Winnie until it was safe to come home. She told me she was taking her to the last place my mother would ever think of looking. Since I wasn't an idiot, I immediately figured out that she'd taken our niece to my half-brother for protection. Alistair was a perfect choice. He had a weird loyalty to the name Halliday, even if our family refused to acknowledge him. Winnie was technically his niece, too, so it was unlikely he would let anything happen to her. The kid had enough money to make sure she was well protected, and he owed me a favor neither of us ever mentioned.

I saved his sister when there was no hope. He would never turn down the opportunity to repay that massive debt.

Channing was correct. It was the last place my mother would look for Winnie. She firmly considered the bastard an adversary. It would never occur to her that he might be one of our most important allies instead.

I didn't want Channing to stay with them, but until I figured out what was happening at my home, I didn't have the right to force her to stay. Losing her hair was one thing. If someone got close enough to touch her with scissors, they were close enough to use that instrument in much more harmful ways. She was lucky her throat hadn't been slit while she slept.

I shoved a hand through my hair and continued to glare at my friend. "Did you at least get my mother's financials?" If there was no sign of my mother's staff taking money to fuck with everyone I cared about, I needed to look in my backyard. It was possible the people I trusted weren't as dependable as I thought.

Conrad shifted in his seat again, which made me narrow my eyes. He'd been extra anxious since I focused more on personal matters and less on what was happening at Halliday Inc.

"I sent her personal financials to your email. She has a few businesses that are subsidiaries of Halliday Inc., which have been harder to locate. They were established when your father was at the helm. Most of those have used offshore banks since inception. You know how difficult it is to track anything with those types of accounts."

"No familiar names popped up in your investigation?" I tried to keep my voice even, but I could hear the hint of accusation in it.

"No." Conrad kept his eyes on mine, but I noticed a small tremor in his hands. "I still think it's absurd that you're suspicious of the staff you handpicked. There isn't any universe in which Rocco, or I, would ever betray you."

I hummed a slight sound of agreement while I watched him with unblinking eyes.

I told him to double check everything and excused him from my sight with a wave of my hand. I was very dissatisfied with his lackluster performance as of late. Once Conrad vacated my office, I called Rocco in. He didn't take the empty seat. Instead, he stood in front of me with his hands behind his back like he was still in the military.

"What did your people find?" I asked Rocco to have his team investigate all the same things as Conrad to see if the information lined up. I wasn't ready to share my doubts about Conrad until I had empirical proof that he wasn't being honest. I couldn't explain why I harbored suspicions toward my friend, but something hadn't sat right ever since he was adamantly against my marriage with Channing. No one had protested as much as Conrad, aside from my mother. Rocco picked up on my ulterior motive before I had to explain anything to him.

"I found the plans from before your great grandparents renovated the manor. There is a network of passageways and tunnels underneath the main house. They lead all the way to the cliff face. Your grandparents and parents had most entrances and exits sealed with modern framing and drywall once they took ownership."

I swore under my breath and knocked a fist on the top of my desk. "Then explain how someone is moving unseen throughout my house."

Rocco frowned, and his gaze sharpened. "I'm not certain, it's just a guess, but I think you need to look at the flooring. That's one part of the manor that hasn't been ripped up and replaced over the years except in the burned wing." Our eyes met and I could see that he was recalling something unpleasant. "When I was deployed overseas, one of the most common places for the opposition to hide for an ambush were dugouts under the floor. The estate has been around since the Revolutionary War. I have a feeling there are connected hidey-holes underneath every room for a quick escape. When Channing scouted everything, she never looked under the rugs and floors."

I sighed, understanding that Conrad had indeed skipped vital information in his debrief.

"What did you find out about my mother? Is she paying off anyone on *my* staff?" If her staff was clean, mine must be dirty.

Rocco shook his head. "It's hard to tell. Her personal transactions are murky. She moves money through a lot of untraceable accounts and shell companies. It's possible, but I can't say anything is one hundred percent certain." He coughed and waited until I looked up and caught his gaze. "One of the most suspicious subsidiaries she's in charge of is a long-term medical care facility. It looks like she invested in it around the time your father's health started to fail."

I nodded. "She did. She wanted to make sure he spent his final days surrounded by people under her control." I laughed. "She was paranoid that someone would coerce him to change his will while he wasn't in his right mind. Little did she know he amended it to include DeVere."

Rocco nodded, his expression grave. "But she bought the facility long before your dad fell ill. She started sinking money into it not long after the fire." He paused for a brief minute and frowned. "This is going to sound like a reach, but are you absolutely sure your brother is buried on the estate? The funeral was rushed. You never saw the body. Your mother never seemed to grieve and was annoyed

Winnie was such a mess. None of that is normal when your child dies. Even for a Halliday."

I blinked because I was too stunned to speak. I had to drink some water before my suddenly parched throat could operate as normal. "Is that a serious question?"

Rocco frowned and lowered his head so that he was looking at the tips of his polished boots. "Colette handled everything after Archie died. There was no autopsy. The death certificate is signed by the coroner who just happens to be married to the mayor of the Cove. The mayor Colette helped get elected. I've seen pictures of the damage after the fire. There wasn't much fuel to feed the flames. I saw Willow's condition when the firefighters pulled her out of the house. She was injured, but it didn't appear to be fatal. My guess is that if someone reached her and Archie in time, they would've been badly burned, but alive."

I felt my heart squeeze, and I forgot how to breathe for a second. My vision blurred. I remembered the sorrow that felt suffocating since my brother died. The blame and accusations were sharp spears that were stabbed into my vulnerable places. I never understood why Archie's choices had anything to do with me. My mother always asserted that if I hadn't left, things never would've spiraled out of control, as if I were responsible for making sure Archie didn't fall in love with a Harvey.

"Are you trying to tell me that you think my brother is still alive? That my mother is keeping him in the same place she kept my father when he was dying?"

"I'm saying it's a possibility we need to investigate. Things don't add up when you scratch beneath the surface. We've always accepted your mother's version of events because you weren't home. I think she's gotten too comfortable. Colette has always insisted Willow drugged herself and Archie, then set the fire. She claims no one at the estate knew that Winnie was with Channing that night. None of those assertions are based on fact. If Willow drugged herself when she supposedly drugged Archie, she couldn't have started the fire.

She was smaller than him. It would be nearly impossible for her to wait for him to pass out before she could ignite anything that would burn. If she took something after Archie was knocked out, then she would've been alert when the fire started. She would've been aware that she was being burned alive. If that were the case, there would've been signs of escape or a struggle to survive. No regular human can sit there and let themselves be torched. It's like they both went to sleep and never woke up, even as the manor burned around them. Smoke inhalation killed Willow. Since there was no autopsy done on Archie, there's no cause of death on record. The entire situation is suspicious as hell. Especially since the law enforcement in the Cove is under your mother's influence. This should've been discussed long before now."

I rubbed a hand across my chin and felt my perception of one of the most defining moments of my life shift. "You're telling me you think my mother drugged them and started the fire, then somehow managed to get Archie out and left Willow to die? Do you think she murdered my brother's wife? And tried to murder my niece, as well?" Unfiltered disbelief colored every word, not because I couldn't imagine my mother as a killer, but because this questionable behavior happened underneath my nose, and I never realized it. How was I fit to run a multibillion-dollar empire if I couldn't keep my home in order? And how could my mother ever call anyone else crazy? If any of this actually occurred, she wasn't right in the head. I never questioned the tragedy surrounding Archie and his family. I didn't have time. My dad's health failed so quickly after my brother's death. Then I was trying to fill his shoes at Halliday Inc. Amid all of that, my mother started threatening to hurt herself if I didn't do exactly what she wanted. I was strung so tightly for so long, it never occurred to me that the pressure from the past might be a smoke show to keep me from taking a closer look at my mother's nefarious intentions. If I was too busy running the company to question what was happening at home, she would benefit from my inattention. A prick of doubt jabbed into my churning thoughts as I wondered if my father's sudden decline was as unpreventable as I always believed.

Rocco's voice pulled me out of my dark thoughts. "I need some time to ask around. I want to check out the medical facility. Privacy laws will shield most of the staff, but I know how to get the information I want. I'll try to keep things quiet but your mother has eyes and ears everywhere. If I kick over the hornets' nest, the queen is going to attack."

I let my head flop back so that I was staring sightlessly at the ceiling. It felt like icy cold fingertips were crawling up my spine. My stomach clenched. I worried I might throw up.

"Rocco, even if by some miracle Archie survived the fire, what does that have to do with someone sneaking around my house?"

The big man shrugged a meaty shoulder. "I can't answer that. But Winnie is his daughter. If I was lucky enough to come back from the dead, the first thing I would want to do is see my loved ones."

I barked out a hysterical laugh. I always felt like my life wasn't real. I often imagined I was mechanically playing a role I'd been assigned from birth. Nothing was mine. I was just a placeholder until a real Halliday came along. These fresh revelations made me feel even more distant from the man I was supposed to be. My mother was cold and unfeeling. I'd been aware that nothing mattered to her more than the name Halliday and all that came with it. It shouldn't come as a shock that the woman might be capable of murder. But the thought of her letting me grieve all these years was astounding. And Winnie. How could she ever justify depriving an emotionally delicate child from her parents? If Rocco's conjecture had any truth to it, my mother was a monster.

"Now that we know Conrad isn't being upfront with me, figure out how deep he's in with my mother. Get an idea of how long he's been selling me out. I need solid proof to confront him." The man had too much access to me to let him go without leverage. "I always knew his refusal to cut off his family was going to be his downfall. All these years, they've never been happy with what he could provide.

They always wanted more. That's a weakness my mother couldn't help but exploit. I'll bang around the floors at the manor myself to keep any suspicion to a minimum. This is un-fucking-believable."

Rocco nodded and quietly asked, "What are you going to do if Archie *is* alive?"

I could only shake my head. What was the proper reaction if a beloved family member came back from the dead? And how would I explain any of this to Winnie? My heart rampaged in protest when I imagined trying to tell Channing. For years, she'd had to live under the stigma of being the sister of the woman who ruined the youngest Halliday. She listened as her sister was blamed and defamed. She watched her family fall apart as the only piece of Willow that remained was forcibly ripped away from her. She always said she hated me, and I let it roll off my back. Now, she would have a legitimate reason. How could she care about the man whose mother murdered her sister? It was no different from having anything to do with the woman whose sister supposedly killed my brother. There didn't appear to be a scenario where she and I made any sense together.

I sent Rocco off to bring me facts. I was searching around my desk, looking for painkillers, when an assistant called to let me know Channing was at the front desk and wanted to come up to my office. I informed everyone in the building to let her up if she made an appearance. Channing refused to accept special treatment and waited until she had permission to see me before stepping into the executive elevator.

I ran through everything I'd just learned before she opened the door. I wasn't sure how much I should tell her since nothing was verified. I didn't want to face off against her and my mother at the same time. I'd gotten used to having her on my side as my reluctant teammate. I was loath to lose her.

I decided I would tell her about the possibility that trapdoors were under the floors. She was hellbent on finding the secret passages. It felt like a reasonable compromise for the time being.

When she entered my office, it felt like the sun peeked out from behind the darkest rain clouds. Her short hair was ruffled from the wind, and she was dressed casually, as always. She didn't fit in with the people working in this billion-dollar skyscraper.

Because of her, I now understood that neither did I.

Chapter Nineteen
channing

I sauntered across Win's office like I owned the place. It was another one of his personal spaces that was predominantly gray with lots of glass and black accents. His big desk was a warm mahogany that managed to give a little life to the surroundings, but everything else was industrial and boring. It was the perfect backdrop for all the glossy magazine covers that his handsome face graced, and not much else.

I dropped a bag of pastries from a popular bakery in front of him and propped a hip on the corner of the massive piece of furniture. I tapped the surface with my knuckles and gave him a playful smile. "This is a nice piece. I was so angry the last time I was here, I didn't notice. It doesn't seem to fit with your usual aesthetic." I bet it still cost a fortune and came with a royal lineage rather than a familiar designer name.

Win reached for the bag of pastries and the harsh lines around his mouth softened when he saw the sweet confections inside. It baffled me that none of his ardent suitors had figured out the way to his icy heart was directly through his sweet tooth.

"The desk was my father's. Supposedly, it belonged to Napoleon." He made it sound like there was no difference between owning a piece of history and buying something from IKEA. "I didn't inherit it. He left it to the next CEO. It belongs to Halliday Inc." Win's voice was devoid of emotion. His features were tight. I could tell he'd been running his hands through his messy hair. The knot of his tie was loose, and his suit jacket was tossed carelessly on top of a bar cart in one corner of his office. There was no missing that the man was having a rough day.

I reached out and ran my hand over his hair to help smooth some strands back in place. "What's the matter, Chester? Did you only make a couple million dollars today instead of a couple billion?"

I was surprised when he caught my hand and pulled me in front of him. I was pressed against the edge of the desk. He was sprawled in the matching chair in front of me, looking like a defeated king who was ready to abdicate the throne. I jolted when he moved forward, pressed his forehead against my stomach, and wrapped his arms loosely around my waist.

"I've always known that I was lying about who I am. It didn't occur to me until recently that everybody else in my life is lying, as well. What's the point of anything I've done if none of it is real? Why did I have to give up everything for a fabrication? How long am I required to keep the farce going? What if there is no end? Am I going to end up like my mother?" He heaved a breath that made my stomach clench. "I'm not as worried about Winnie's future, because she has you."

I stayed as still as possible while he cuddled into me. I stroked his head and ran my nails across his neck. I could feel how tense he was.

Unsure of what had him in such a morose mood, I quipped, "You have me, too. At least until our contract is up."

Win's hold on me tightened, and he lifted his head. His gray eyes were as fierce as a thunderstorm. "What if I want to keep you longer, Channing?"

The intensity of his stare was unnerving. I put my hands on either side of his face and rubbed my thumb across his lips.

"There's always room for negotiation. Isn't that what you told me? You've got time to convince me that it's worth it to return to the bargaining table when our time is up." His mood was strange. I could see his turbulent emotions in his cloudy gaze. "Do you want to tell me what's gotten into you today? You're acting like that lion with a thorn in his paw."

Win captured my hand and placed a tender kiss in the middle of my palm. "Does that make you the mouse who's going to pull it out? Then I'll be in your debt forever." He sighed against my hand before placing it on his shoulder. Win got to his feet and stepped closer to me so that he was standing between my legs. Our eyes locked and his voice was barely above a whisper when he warned, "I'm trying to figure some things out, Harvey. Once I do, there's a real chance it'll be the end of the road for us. If that happens, and we go our separate ways, don't forget that I owe you for getting out that fucking thorn. You can always come to me — for anything."

That was a pretty hefty trump card to have in my pocket. There wasn't much Win couldn't handle. It felt like I'd just been handed a cheat code in the game of life.

Win lowered his head to kiss me. I wrapped my arms around his neck and let him guide me until I was sitting on the edge of his desk. I was wearing a flowy, ruffled skirt that lifted easily under Win's hands. I set my hands to work on Win's suit, while he kissed me breathless. We were both in a state of disarray when he used his leverage to lean me all the way back in front of him. His hands ruffled my short hair as his knee moved purposely between my legs. I tossed my head and stretched out my hands, knocking that stupid brass nameplate to the ground. Win pulled his tie the rest of the way off and let his perfectly pressed shirt fall open on either side of his chiseled chest.

"Lift your ass, Harvey." I chuckled at the crude words coming from his refined mouth. I followed orders and arched just enough for him to slide the poofy skirt and lacy underwear over my hips and down my legs.

"I never thought I would willingly walk into this office." I giggled as his hands skimmed my ribcage, moving to take my t-shirt and bra with them. I stopped by because I wanted to see his face. He'd been so busy lately, and every time I spoke to him on the phone, he sounded like another piece of his soul was chipped away. I used the excuse of asking about the manor to see him. This visit could have been a text message. I was worried about him. Which made me worry about myself. Win wasn't someone who should elicit sympathy from anyone. "If you told me I would end up naked on your desk, I would've laughed you straight out of the city."

Win grunted and suddenly moved so that he was on his knees in front of me with a perfect view of my exposed pussy.

"You look good on my desk. You look good wherever you are." I sensed the sincerity in his words. It wasn't an empty compliment.

"That's because you surround yourself with stuff that's expensive, but ugly. There is only so much gray one person can take." My words skipped when I felt him kiss the inside of my thigh. His hands grabbed my butt and pulled me closer to his face. Every breath he took hit my bare center. I grabbed a handful of his hair and tugged him closer to the place I'd imagined having him when we were separated by an ocean. "The manor is beautiful on the outside. It's what goes on inside that makes it so hideous. You can change your view, Win. The only one keeping you trapped in that flavorless life is you."

"I have no complaints about my current view." I felt his words whisper against my damp folds.

Neither did I. Looking at the stark metal ceiling of his office, the hazy mirrored image of Win between my legs was reflected back at me. The image looked like an erotic painting. I watched him move closer and gasped when his tongue traveled from the top of the quickly warming slit to the lowest point. My ass clenched in surprise. I sucked in a breath because I was stunned Win would get so sexually adventurous in the middle of his workday. I had no clue what was going on with him today, but I was happy to be the beneficiary of his unusual mood.

Win pressed forward and inhaled me. His tongue was everywhere and felt deeper than it should be able to reach. His hands locked me in place as he devoured me. I gasped his name and arched my back. Pens and paperwork scattered beneath my writhing body. Pleasure pulsed in time with his movements. The surreal version of myself on the ceiling showed my wanton and unfiltered reactions. Win was correct. I looked good spread out across his desk like this. I couldn't remember the last time I saw my reflection look so truthfully enamored and consumed by a man. I always gave my all in every relationship, bending over backwards to be loved and appreciated, time and time again. I became a lesser version of myself to avoid being abandoned.

None of that applied to Win.

Since our relationship was fake from the get-go, I never had to pretend with him. I didn't try to trick Win into liking me or worry about being too much for him to handle. Because I agreed to the ridiculous marriage pact, I never hesitated to ask Win for whatever I needed. I gave him enough. It didn't bother me to take what he offered. Despite the glaringly apparent class difference between us, being with Win was the easiest relationship I'd ever had. Minus his evil mother and the ghost who kept stealing my stuff. We weren't compatible on paper, but my blissed-out, thoroughly turned-on reflection said otherwise.

I scratched my fingernails against Win's scalp and heard him grunt in response. A phone rang somewhere, and a computer beeped repeatedly. The common office noises made me laugh, which should've ruined the mood. They didn't. Win never broke focus and turned his attention to my throbbing clit. I squirmed when he licked it like a piece of candy, and I nearly came undone when his tongue stiffened and circled the tiny hot spot more forcefully. His fingers caressed my thighs until they quivered under his touch. I was at the point where my head was rolling uncontrollably, so I used my hold on his hair to pull him to his feet.

I helped him push his shirt off his shoulders and watched with hungry eyes as he shoved his pinstriped pants and designer boxers down below his remarkably firm ass. The more of him I saw, the more I understood why he was among the world's most sought-after bachelors.

I was on birth control, and considering Win's sex life was as boring as every other part of his life, being cautious wasn't much of an issue between us. In fact, I could've sworn there was a flash of regret in Win's eyes when I told him we were good after the first-time things got heated and moved faster than either of us expected. It was almost like having an accidental baby wouldn't turn his perfectly planned life upside down. I was certain any offspring of the sole Halliday heir would come from a lab after Colette genetically engineered her ideal grandchild.

I snorted a laugh at the thought and was forced to focus on Win when he grabbed my chin and held my face still. He didn't bother to ask me what I was thinking. He told me not to bring up his mother while we were having sex. I just couldn't stop my mind from wandering to the awful woman whenever I was desecrating her perfect son. It was the only thing I could hold over Colette until the day I died.

Win slapped a hand down next to my head. Before he pushed himself inside of me, I turned over so that I was on my stomach. I pressed back against his rigid flesh and wiggled my butt in invitation. I couldn't look at myself drowning under waves of satisfaction any longer. If I did, I would get ideas that were better left buried in the very back of my mind.

I didn't have long hair for him to grab anymore. Win settled for placing one of his hands on the center of my back while he used the other to guide his cock into my now drenched opening. We both let out a strangled sound as he sank deeply into my aching body. I felt my pussy clench when he moved.

His hand ran up and down the length of my spine, like he was petting a large cat. I shivered at the caress and moaned softly when I felt the touch of his lips on the back of my neck. I wanted to tell him it was fine for him to rail me into oblivion so he could get back to buying and selling half the world, but I couldn't find the words. I liked it too much when he treated me like a real lover and not a convenient hole..

I moaned as he pulled out and pushed in with more force. The motion moved my body across the desk, making a bigger mess as more stuff scattered. I was sure I'd never felt this full, or this thoroughly fucked in my life.

Win slid a hand between my waist and the ancient wood. I thought he was going to hold me away from the edge to soften the blow as he hammered into me. My whole body shuddered, and my toes curled. I felt electrified when his fingers slid down until they stroked against my clit. Sensations rampaged throughout my body as I panted against the polished surface. My body thrust backward to meet Win's movements. I heard him swear and felt the edge of his teeth lock down on the curve where my neck and shoulder met. There were going to be bite marks to go with the finger-shaped bruises he left on my thighs.

Win moved faster and started hitting places that were deeper and more sensitive. It was so good, my eyes watered and I moved with him blindly. It was rough and nearly animalistic. My body throbbed around his, making everything wet and slippery. The sounds we were making were second in lewdness only to the sounds from our joined bodies. Win swore softly against my skin, then shifted so his lips landed lightly behind my ear. Easy access to one of my favorite places to be kissed was an unseen benefit of my new hair. When his index finger rubbed circles around the tender little bud he was stoking, my orgasm was inevitable. We'd barely kissed, and I was on the edge of starting to come. I wasn't sure if that said more about his skills or my response to them.

I reached behind my head so I could grasp a handful of Win's hair. He lowered his chest until I could feel his heartbeat on my back.

"I'm going to come." I turned my head and moved with more enthusiasm, meeting him thrust for thrust.

Win licked a line around the shell of my ear and made an outlandish promise. "I'll always make you come, Channing. I never do anything halfway."

I laughed through tremors of desire and satisfaction. My pussy quivered excitedly around his heavy length and surrounded him in heat. I was breathless as I teased, "Do you think Napoleon ever said something like that when he had this desk?"

Win grunted before straightening up. He kept moving behind me and I found my completion. I laughed when one of his hands smacked my ass right before he released in a heated rush shortly after.

"Napoleon wasn't tall enough to fuck anyone on this desk." He sounded fully satiated when he grumbled the words into my ear. We made the same sucking sound when he pulled out. Thank God his office had an executive bathroom because we were both a mess.

Once we put ourselves back together and were snacking on the long-forgotten pastries, I finally got around to asking him if he'd learned anything new about the manor. The dark expression on his face gave me chills. There was clearly more to the story. He said curtly, "We have to check the floors. Rocco said there are probably safe rooms under the floors from back in the Revolutionary War era. You keep Winnie away from the estate for now. It's not safe for either of you."

I frowned and pointed my finger at the end of his nose until he bit it. "Your brother has Winnie under lock and key. He's taking her safety very seriously."

Win snorted and muttered, "Half-brother.."

I flicked his forehead and reminded him, "We both have ghosts inside that house that need to be exorcized. The more you want me to stay away, the greater my desire to pull that manor apart stone by stone becomes."

He sighed heavily and tugged me closer to cuddle me. "I swore I would protect you from my mother. I didn't know how difficult it was going to be to keep that promise."

A million different thoughts ran through my head at his defeated words. Everyone underestimated the lengths Colette Halliday was willing to go to.

The bar was in hell when it came to that woman. It was impossible for it to get any lower.

The emotion that came out of left field was the sudden urge to keep Win safe from all the damage his mother could cause.

What rattled me the most, though, was that the man had everything.

The last thing he needed was my heart.

Chapter Twenty

win

"You can't tell me that you're surprised your mother might be capable of murder." A dry laugh followed my half-brother's words.

I met his gaze, which was startlingly similar to my own, and wondered why I felt the urge to blurt out my worst fears to the young man I swore I'd have nothing to do with. I had no idea how Channing got me to agree to come to Alistair's townhouse for dinner. I had to do a whole song and dance to make sure I wasn't followed, because I still didn't want anyone to know where Winnie was. It was probably because she invited me right after I convinced her to go down on me in my executive bathroom while we were taking a shower after demolishing my desk. She used my niece as bait, claiming that Winnie really wanted to see me. However, once we reached the stylish home, Channing and Winnie became engrossed in some anime show Alistair had introduced them to.

When the younger man offered to get me a drink, I accepted and followed him to the secluded garden on his building's rooftop. It was a private, calm oasis in the heart of such a busy city. I begrudgingly told him, "You have a beautiful home." It was far more tranquil than the manor.

Alistair sipped his drink and watched me over the rim of the glass. His eyes crinkled at the corners when he grinned. His expression reminded me so much of Archie, it made my heart twist. It was weird to have so much animosity for someone I could see myself, and my brother, in.

He failed to respond to the compliment. Instead, he asked, "Did you know your father was deathly allergic to peanuts?"

It was such a random change of subject that I had to take a moment to keep up. "How do you know that?" We'd always had a chef on staff. My mother never cooked. I didn't even learn how to make the basics until I was in charge of Winnie's care. I couldn't recall my father ever having an allergic reaction to anything. But he always traveled with an assistant who handled every aspect of his life, including his meals. I couldn't remember the last time I ate anything as basic as a peanut butter and jelly sandwich. It seemed to be a cabinet staple that was missing from my childhood.

"My father fed me a peanut butter and jelly sandwich one time while my mom was at work, and I almost died. No one in my family has allergies, so I always thought it was weird that I was the only one who did. After I learned I had Halliday blood, I did a lot of research. The same thing happened to your father when he was young. His school wasn't careful about allergies and provided peanut butter in a snack. He nearly died, and your grandparents shut down the school. It's a well-known fact in the upper circles of society. Peanuts were pretty much banned from all the places he frequented." Alistair chuckled, but there was no humor in the sound. "Colette wasn't his first choice for a wife. The Hallidays hand-picked her, but he had his eye on someone else. Someone no Halliday would approve of. He wanted to run away with her and leave the family fortune behind."

"The same way Archie did." I couldn't help but make the connection.

My half-brother nodded and kicked his feet up onto the edge of a large fire pit that looked well used.

"Your dad never made it out of the Cove. He had an allergic reaction and ended up in the hospital for weeks. There are rumors that his allergic reaction was so bad that the lack of oxygen when his airways closed caused serious damage to his organs. By the time he was back on his feet, the girl he loved so desperately had disappeared without a trace. He wanted to track her down, but Colette was by his side twenty-four-seven. Between his physical weakness and his parents' persistence, there was no way he could avoid getting hitched to your mother. And when her parents died in the midst of all that, he felt responsible for her. I know how intelligent you are, so I won't bother asking if you can come up with someone other than Colette who would benefit from poisoning your old man in such a timely manner. If you ask me, the timing of your grandparents' accident is weirdly coincidental. Things lined up in a perfect way to give your mother exactly what she wanted."

I chugged back the amber liquid in my crystal glass. The liquor and suspicion made my brain buzz. "How do you know all of this? No one in my family has ever talked about my father nearly dying from allergies."

Alistair laughed again. This one sounded even more bitter than the first. "A few weeks before your dad died, someone brought tainted food to my college dorm room. I ordered from a place that was well aware of my allergies. I failed to check it before I dove in. After the first bite, I went into anaphylactic shock almost immediately. Fortunately, I had a roommate who was pre-med and knew exactly how to use an EpiPen. I was hospitalized for several days, but I could've easily died. I was just a kid. I was completely clueless about the world and the Hallidays. I couldn't have been any less of a threat to Colette. When I tried to track down the delivery person, the restaurant was shut down, and the ownership changed hands. There were no records left behind. I don't eat anything that isn't prepared by my private chef anymore. I'm never going to give your mother an easy opening again." He tilted his head to the side and stared at me. "No one in your family talks about what happened to your father. The Hallidays could've stopped Colette at any point, but they didn't. Imagine knowing your parents would rather have you dead than married to someone they don't approve of."

The liquor loosened my tongue just enough to taunt, "Isn't he *our* father?" After all, his parentage was the reason he was on my mother's radar.

"I don't know that I want to claim such a coward. He did what the Hallidays wanted but kept sleeping with simple, kind women. Women like my mother. He knew what Colette was capable of and did nothing to stop her. Sure, it's possible your father died from prolonged heart failure. But if you're asking if I think Colette Halliday can commit murder to get what she wants — the answer is unequivocally yes."

I tapped the side of the crystal glass and stared at the sky. It was dark, but the lights from the city turned everything a dark, muted gray. I was really starting to hate everything about that damn color.

"Why are you so determined to connect with a Halliday if you think my mother tried to kill you? Isn't it stupid to provoke her?"

Alistair dropped his feet and leaned toward me. "Colette is only a Halliday through marriage. I think everyone forgets it was a name she was given, not one she was born with. I'm more of a Halliday than she is. Why should I let her stop me from learning about where I came from?" He snorted. "She has you to control. That should be enough for her."

Feeling particularly exposed, I couldn't help reminding him, "I gave you money when your sister was sick. My mother doesn't get the final say in everything I do."

"If that was true, you wouldn't be *fake* married to Channing. You would've had a normal relationship and asked her to marry you because you love her. Anyone with functioning eyes can see you are down bad for her."

I couldn't refute his astute claims. "Channing thinks I'm a menace. I haven't been very kind to her. Our family history isn't conducive to simplicity between us. Even without my mother in the picture, a normal relationship isn't in the cards."

"Give it all up." Alistair's tone was suddenly serious. "Get rid of everything that makes being together difficult. Your father was willing to do it. So was Archie. Channing deserves a man willing to choose her over everything else. I had no intention of being associated with the Hallidays until my sister got sick. If I hadn't needed the money, and if my parents managed to work things out, the only thing I would've asked for is the chance to get to know you better. I went into design because of you, Win. I admired you long before I learned we were related."

I lifted my eyebrows and watched the younger man thoughtfully. "Could you walk away from everything now that you know what it's like to have more money and power than you ever imagined?" Who in their right mind would willingly go from extraordinary to ordinary?

My half-brother sat back in his chair and gave me a bright grin. "Winnie told me that Channing said that having more is always better than not having enough. There is some truth to that, but my life was turned upside down when I found out I had another parent. I think we should strive to have just enough to be happy. The more money and power you accumulate, the further away you get from what you actually want." He had a point. Channing was always perfectly content with her ordinary life, which is why I found her to be extraordinary. "It doesn't matter if your relationship with Channing is real. Colette won't accept it. She's been in danger ever since you started to show the slightest interest in her. Eventually, you're going to have to choose."

Alistair climbed to his feet and patted me on the shoulder when he walked past me. It was almost time for dinner to be served and he left me alone with my thoughts and the faint stars struggling to shine through the light pollution.

Most days, I felt like I could cover the sky with a single hand. Not today. For once, I realized how ridiculously small and irrelevant

I was. I pushed to my feet and turned to head inside. My steps faltered when Rocco called me.

I walked toward the balcony and looked down at the sprawling city below. My voice was strained when I answered the call. "I'm assuming you found something." He wasn't the type who let something go once he sank his teeth into it. It was one reason we worked so well together.

"The medical facility is abandoned. It looks like the place was emptied and scrubbed clean in a hurry. I'm tracking down anyone who was on staff. So far, there are no records of employment or government license. Is it possible your mother was running a ghost business all these years?"

I suddenly wished I were a smoker. Or that I had another drink in my hand. "I'm fairly certain I've been living my entire life in the dark. I don't think there is a line my mother wouldn't cross to make sure everything and everyone acts according to her wishes." I closed my eyes and rubbed them with my free hand. "While you're trying to locate the employees, see if you can find anyone who worked at the main hospital in the Cove before my parents were married. Someone mentioned my father was incredibly ill right before they got engaged. It seems like my mother might've been manipulating things behind the scenes long before Archie and I were in the picture."

Rocco sighed. "I told you it wasn't wise to move home after your dad died. Things have been off in your family for a long time."

I chuckled and opened my eyes. It was well past time I needed to see things clearly. "I'm what is off." There was no excuse for blindly following the path laid out for me before I was born. Sure, it was paved with gold and lined with any extravagance a man could ask for. All I had to give up was a mind of my own.

Rocco's low laughter filled my ear. "Never would've thought billionaires had bigger burdens than the average Joe. I'll keep poking around until I have something solid." There was a pointed pause before he asked, "Are you positive Conrad is your mother's insider? That's a lot of years of friendship to throw away if you're wrong."

"And if I'm right..." There was no telling how much of my day-to-day life was being guided by my mother's specifications. I followed Conrad's directives without question because I truly believed we were cut from the same cloth.

"If you're right, I can bury him in a hole so deep, he'll never be found." I couldn't tell if the former military man was serious or not. I decided it was in my best interest not to ask questions.

I hung up the phone and stepped into the townhouse. The sound of laughter greeted me as soon as I opened the door. Winnie sounded lighter and more cheerful than I'd heard in a long time. She sounded like a kid who knew how to have fun. If I didn't act now, she would have joy stolen from her the same way I did. I couldn't allow that to happen.

When my gaze met Channing's, I noticed her eyes were brighter than the stars outside. The way she smiled at me made me feel like a million bucks. It was insane that the weight of her smile carried more weight in my heart than my money.

I ruffled Winnie's red hair and dropped a kiss onto Channing's. My half-brother caught my eye and gave me a knowing wink. He gestured to the table full of food and encouraged everyone to eat.

Halfway through the meal when Winnie asked, "How much longer am I going to stay in the city?"

I stiffened involuntarily. Channing noticed my reaction and leaned over to bump Winnie's shoulder with her own. "Are you bored? We haven't even gone to my favorite pizza place yet."

Winnie bumped her back. "I'm not bored. But going back and forth to school is a hassle. I have to get up so early to be there on time." She gave me a wide-eyed look. "It wouldn't be so bad if I could travel by helicopter."

Alistair let out a low whistle. "You have a helicopter. Impressive, Mr. Halliday. I see I'll have to up my corporate game to keep up."

"He has a private jet as well. I flew on it once when Uncle Win took me to Paris." Winnie was just stating facts, but her revelation made Channing look like she was sucking on a lemon.

"For now, you can commute by car. Once I get some personal things ironed out, we'll discuss if it's better to keep you in your school or move you to one in the city." Thinking about all the choices I hadn't been allowed to make for myself I promised her, "Let us know what you prefer, and I'll do my best to accommodate your wishes."

Winnie nodded, but her playful attitude faded. "Are you going to explain what's going on? I keep asking Aunt Channing, but she won't tell me anything." She pointed at the young man at the head of the table. "Neither will Uncle Alistair."

I felt a pang in my chest when she referred to someone else as 'Uncle.' That was an honor specific to me for so long, I wasn't sure I wanted to share it.

Sensing my internal struggle, Channing chimed in. "I told you that you aren't using a helicopter unless it's an absolute emergency. We're dealing with some complicated adult stuff you don't need to worry about right now." She smoothed Winnie's hair that I'd ruffled. "You remember that your uncle and I are going to protect you no matter what, right?"

My niece reluctantly nodded.

Channing grinned at her. "Trust us."

Winnie pouted in protest until Alistair poked his fork onto her plate to steal some of the potato tarte tatin she'd been hoarding to eat at the end of her meal.

The tension snapped that easily.

It sank in that this was the first family dinner I'd ever experienced. I wanted to memorize every moment, because it might be my last shot at something so normal and heartening, when all the ugly secrets my family had silenced over the years were given a voice.

Chapter Twenty-One
channing

"Where do you think you're going?"

I stopped in the middle of the winding stairway and turned to look down at Colette, who was glaring up at me.

I agreed to wait for Win before storming the Halliday manor, but he got caught up with an emergency business meeting and couldn't get away. I hitched a ride back to the Cove with Winnie's security detail and rushed to the estate after stopping to purchase the sledgehammer that was slung over my shoulder. It was mostly for show and to aggravate Colette. Not that I would hesitate to smash up the floor if I found something. It could come in handy for opening the locked doors of the forgotten wing. Win didn't want me to confront his mother alone. He said it might be dangerous. I refused to cower in front of the woman who made both my sister and my niece feel like they weren't worthy. I was determined to put an end to Winnie's nightmares and ghost stories once and for all. Win would just have to catch up once he was free from his endless obligations.

"This is my house. I forbid you from taking a single step further. I'll have you arrested, Ms. Harvey."

I rolled my eyes. Colette's arms were crossed, and she was tapping one foot impatiently. Several of the staff members were standing protectively behind her, looking like they wouldn't hesitate to pull me down the stairs if so ordered.

"But it's not really your house. Is it, Colette?" I flashed a vicious smile and tilted my head to consider her condescendingly. "Isn't this house like everything else attached to the Halliday name? It's the property of Halliday Inc., which makes it Win's house. Just like that exquisite desk in his office. Nothing is yours; it belongs to the company and the name Halliday. I finally understand why you were so desperate to make sure Win followed in his father's footsteps. It makes perfect sense why you pretended to be suicidal to get him to move back to the manor. Without him, you haven't got a claim to anything other than that stupid last name."

Colette's face flushed, and I could see that she was clenching her teeth with suppressed fury.

"Come down here right now or I will have you dragged down." Colette bit out each word. She was so angry, I expected cartoon smoke to come out of her ears at any moment.

"You can drag me down these stairs and stop me. But I'll come back with Win as soon as he's free. When that happens, I'll bring a jackhammer. And the damage won't be isolated to your son's wing. I'll smash every valuable relic you cherish so damn much, and you know Win will not only let me, he'll encourage the destruction. He hates this house almost as much as I do." I lifted my eyebrows in a taunting manner. "As you Hallidays are so fond of saying, we can do this the easy way or the hard way." I laughed in the face of her fury. "Please, I'm begging you, pick the hard way."

"I don't know how you've bewitched my son and granddaughter, but your influence isn't as all-powerful as you seem to think, Channing." Colette narrowed her eyes. "I bet you thought you were clever taking Winnie to that bastard's house." It was her turn to smile when I frowned. "Of course, I've always known where she was. I have eyes and ears everywhere. Win might be the face of Halliday Inc., but everyone knows I'm the brains and the heart of the corporation. I think you've forgotten the pull that I have at Winnie's school. If I wanted to bring her home, I would have. Since Win started spending time with you, he seems to have forgotten exactly how things work in our world. I taught that boy everything he knows. He'll never be able to use my own methods against me." She sniffed dramatically and turned on the heel of her designer loafer. "Do whatever you want in Win's wing of the house. He can afford to repair whatever you plan to destroy. You don't even know what you're looking for. Ghosts and goblins aren't real. The monsters are all in Winnie's head."

I scoffed. "They aren't *all* in her head. There's one standing right in front of me."

Colette walked away, her legion of employees trailing behind her as she barked orders. She gestured toward the abandoned wing of the house and sent several staff running in that direction. I adjusted the sledgehammer and continued to Win's suite. I was admittedly surprised that she figured out where I'd stashed Winnie. I thought Win's obvious dislike of his half-brother was the perfect cover. I should've known better. Colette was likely monitoring Alistair long before I befriended him. He was the only person who could prevent her from keeping her iron grip on Halliday Inc. If Win abdicated his CEO position, and Winnie refused to take the reins when she got older, Alistair was next in line for the position. Everything Colette coveted would be his if she didn't play her cards right.

Once I was inside, I set down the sledgehammer and started moving the rugs and furniture. Some of it was too heavy, like the bed frame. I had to make do with lying on my stomach so I could knock on the floor beneath and listen for anything that sounded hollow. I crawled around on my hands and knees for hours with no results. I didn't see anything that looked like a handle or hear anything that might be a vacant hiding space. I was sure I looked like a lunatic on the security cameras that recorded my every move. Frustrated, I climbed to my feet and sat down on the large windowsill where my plants used to live. I scanned the entire suite, looking for any area

I might've missed when the wood underneath me suddenly creaked and moaned in protest.

I jumped up, afraid my weight was too much for the old alcove to bear. The whole thing squeaked like there was a rusty hinge somewhere. I tossed the decorative pillows that had replaced my beloved plants out of the way and banged on the spot where my ass had been. My eyes popped wide with surprise when I heard the empty, dull thud I'd been searching for everywhere. I scrambled to lift the edge. It was heavier than I expected. Once I hefted the wood up, a dark, empty space loomed before me. The area was pitch black, but I could see the top of an archaic staircase. Down into the cavern, metal sconces lined the walls from the time when candles and torches were used for light. The sounds Winnie and I kept hearing were coming from underneath our feet, not the walls.

"Holy shit!" I couldn't keep the exclamation from slipping out. Unknowingly, I turned to look at the security camera so there was documentation of my incredible find. I found something to prop open the entrance to the passageway and ran to Win's room. There wasn't a large window in the primary bedroom, but there was a fireplace. It took a bit of poking and prodding, but sure enough, there was another hidden entrance underneath the ornate hearth. It was smaller than the one in the living room, but it had the same old stairway leading into an abyss. No wonder Colette didn't forcibly stop me from entering the wing with a sledgehammer. These locations were nearly impossible to locate unless you were looking with absolute focus. That terrible woman probably believed I was too stupid to find them. I was certain she thought I would give up my quest after I demolished Win's expensive floors. She always criminally underestimated the Harveys.

Overly excited, I dashed to Winnie's room and searched for another secret entrance. Her room wasn't as big or extravagant as the rest of the remodeled wing. I spent a lot of time combing over every inch, but I came up empty. There had to be something, somewhere. Winnie hadn't imagined a monster in her room because she had a fever. I firmly believed she wasn't alone that day, and the supposed ghost was using the secret stairways to move around undetected. When I stepped out of the teen's room, I realized it was directly across from Win's home office.

I pushed into the only part of the house I'd yet to explore. This room was much nicer and warmer than the office he used in the city. There were rows and rows of books behind his desk. There was another fireplace and an enormous window facing the garden. It looked like it hadn't been touched since it was built at the turn of the century. There were so many options for an entrance, I wasn't sure where to start. I wanted it to be a passageway that opened when you pulled a specific book or turned one of the decorative items, like in the movies. It wasn't. There wasn't an opening in the fireplace or on the windowsill, either. Once again, I searched on my hands and knees, banging on the floor. Only this time, I found something. Underneath the heavy desk was a section of the floor that echoed when I knocked. Win was sitting on top of the answers all along.

It felt like a metaphor for the man's entire existence.

I texted Win pictures of all my findings and a halfhearted apology. I'd promised I would wait for him before doing anything dangerous, but I couldn't resist exploring the unknown. It never dawned on me that venturing out to hunt ghosts on my own would make him worry. It certainly never occurred to me that Win would lose his ever-loving mind when he belatedly saw my messages.

I contemplated taking the sledgehammer with me as an intimidation factor, but the stairs were narrow, steep, and precarious. I had to hold my cellphone for light in one hand and use the other to keep my balance. It was a suffocating journey. The darkness seemed to stretch out forever. The enclosure smelled damp and musty. I'd lived in the city long enough to know the scratching and scurrying I heard belonged to mice or rats. I felt like I was transported back in time, and any second I could stumble into a dungeon. I could hear the ocean crashing against the cliffs remarkably well. The deeper I wound under the manor, the more I felt like a character in a video game about to face the boss in the last level. And I seemed to get closer to the water..

Eventually, I came to a large open area where several stairways led. There was a long tunnel with a faint light at the end. Instead of taking the route that would surely lead to the way out, I picked a stairway that went back up to the manor. This specific passage had a newly installed handrail, and as I took the first few steps, motion sensor lights glowed near my feet. It was clear this path was frequently used by someone. I couldn't picture Colette down in the bowels of her dream home, but clearly somebody traveled this way enough to require modern updates.

I moved lightly and soundlessly. I couldn't guess what, or who, I might encounter. Keeping the element of surprise was in my best interest. So, I practically tip-toed to the hidden opening at the top of the stairs. This one looked the most like a regular door. I twisted the knob and blinked in shock when it turned under my hand. Why go to the effort of concealing all other ways into this hidden chamber but not even lock the one that was most used? It felt like a trap, but that didn't stop me from pushing the door open just enough to slip inside.

I thought I would end up in an unfamiliar part of the estate or even somewhere outside, perhaps the gardener's workshop or a garage. The last place I expected to step into was Winnie's old nursery. I let out an audible gasp when I saw the familiar room.

"What in the world?" I was so confused, I spun in a circle. "Is this why she had this wing sealed off? Was she hiding how her people moved around under Win's nose?"

I asked the questions into the air while my mind scrambled to make sense of the bizarre situation. The nursery looked the same as the first time I'd been here, like it was frozen in time. I wandered around aimlessly and sent a message to Win about what I'd found. He had yet to respond to the first few. I assumed he was still caught up in whatever business kept him away in the first place. I didn't forget to mention all the windows and doors had shiny new locks on the inside, as well. I was positive Colette ordered the staff to make sure this area was secure after our confrontation.

I was about to go back into the hidden passageway and try another staircase when I noticed Winnie's stuffed animal that was often laying around Win's suite. It was tucked into the miniature bed as if it was waiting for its owner to cuddle it to sleep. There was zero possibility that Win moved the doll in here, and even less chance my niece revisited the place where all her nightmares stemmed. Someone brought the fluffy toy to this time capsule on purpose. I sincerely doubted it was Colette. The Halliday matriarch had no clue what her granddaughter liked. She would never know this specific item was Winnie's security blanket.

"This is so messed up." I muttered the words under my breath and turned to unlock the door that would lead to the main part of the house. I planned to take this piece of evidence to Win and let him figure out what he wanted to do with it. One thing was certain: he needed to get Winnie out of this house. She was obviously the target of whatever creepy things were happening.

Just as I was sliding the chain latch that was newly adhered to the door, a large hand wrapped around my mouth and a bony arm pulled me backward and trapped me against a thin chest. I tried to scream and bite. My feet kicked wildly, and I thrashed around, which caused my phone to fall to the floor. I was a city girl. I thought I was ready to fight against a sneak attack from behind, but I was regrettably unprepared.

The skeletal but shockingly strong body behind me hauled my struggling form to another locked room in the barred-off wing of the manor. The automatic lock popped open after a code was hastily entered. It sounded like it took a couple of tries to get the correct numbers. I started to see signs of life everywhere, and weirdly, I recognized Willow's things mixed in. There were pictures lining the walls from the time when Willow met Archie to family photos taken right before my sister died. I could see her smile dim and her figure start to fade away as the time progressed. There was no way Colette would've kept anything of my sister's after the fire. She wiped out everything during the remodel. I remember being heartbroken that there wasn't so much as a trinket to pass down to Winnie from her mother.

I was dragged into an enormous bedroom that was a twin of Win's but decorated much differently. High-tech medical equipment was pressed against the walls and was beeping rhythmically. On the bed, there was something that resembled an antique mannequin that sported all my missing stuff. My earrings. My shoes. My hairbrush sat on the nightstand, and on the mannequin's head was my shorn hair. It looked as if someone had created a life-sized voodoo doll that bore an uncanny resemblance to me. I was so freaked out I almost threw up against the hand that was blocking my mouth. The metal ring on one of his fingers dug into my lip, and I tasted blood.

Realizing this ghost hunt was far more serious than I thought, I reached behind my head and attempted to scratch the eyes of my attacker, but I went totally still when my hands landed on something that felt like melted wax. It was lumpy but oddly smooth. I silently wondered if the person holding me captive was wearing a Halloween mask. It didn't feel human.

I pulled frantically at the arm locked around my head and tried to remember every trick to free myself from stranger-danger. Images flashed through my mind too quickly to land on anything that might help. Just as I was about to go totally limp in the hopes my deadweight would be too much for my assailant to hold upright, I felt a sharp prick and a burning sting on the side of my neck. My whole body began to feel heavy, and my vision narrowed to pinpoints. The arm holding me abruptly let go, and I sank to the ground.

A hazy figure leaned over me. I couldn't make out any distinct features except a familiar pair of gray eyes. The injection made my brain too fuzzy to fit the puzzle pieces together. But the last thing I heard before I slipped into a drug-addled blackout was, "Willow. I've missed you so much. I knew you would never leave me. Now that you're back, we can be a family again."

Chapter Twenty-Two

win

"It was a strange job. Very secretive. But we got paid cash under the table, and it was easy. There were only a couple patients. One was a long-term case: a guy who'd been in a coma for years after an accident. The rumor was they kept him asleep the whole time he was at the facility because he was injured so badly. When he woke up, he couldn't take it and had a breakdown. The other patient was an older gentleman who only lasted a week. He seemed to be all right when he arrived, but he quickly deteriorated. All I did was clean the floors and empty the trash. I can't give you any legit medical details. Not that the doctor in charge ever shared anything with anyone but the lady paying the bills. Like I said, everything was a big secret."

Rocco and I exchanged a look. It hadn't taken him long to track down someone down from the medical facility who was willing to talk. He just waved a handful of money around and promised to keep anyone who came forward anonymous. A few people took the bait, and the most reliable one was sitting in the back of my SUV in a sketchy part of the city.

"Did you ever see this woman visit either of the patients?" I showed the former janitor a picture of my mother on my phone. I had to clear the message notifications from Channing before flashing the image. The man stared at the screen for several minutes before lighting up like a lightbulb.

"She didn't visit them, but she picked up the body when the older one died. And she picked up the younger one when he finally woke up. I remember because she didn't speak to anyone and hardly bothered to look at the doctor when he took her in to see the patient. After the guy in the coma went home the entire operation was shut down in a matter of hours. A group of scary men in suits came around and reminded everyone not to say a word about the facility. I wouldn't have thought much of it, but the nurse who took care of the guy was murdered recently. I heard she was looking for a new job and reached out to the wrong people when she asked for proof of employment. We were supposed to disappear." I frowned. Rocco stiffened and told me he would look into the astonishing claims. I didn't need more proof. All the puzzle pieces were locked in place and revealed an extremely dark picture.

I scrolled through to a picture of Conrad and asked, "What about this guy? Did you see him at any point?"

He nodded vigorously. "That guy was always around. He was in charge of paying us and making sure everybody kept things on the down-low. He's a nice dude. He spent a lot of time talking to the guy in the coma. I always wondered if they were related."

I bit back every nasty thing I wanted to say about my longtime friend and forced myself to stay on topic. "When the older gentleman was admitted, did anyone mention he had a nut allergy?" I don't know why I asked. I couldn't help searching for something that might redeem my mother.

The custodian laughed like I'd just told the funniest joke he ever heard. "No. We didn't even know the patients' names. How would we have personal information like that?" He tapped a finger against his chin. "In fact, the nurse I just mentioned, she used to bring cookies and other baked goods for the staff. Her peanut butter and chocolate cookies were a fan favorite."

I sat in stunned silence while Rocco kicked out the informant and paid him the promised reward. Once my head of security climbed back in the SUV, he gave me a concerned look. "We don't have to keep going, Win. We can stop right here."

"Did I not see what was happening to my family because I didn't want to? Doesn't that make me as culpable as my mother?"

"How could you see what was happening at home when she purposely diverted your attention elsewhere? Those things had to happen to convince you to leave the city and come home. Your mother is playing chess, and you're playing checkers. You're just a pawn, and everyone else on the board protects the queen. I've worked with you from the start. Halliday Inc. has kept your head underwater since you took over. You're drowning, Boss."

I sighed as I spun my phone around in my fingers. "That's not an excuse. I should've done better. Should've been better. Maybe if I was…"

Rocco snorted and started the SUV. "Nothing would've changed who Colette Halliday is. You can't take responsibility for her actions. She was up to some shady shit long before you and Archie were part of the picture." Our eyes met in the rearview mirror. "I think you should focus on the fact that your brother may be alive. Isn't that excellent news?"

I hummed absently and remembered that Channing had been sending messages for the last couple of hours. I didn't get to the first one because I was in a board meeting. The second came while my attention was on the janitor. I clicked on the text and responded to Rocco. "I thought I would give anything to have Archie back after the fire. Now, I'm not so sure. The circumstances don't feel right. My mother is clearly hiding something. She would never let Winnie be next in line if Archie could take over. She's always resented that Winnie is far more Harvey than Halliday." I didn't have a good feeling about my brother's condition. I paused to scroll through Channing's messages and swore in surprise when I came across the pictures of the hidden doors all over my house. "Channing found the passage from the plans you located. It looks like it drops right into the interior of the cliff from my fucking living room." I wanted to smack myself for being so obtuse. "Why did I let my mother find the contractor when I remodeled the wing? I've been sleeping over more secrets than I could've imagined."

I felt sick inside. And guilty.

I never should've questioned Winnie when she told me she was scared. It was another instance where I only saw what I wanted to see because it was easier than the alternative.

Rocco chimed in from the driver's seat. "Tell Ms. Harvey not to go exploring on her own. There is no telling what condition those hideaways are in. They're ancient and I doubt anyone has maintained them. With erosion and the change in weather patterns, who's to say the ocean hasn't eroded away the supports?"

"It's obvious you haven't tried to tell Channing anything. If I suggest she wait until I get there, she'll do the opposite just to spite me." I couldn't hide the smile that tugged at my mouth when I thought of the stubborn redhead. She was the first person who was brave enough to openly defy me.

I nearly dropped the phone when I realized Channing was doing exactly what Rocco thought she shouldn't. I immediately called her. It rang and rang with no answer. I texted her that I was on the way and still didn't receive a reply. I called her again, and this time it went directly to voicemail. My stomach sank and unease settled heavily in my heart.

"Channing's not picking up the phone. I think something is wrong. We need to reach the manor as soon as possible."

Rocco sped up the SUV and joked, "Do you think this qualifies as an emergency and we can use the helicopter without pissing off Ms. Harvey?"

It was the fastest way to get to the Cove. I was going to use it, even if I had to make it up to Channing later.

I called my mother and became even more anxious when she didn't pick up the call. I could tell something was wrong, and I didn't like the direction my mind was taking me. My mother had proven she could do horrendous things, and Channing wasn't a woman who would back down from a fight. If she pieced together that my mother was behind the fire, she was going to tear the woman apart. Especially if she learned my brother survived my mother's scheme and Willow didn't.

In desperation, I called Conrad. He was supposed to be at the office in the city handling the follow up from the board meeting this morning. Icy fingers of fear gripped my spine when he didn't pick up, either. It seemed like the other side was setting up an ambush and the odds weren't in Channing's favor.

"Drive faster. I can't get a hold of Conrad, either. Have any of your guys who are in or around the Cove get to the manor ASAP. I want him stopped if he's going to the house to help my mother with whatever she has planned." I scowled out the window as the buildings blurred by. "We need to make sure Winnie is safe. I can't afford to have my attention divided." I messaged Alistair to give him a heads up since he was actively involved in protecting my niece. It never occurred to me that my forsaken half-brother would become one of my best allies in a war I never imagined waging.

Rocco grunted and the SUV hurriedly lurched forward. "Do you think your mother would sink that low?"

I wanted to say no, but I couldn't. If the woman had no qualms about hurting her husband, and possibly her own parents, why would her granddaughter be off limits?

"It's better to be safe than sorry." My voice trailed off as I recalled Alistair's warning that I was going to have to choose. If the decision was between my mother and Channing, I could pick with ease. Specifically, now that the depths of my Mother's diabolical nature had been exposed. The choice was impossible between my niece and her aunt. I wouldn't survive without either of them.

The helicopter launch pad was on top of the Halliday building. By the time we reached it, the pilot was waiting. The flight took a fraction of the time as the drive, even though we had to land at a private airstrip and drive to the manor. When we arrived at the house, there was a standoff in the pristine gardens. Rocco's security personnel faced off against Conrad and my mother's staff. Obviously, the highly trained security team could've easily stormed in, but no one wanted to hurt people who were just trying to do their jobs. Conrad stood between the two factions. It wasn't clear if he was trying to keep the peace or provoke chaos.

I was stunned at how disappointed I felt. I had so few people I could count as genuine friends, and even fewer I let myself trust. Conrad's betrayal burned deep.

"You take care of this mess; I'm going to find Channing." I barked the order at Rocco and pushed through the crowd toward the steps. Conrad grabbed my arm as I rushed by.

I didn't hesitate to swing at him. My life never required me to fight for anything. It was handed to me on a golden platter. For my niece and Channing, I was willing to do a lot of things I'd never had to do before. I rushed toward the house, but Rocco tried to stop me. I shook him off and reminded him that my mother couldn't hurt me. I was the CEO. If something happened to me, she would lose everything attached to my bullshit title. I was literally the only person who was safe from her.

Conrad swore and clutched the side of his face that was quickly turning bright red. He gave me a pleading look that I ignored and yelled at my back,

"You don't understand, Win. I have to take care of so many people. There is so much pressure on me. I'll never be a CEO like you. I'm supposed to be building a family fortune. It was impossible to turn down your mom when she suggested I work for her on the side to make some extra money. It started out small. She just wanted to know what you were up to and how you were doing while we were in college. When you moved to the city, she asked me to keep tabs on you for your own good. Before I could comprehend what happened, I was doing more for her, and she was paying me more money. I was in too deep. My family relied on the extra income too much."

I paused at the top of the stairs and turned to give my former best friend a frigid look. "It never occurred to you to ask *me* for help? I thought we were friends, Conrad. I would've done my best to keep you from sinking under the pressure from your family because I know exactly how that feels." I narrowed my eyes and asked, "Do you think there are no consequences for helping my mother keep quiet about what happened to Archie and my father? Even if my mother manages to get away with all the terrible things she's done, you won't." Conrad looked stunned. I couldn't imagine he was naïve enough to believe my mother would watch any back but her own.

I left my former friend to Rocco for clean up, and I dashed through my childhood home. It felt so empty and creepy with all the staff outside. I heard waves crashing on the cliffs behind the house and, for the first time, the familiar sound felt ominous.

My first stop was my wing of the house. The place was a wreck from Channing's search. When I saw the trapdoor underneath my desk, I felt like a fool. I was sitting on top of the worst Halliday secrets and had no clue. I felt thoroughly violated. It felt like my mother forced me to come home not only to control my every move, but also to laugh at me and lord over me about how little I understood my place and my family.

Instead of following Channing's cookie crumbs into the bowels of the house, I ran to the burned wing. Rocco had said that he would want to see his loved ones, first and foremost, if he came back from the dead, and it resonated with me. If Archie was indeed alive, I was sure he would feel most comfortable in the last place he got to hold his wife and daughter.

I kicked in several locked doors until I saw proof Channing was here. Her phone was on the floor of Winnie's nursery, and the notifications from all my missed calls and texts were going crazy on the screen. I picked it up and charged into the hallway. I was stunned when I saw that the space looked almost the same as when Willow and Archie lived there.

I started calling Channing's name, pushing open all the doors that led to different rooms along the way. After five minutes of searching, I heard a faint beeping sound and a low moan coming from the primary bedroom. It was the area that had taken the most damage during the fire. It was where my brother and Channing's sister were supposedly found. The space was completely off limits after the tragedy, but as soon as I opened the door, I saw how well lived-in everything appeared.

A pair of running shoes were tucked under the edge of the bed. A hoodie was hanging on the back of the door. Discarded snack packages and empty drink bottles were scattered about. The lights were low, but the medical equipment gave everything a soft glow. It would be a comfy vibe if it wasn't for the grotesque doll on the large bed. I instantly recognized all the items stolen from Channing's stay in my suite.

While I grappled with my shock over the macabre scene, another moan came from the floor next to the bed.

"Channing!" I yelled her name and leaped across the distance, trying to reach her. "Are you okay?" She was prone on the floor and completely still. I didn't see any blood or bruises, but her hands were scratched and there was a large red mark on the side of her neck. I quickly surmised she'd been drugged.

I bent over to pick her up. She was limp as a noodle in my arms. Her rust-colored eyelashes fluttered, and she kept making sounds of pain. I needed to get her out of this fucking house as quickly as possible.

When I turned to leave, I noticed someone in the doorway.

I always thought I would recognize my little brother under any circumstances. We shared a special bond. I was the only one who supported him when he left and when he returned.

The person blocking me barely looked human, let alone like my kind-hearted, sweet younger brother. Archie may have survived my mother's murderous plans, but the cost was astronomical.

It wasn't the burn scars or the deformed facial features that threw me off. It wasn't the thin frame or the missing patches of dark hair. He'd been through hell and back, and it was easy to see. The biggest change was his eyes. They used to be a gentle, soft gray. A color closer to Alistair's than mine. They once were warm and welcoming, full of endless optimism. Now they were cold and nearly devoid of life. They looked right through me with zero recognition.

Those were the eyes of someone who'd lost everything and would do anything to get it back. Including turning his deceased wife's sister into a morbid substitute.

"Archie..." My voice broke and tears stung my eyes. I wasn't sure what to say. I doubted there were any right words for this situation.

"Where are you taking my wife? I just got her back. Give her to me." The words were slurred and choppy. Archie didn't use my name in his confused demand. I wondered if he even knew who I was.

"This isn't Willow. It's her sister, Channing. This is Winnie's aunt. You're confused, little brother. I'll help you remember. I'll help you with everything."

The twisted, misshapen facial features shifted to frown at me. "She's mine. So is Winnie. You can't have them. Mom promised me I would get my family back when I came home."

I wanted to dropkick something. That woman was always at the center of every fucked-up scenario.

"I'll bring Winnie to see you, Archie. I'll make sure you get everything you want, but you can't take Channing. She's mine. I'm sorry about what happened to Willow, but they aren't the same. Don't listen to anything our mother promises you. She's been lying to both of us for a long time." I took a deep breath and held Channing close to my chest. She was still limp and lifeless, but the soft moans stopped, and her eyelids were fluttering. "Mother started the fire. Do you remember?"

I wasn't sure how Archie's mental state was after all the trauma he'd suffered. I hoped I might trigger his memories with the right prompt.

Before my brother could respond, a muffled *bang* echoed throughout the large estate. I wanted to run, but I was hesitant to hurt my younger brother.

"Gun." Channing whispered the word so softly I barely heard it.

At first, I thought she was trying to tell me that Archie had a gun. I should've known. My innocent, simple little brother would never have the heart to shoot someone, no matter how damaged he was. My mother, on the other hand — she didn't have a heart at all.

I was certain of the fact as she stepped around a frozen, befuddled Archie and pointed a weapon directly at me.

Chapter Twenty-Three
channing

My limbs felt like they were made of soggy pasta, and my head felt like it was full of cotton candy. I could barely keep my eyes open, but I was no longer alone with the creepy doll and my attacker. I didn't see Win, so much as I sensed him. A lot of the panic and fear that rose to the surface once some of my awareness came back online was tempered by the feel of powerful arms holding me and the steady heartbeat underneath my ear. I sensed Win was tense and angry and was trying to unwind his words in my fuzzy brain. It sounded like he was carrying on a conversation with his dead brother. Which was concerning, but not as much as the gunshot echoing through the halls of the massive estate. I'd lived in the city long enough to be intimately familiar with the noise.

I attempted to warn Win that his rescue was about to go tits up when I heard him ask, "Where did you get that gun, Mother?"

Colette laughed like Win just told the best joke in the world. I never thought the woman had a sense of humor — and I was right.

"If you were more invested in the legacy that comes with your last name, you would know this pistol has been handed down to every generation of Hallidays since the nineteen-twenties. It was a gift to your grandparents from the Winchester heiress before she died. It's where your father came up with your name."

Win's dissatisfaction rumbled from his chest. "Isn't the Winchester heiress the woman who lost most of her family and built a never-ending mansion out of guilt because she was compelled by all the souls lost to her family's firearms?" Even through the fog filtering around my brain, I could hear the irony in his question.

I wiggled my fingers and got the faintest response. Whatever anesthetic my captor pumped into my veins was slowly starting to dissipate. I needed to be mobile so Win didn't have to fight two-on-one. Without the gun pointed at him, he could take them. With the weapon in play, the other side had a distinct advantage.

"There isn't time for a history lesson, Winchester. You've made quite a mess of everything, haven't you?" Colette sounded as arrogant and unfeeling as always. It seemed holding her beloved heir at gunpoint barely fazed her.

"I heard the gunshot, Mother. Who did you shoot at?" Win's voice was strained, and I realized he was trying to buy time. Rocco was undoubtedly close behind. He was waiting for the rescuer to be rescued. "I know there's no chance you'll pull that trigger while you're facing me. If you do, you risk losing everything you've worked so hard for."

My head lolled to the side, and I saw Colette pat the thin shoulder of the man who dragged me into the bedroom.

"I've always had two sons. Of course, I wanted you to be obedient and marry someone suitable. I wanted you to give me a high-quality grandchild who would eventually take your place. But you've always been difficult and stubborn, and Winnie takes after her mother far too much for my liking. Your brother is much easier to deal with. Why do you think I've been taking care of him all this time? It was out of necessity." She walked fully into the room and pushed the silent man behind her who was still staring at me obsessively. "If you anticipate your security team riding bravely to your rescue, I'm afraid that won't be possible. I ran into Rocco. He's currently incapacitated and won't be able to save you or alert the rest of the team that there's a problem."

My skin prickled like a thousand needles were stabbing me at once. Colette was evil. It was still shocking to hear just how conniving and vile she could be. Could you even be called a mother if you were only keeping your child alive for spare parts? How could Colette see her own flesh and blood as nothing more than a tool for breeding? It was disgusting on so many levels.

I moved my head and caught Win's eye. He hugged me closer and nodded when I mouthed, "That's Archie?" I was baffled. How had he survived the fire when my sister didn't?

"Mother." Win paused, took a deep breath, and changed how he addressed the deranged woman holding him at gunpoint. "Colette. How do you think you're going to explain this? Bodies keep adding up where you're involved. And even the Hallidays don't have the power to bring back the dead. People are going to ask questions about the fire. When they do, all the skeletons in this manor are going to fall out, one after the other."

I tugged on Win's sleeve and tried to get him to look at the oxygen tank by the bed. When I was on the floor, I'd been tangled in the cannula tubing. If the canister was open, there was no telling how long it'd been leaking into the room. If Colette fired the antique pistol, there was a chance the entire room would blow up. I gained enough feeling in my hands that I could worriedly clutch the hem of Win's sleeves. I was nervous. We needed to find a way out of this room, this house of insanity, in a hurry.

"No one bothers to look below the surface when the right people and enough money are involved. It's no secret Ms. Harvey hates our family. It's not a reach for people to believe she married you to seek revenge. Once she integrated into your life, she concocted a murder-suicide plot that sadly ended both of your lives. Your head of security tried to intervene. He died a hero, trying to protect the CEO of Halliday Inc. I'll have my hand-picked replacement fill in for you until your brother provides me with a suitable heir." The smile that crossed the older woman's face was Machiavellian. She spoke of murder as if it was nothing more than the price of doing business.

"No one outside the house has to know that Archie survived the fire. This family has a history of bastard children appearing out of the blue. As long as I recognize the progeny as my grandchild, the rest of the world will be none the wiser."

Win scoffed. "Let me guess. You promised to make Conrad the interim CEO while this madness plays out. That's why he agreed to be your lackey for so long."

"He follows directions well. It's a shame his family isn't more noteworthy. He could achieve great things with the proper motivation and backing." She gave Win a disgusted look. "I don't understand why I was cursed with such disobedient children."

"Maybe because you tried to murder their father because he dared to love someone who wasn't you." Win's words were as frosty as the Arctic.

It sounded like Colette had everything perfectly planned. Win was shaking where he held me, and the man whom he identified as his brother seemed frozen in place. Archie's injuries were pretty horrific. However, when his eyes caught mine, I could tell the damage done to the inside was worse. I couldn't imagine what it felt like to rise from the dead and realize you lost everyone you loved. I wondered if Archie would be so compliant if he comprehended that his own mother made him like this.

I tried to motion with my eyes that Win should put me down to fully confront his mother. The situation was getting more dangerous the longer the two bitterly argued. If flammable gas was leaking into the air, and so much as a tiny spark ignited, all of us were doomed to be caught in a fiery inferno — and there'd be more deaths attributed to the cursed Halliday manor.

Win gave me a squeeze to stay still and ignored my silent pleas. He turned his attention to his younger brother and asked, "Archie, do you remember what happened the night of the fire?"

The other man tilted his head as if trying to process the question. Colette reached out and grabbed the arm of her youngest. "Go to the nursery and wait for your daughter. Mom will make everything better. Remember who took care of you when no one else was there?"

"No one was there. No one knew you survived the fire, Archie. She's the person who hurt you. She killed your wife."

I was stunned. I always knew Colette had a hand in orchestrating my sister's death, but what Win just said made it sound like she outright murdered Willow. There was never an accident. It was a manufactured tragedy. Willow had been a scapegoat all along. When I got full feeling back in my limbs, I was going to tear Colette Halliday to pieces. Well, I'd seek vengeance if I survived the impending explosion.

"My wife?" The muffled words were hard to understand. The shaky finger pointed in my direction was much easier to decipher. "Willow."

I tried to get Win to put me down once again, but his attention was fully on his brother.

"This isn't Willow. This is Channing. Willow is gone because Mom killed her. She started the fire but only saved you. Remember, Archie?"

"Enough!" Colette barked the word and marched threateningly toward Win. It seemed surreal this was playing out in one of the most well-known colonial estates in the country. The lifestyle of the rich and famous was supposed to be above something as mundane as murder. Though, it made sense that the more you had, the more you were likely to lose. And the less ethical and rational you became to keep it all.

Win reluctantly set me down so I wasn't an easy target pinned to his chest. My knees were too gooey to hold my weight. I slumped to the floor and noticed I was right next to the fireplace. Silently, I started to feel around for a ledge, thinking there might be another hidden entrance in the hearth. We had to get out of the room, and going through Colette and her gun didn't seem like an option. The woman had our demise perfectly planned. We couldn't out-calculate her. And while Win could definitely overpower her, the space was small enough that there was a real danger of a wayward shot hitting either me or his brother. Plus, Win wasn't exactly familiar with brute force. His life up to this point was too soft. If we managed to survive this, I was going to nag him to learn how to hold his own in a bare-knuckle fight. It was a useless skill for a billionaire, but any man as annoying as Win Halliday should possess it.

Without warning, Archie moved. He grabbed his mother from behind, his thin hands clamping down on her arms to reach for the gun.

"Fire. Hot. Burning. Willow sleeping. Why won't she wake up? Where's Winnie?" The questions were garbled, and his lifeless eyes suddenly glowed with vengeance. "She wanted to leave. You wouldn't let her!"

"Let go of me! Be a good boy, Archie." The gun swung wildly as the two wrestled.

While they were distracted, I grabbed Win's hand and pulled with my limited strength. "Open this passageway! Hurry!" I pointed to the oxygen canister. "If that's open, and the gun goes off, we're all going to die."

He was much faster on the uptake than I would be. He dropped and helped me lift the heavy marble hearth. It opened easily, indicating frequent use. Colette screamed like a banshee and demanded her younger son let her go. Archie couldn't put up a lengthy battle. That's why he had to incapacitate me with the same drugs his mother used to keep him docile. No wonder he was haunting his childhood home in the dark. He wasn't a ghost. He was searching for one.

"I'll kill what's left of your family, Archie! Behave! Why are you stupid boys always messing up my plans? This family would be nothing without me."

As soon as the gap in the floor was visible, Win shoved my sluggish body into the dark hole. I reached out to clutch his arm, trying to pull him down with me. His stormy eyes locked on mine with regret, and the line of his mouth was ferociously grim.

"I can't leave my brother behind again. Get somewhere safe and wait for me." He squeezed my hand and tried to straighten up. I kept my tight grip on him.

"Now is not the time for you to be a hero. One wrong move and no one is making it out of this fucking cursed house."

He kissed my fingers and pried them off his arm. "I missed every other time I should've been the hero, Channing. I can't let my little brother down." I argued as he started to close the hidden entrance, but he ignored my pleas and muttered, "Maybe the best thing is for the Halliday name to go away for good. Winnie has always been more of a Harvey, anyway."

I wanted to scream and climb out of the security of the subterranean stairway, but the drug still coursing through my veins slowed my actions. I tried to crawl toward him. It didn't do any good. Win seemed determined to lock me away from the massacre unfolding a few feet away.

Suddenly, a new voice joined the fray. I wasn't familiar enough with Win's assistant to recognize him by sound alone. It wasn't until Win called Conrad's name and told him to put down yet another gun that I realized the situation had taken another turn for the worse. I attempted to crawl to the top of the stairs, but it was slow going.

"Conrad, this room is filled with flammable gas. If anyone fires a weapon, we're all going to die." I heard him exhale a long, slow breath. "While my mother and I might deserve such an ending, my younger brother doesn't. He's had half his life stolen from him. He's not well. You need to let him go."

"I don't need to do anything. I've got a gun I took from Rocco. Serves him right for always thinking he was better than me. I swear, rich people are so incompetent. You all think you're untouchable. The truth is, you're all so fucking fragile. The minute something doesn't go the way you want, you're ready to burn the world to the ground rather than think of a compromising solution. I've had enough of the entitled bullshit to last a lifetime."

By the time I managed to peek over the lip of the opening, the dynamic in the room had changed drastically. Win's mother was now pointing her gun at his assistant, screaming that he was messing up her plan. If there were extra bullets at the scene, a murder-suicide would be a harder sell. Win stashed his younger brother protectively behind his body. There was still a weapon directed at the center of Win's chest, but the threat had changed.

Even though I was bitter about the abduction, I stuck out my hand and grabbed the bottom of Archie's sweatpants. I tugged until the incoherent young man responded. Fortunately, he was familiar with the secret passageways, so getting him to duck down into the safety underneath the toxic manor went smoother than any part of the rescue mission thus far.

Colette was arguing with the man she'd hired to subvert most of Win's life. They were screaming about who was responsible for all of the Halliday's great achievements, forgetting that the Halliday who actually put in the work was directly in the line of fire. Once Archie was fully out of sight. I whisper-yelled that it was time to retreat, but Win refused to acknowledge me.

"Didn't you just tell me you would never be a CEO, Conrad? Haven't you been planning to take my spot since my mother first approached you?" Win shook his head, but finally stepped backward, closer to the opening. He was too far away from me to grab without exposing myself. I made a mental note to chew him up one side and down the other for being so unnecessarily heroic. I understood the man had regrets about the way he'd lived his life until now, but catching a bullet wasn't the correct way to make amends.

"You never should've been in charge of Halliday Inc. You think it's a burden. You treat the company as if it's boring and redundant when it's the lifeline for so many. It's not your dream; it's worthless to you. You aspired to be a musician and you've been crying about your mommy making you give up the violin for years. You're pathetic, Win. You've never appreciated anything you have. Colette should've taken you out instead of your father. At least he showed up and played his part without complaint."

I gasped. I'd never expected to find out Colette was behind multiple murders when I went adventuring under this cursed house. Marrying Win was bringing me truths that I never would've imagined were possible.

Lady Halliday was a killer.

"Enough." Colette whipped around and pointed her gun back at her son.

Win stood still, just out of reach.

Desperate, I looked down at the pitiful youngest Halliday and asked, "Do you want your brother to die?"

The hollow eyes seemed to flicker with some form of recognition.

"Your mother is going to kill him. Just like she killed your wife and your father. And once she's done with Win, she'll go after your daughter." I had no clue if Archie understood a word I said, but he cocked his head and watched me closely. Instead of looking terrifying, he looked lost and alone. "He would've saved you, Archie. If he knew what was happening to you, he would've been there for you. Your mom kept it secret. He's willing to die for you right now to make up for everything he missed. Do you want to let your mother keep taking your family away from you?"

"Willow?"

I screamed in terrified frustration, "I'm not Willow! But I know my sister would want you to help me save Win. Do you understand?"

It was unclear if he processed what I was saying, but the next second, there was a massive bang and the world started to burn. I was pushed violently down the darkened stairs as Archie suddenly burst out of the entrance. I rolled head over heels all the way to the clearing that sounded close to the sea. I was weak, and the impact on my head was too much for my recovering body. A faint shadow moved on the outskirts of my vision. I couldn't tell if it was Archie, Win, or someone wielding a gun.

My last thought before I lost consciousness for the second time that day was that I had a hand in the fall of the Hallidays.

Willow would be proud.

Chapter Twenty-Four

win

I woke up in a tangle of tubes and wires attached to every visible part of my body. My chest felt like there was a fire burning in the center of it, and my head felt stuffed with cotton. My throat and eyes burned with irritation, and I couldn't move without waves of pain crashing throughout my entire being. I was clearly in a hospital, but I had no recollection of how I got here.

While I struggled to get my bearings and piece together what was happening, an annoyingly handsome face flashed into view.

My half-brother gave me a smile and placed a cup of ice chips on a little tray within arm's length.

"You're awake much sooner than the doctor told me you would be. Winnie will be relieved. The poor thing has been crying her eyes out for days. It's a good thing I grew up in a house full of sisters, so I'm used to it."

I attempted to ask the bastard what was going on but my throat seemed to be lined with sandpaper and razor blades. I couldn't make a sound, and when I tried, it burned badly enough to make my eyes water.

Alistair nudged the ice toward me. "You were intubated until an hour ago. I'm sure your trachea feels like raw meat. You're going to have to learn how to take it easy for a bit, big bro." His eyebrows lifted as I frowned at him. "You were shot, Win. Twice. And you've got significant burns all over your front side. The burns on your hands and arms are bad enough you're looking at more surgery in the future. You've been knocked out on the best heavy-duty drugs for over a week. The burn specialists felt a medically induced coma was the best way for you to recover. It was touch and go a couple times. Your blood pressure bottomed out during the emergency procedure to remove the bullets. Winnie and Channing have been on pins and needles until yesterday. You turned a corner pretty suddenly and finally started breathing on your own. It took a few days for your blood pressure to even out. I think you better get used to the hospital, because you aren't going anywhere for a while."

I looked down at the length of my prone body and took in all the gauze and bandages I was wrapped up in. I looked like a mummy.

Alistair waited until I moved my gaze back to his. I tried to motion to him to keep talking, but I couldn't even wiggle a finger without feeling like my skin was going to peel off. Fortunately, he was quick on the uptake. He moved closer to help me with the ice chips and kept talking.

"Colette tried to shoot you in the heart. She got close. But that antique gun she was so proud of hadn't been cleaned or maintained in years. She used it to take a shot at your security guy, it misfired, and the bullet went wide and hit you in the shoulder. It ignited the flammable gas from Archie's medical equipment. The police aren't sure if your assistant purposely shot at you or if he just fired in surprise when the room exploded. His bullet caused all the problems. It tore through most of your major organs. You're down a kidney and missing a couple feet of intestine." He sighed and his tone turned somber. "Neither of them survived the explosion. You wouldn't have either if Archie hadn't pulled you into the secret stairwell. He saved your life. Both he and Channing ended up battered and bruised, but you took the brunt of the blast. You and your security guy both have brand new bullet holes. He was shot in the leg. Nearly bled out since the bullet clipped an artery and Conrad knocked him out while he was down. The firefighters who went in after the explosion saved his life. He told the rescue team to check underneath the manor for survivors. Both you and Channing were unconscious. Archie did his best to protect you."

I gasped in pain while I tried to form simple words. All I got out was, "Wh-er-e?" Getting out the stuttered syllables made me feel like I'd just run a marathon. I was shaking from the effort.

Alistair shoved more ice chips in my mouth. I scanned the room, looking for a particular redhead. I didn't understand why Alistair was playing nurse and not her.

"Channing made sure Archie was situated somewhere safe after the chaos calmed down. He's very receptive toward her. Probably because he still confuses her for her sister. She took him to the same facility that's cared for her mother all these years. He's doing much better with proper medical care. The physical damage might not have the best prognosis at this time, but most of the medically induced fog Colette kept him in has faded away. Plus, seeing Winnie has given him a new lease on life. Archie clearly wants to take part in her life. She's got some major guilt for thinking her father was a monster. Winnie's staying with me for now. I got her an emergency leave from school. She doesn't want to go back to the manor. Who could blame her? Besides, the explosion did a lot more damage than the fire. The structure is compromised. If you want my opinion, you should level the damn thing. Nothing good has come from that house."

Alistair was saying a lot, but none of it answered the question I wanted to ask. Where was Channing? We'd been through a life and death situation together. There were no more family secrets lingering between us. Even if she didn't care if I lived or died, how could she not have something to say about the fact my mother killed her sister?

"Your niece has been climbing the walls waiting for you to wake up."

I choked when Alistair shoved more ice chips into my mouth, and I glared at him when he climbed to his feet. He brushed his hands together and looked down at me. "You're only allowed one visitor at a time. The medical team is trying to keep you in a sterile environment because of the burns. I'll get Winnie ready to see you now that you're awake. She hasn't slept through the night in over a week."

Of course, I wanted to see my niece and reassure her that I wouldn't leave her. But that desire was second to wanting to see Channing with my own eyes. My entire family owed her an apology, at the very least. I owed her so much more. I was getting agitated about not being able to communicate. I had to control my frustration when Winnie ran into the room clad in a blue hospital gown and cap. Her eyes were red, and it was easy to see how deeply she'd been affected by these traumatic events. She sat down next to me and gently placed her gloved hand over the top of my bandaged one.

"I'm so glad you're awake, Uncle Win." Her voice was thick with tears. "I don't know what I would do without you." She sniffed loudly and started to silently cry. "Uncle Alistair helped me plan a funeral for Grandma." Our eyes met, and she blinked wet eyelashes at me. "Barely anyone came. People are calling her a serial killer." She paused for a moment to catch her breath. "Uncle Alistair has kept the press away from me for the most part, but I still get calls from random numbers and shady direct messages. He told me not to respond. He's trying to keep the news that my dad is alive under wraps until you feel better. He says that's your problem to solve."

I couldn't hug her or pat her head the way I typically did. I couldn't even tell her I was okay, not because I wasn't able, but because I really didn't know how I was. I felt very fortunate to be alive.

Since I couldn't get out simple sounds, there was no way I could say Channing's name. Instead, I tried to ask Winnie, "Aoo-u—nt?" It hardly sounded like English. It was close enough. I saw the instant recognition and avoidance in Winnie's eyes.

"Aunt Channing took me to meet my dad and grandma. They were both very nice. My grandma kept confusing me with my mom and Aunt Channing, but she told me that I'm the prettiest girl she's ever seen. She asked me to sing for her next time I visit. I think I'm going to take lessons from Aunt Channing's friend. My dad cries whenever he looks at me. He won't let me see his face. He always wears a mask and a hat. I think he's worried about scaring me. He apologized for sneaking into my room to see me. He explained that he was taking a lot of medicine that made him act weird and messed with his mind. I know he was burned badly. I tried to research what happens to someone who survives a fire to brace myself for when he's ready to show me." She shrugged and looked downcast. "Aunt Channing says everything will take time. She keeps reminding me that we all have to heal. I don't want to go back to the Cove. When you get better, I want to change schools and stay in the city with you."

I tried to nod, but moving my head made my entire body throb. She never responded to my question about Channing. First my half-brother, now my niece. I might be fuzzy-headed and delirious from pain, but I could tell they were talking around the answer I wanted most.

Winnie stayed with me until the medical crew came in and started moving around me, checking all the beeping machines, and messing with the dressings on my wounds. It was too much stimulation and too much pain. It wasn't clear if I fell back asleep naturally or if it was medically induced. My mind was a jumbled mess, and I was exhausted.

I'd been shot. By my mother and best friend.

I was nearly blown up. But my dead brother saved me.

Everyone I cared about made sure I was going to survive the ordeal, except my wife.

While I anticipated the tide to turn when the truth came to light, I never imagined she would ignore me at my weakest.

She was too kind for that.

She might not care for me the same way I cared for her, but I refused to believe there was nothing but that fucking contract between us. It wasn't time for her to say goodbye just yet. I had to let her go first.

I chose Channing.

Above and beyond everything else. I was going to give it all up. Screw being a Halliday. Fuck generational wealth and a lifelong legacy. Those privileges brought nothing but pain and regret with them. Love was priceless. Channing was my first choice. I wanted to tell her that before I set her free.

If she ever found her way back to me of her own volition, I would keep her forever.

Somewhere in the middle of pain-fueled dreams and drug-addled delusions, I felt a cool hand touch my face. I imagined a sweet brush of lips over mine. I doubted it was real. I was certain my brain was only conjuring up what I most desired so I could get the rest my battered body so desperately needed. A soft goodbye drifted on my dreams and left behind a hollow heart and unfulfilled promises.

When I woke up the following day, I still felt like I'd been hit by a flaming truck, but my throat was less raw. While I still couldn't form sentences I managed to ask where my wife was. The medical staff didn't know. Winnie pointedly ignored the question. When Rocco was wheeled in to see me, I thought he would break and give me something useful, but he stonewalled me, as well. As relieved as I was that he survived my mother's murderous machinations, I still threw him out of my room when he refused to relent. He stayed silent, no matter how many times I asked him about Channing's whereabouts.

I was restless throughout the day from the pain, both internal and external. Every time the door opened, I hoped to see Channing walk through it. By the time the day shift turned to night shift, I realized she wasn't coming. It wasn't until Alistair showed up right before I was ready to fall asleep that I finally got an answer.

My half-brother met my questioning gaze steadily as he took a seat next to my bed. Medicine and painkillers were pumping through my veins. I had to struggle to keep my eyes open.

"I bet you're wondering why no one mentioned Channing, even though you asked about her all day." I would've nodded if I'd been able. Alistair sighed and adjusted his protective gown. "We all thought it was best to wait until you made it through the day and were a bit more stable to tell you that she's gone. She waited until you woke up before she took off, so don't think she wasn't worried about you."

"Where...did...she...?"

"I don't know where she's going. I promoted her to the acquisitions department of my design company. I gave her a company credit card and told her to bring me back a suitcase full of treasures. Your contract didn't say she had to stay right by your side. And now that Colette is out of the picture, may she rest in hell, most of the agreement is void anyway. She didn't tell me where she's headed or when she'll be back. But Winnie's birthday is right around the corner. My guess is she'll be back before we know it. She's not going to abandon that little girl." He let out a long breath and gave me a serious look. "She's been through a lot, Win. Channing toughed things out better than anyone else would've in her shoes. I think she needs some time to recalibrate. And so do you."

I tried to laugh, but it turned into a hacking cough. My body shook in agony, and I had to squeeze my eyes closed to keep tears from leaking out.

Alistair got to his feet to leave, as if he hadn't just dropped a bomb in the center of my world. I tried to reach for his hand, but the bandages and the burns underneath made the move limp. Luckily, the bastard was a more compassionate man than I'd ever been. He leaned closer and listened without interruption as I brokenly told him, "I'm giving you the company."

Our eyes locked — his stunned, mine hazy and unclear.

Alistair laughed and shook his head. "I can tell they have you loaded up on some primo stuff. Be careful or you're going to give Halliday Inc. away to someone unscrupulous enough to take it while you're all fucked up."

I once told Channing that when you knew where you belonged, no amount of money or power could remove you from that spot. It was yours and yours alone. Too late, I realized the place I wanted to be was next to her — wherever that might be.

I grunted. "I'm giving it to you. I'm going to sign all my shares over to you and Winnie."

I was about to give up everything.

And come hell or high water, I was going to get my wife back.

The End

(Book #2: The Sound of Secrets *Coming Soon-ish)*

Afterword

What the hell was with that ending!

I know. It took me by surprise, as well.

I've NEVER been interested in writing more than one book about my fictional couples. Not a single story over the course of a decade or forty-plus books. I've always managed to wrap up my novels and be one-and-done.

It was impossible with this book. Channing has so many reasons to dislike Win and his lifestyle. Plus, she has so much baggage tied to their family discord that was never addressed because of everything else going on. I managed to make her fall in lust with Win, and I think she's always been genuinely fascinated by him, but there was no way I could force her to *love* him by the end of book one. She's a woman who truly believes that money is the root of all evil and isn't interested in tying herself to the Halliday fortune. And as much as Win cares for Channing, the man really had no clue how to be anything other than an entitled prick. He needs more time to step out of his CEO shoes. I could've written a different ending to make less work for myself, but that would've made for a super shitty romance that wouldn't have been very romantic at all. So, Win and Channing get a duet to tell their tale, and I am as surprised by the outcome as you are. I am looking forward to this new challenge. (Of course, I've dabbled in duets before, but Rebecca Yarros fielded half the work back then... yes, *that* Rebecca Yarros.) This time, it falls on me to make both books interesting and seamless. It's a bit nerve-wracking, to be honest. If the heat levels in this book feel tame, refer to all the reasons I couldn't tell this book in one go. You'll have to trust that book two will be a different beast all around. I can feel it in my gut.

Don't worry, book two is currently in the works and will be out as quickly as possible. I don't enjoy waiting after and ending like this either! I want to have a satisfying conclusion for the characters just as much as the next reader. I have zero patience for anything.

As for how this grumpy billionaire book came about, I've been playing with the idea forever. I was watching K-dramas, as one does, and the idea of a wealthy heir who hates everything about his life took root and wouldn't let go. I wanted to write a character who embodied the phrase 'money can't buy happiness.' Win should be overjoyed with everything he has, but it makes him so much more interesting that he can't stand the privilege he possesses.

Giving him a tyrannical, psychopathic mother came from the idea of writing a caricature of an overly-controlling parent often depicted in K-dramas. The over-the-top family dynamics reminds me of all the soap operas I used to watch with my mom when I was little. (*General Hospital* was the fave...lol.) So does the plot-point of bringing back someone who was thought to be dead.

When I decided to write an emo billionaire, I knew I needed to pair him with my most relatable leading lady to date. Channing is meant to represent every woman who is thriving just because they are surviving. She rolls with the punches. She doesn't blame anyone for the choices she makes. She succeeds and fails equally. Just like Win thinks of her, she is extraordinary because she is so ordinary. She stands out because of who she is, not because of what she has. Of course, the only way to throw two people together who are very much at odds is to make them get fake married. That's another common plot in dramas from all over the world. Channing is a woman who really loves love. Which is why she's been married more than once. She's not afraid to risk her heart, which makes it telling that she refuses to offer it Win. The ambiguity surrounding her mental health is very deliberate on my part. I want it to remain a question if Channing is afflicted like the other women in her family and just really good at masking. Or is she the odd one out of the bunch? It makes interpreting her actions and reactions a more involved experience.

Along with all the dramas I pulled inspiration from, you'll notice a spooky, haunted feeling throughout this novel.

The Nancy Drew series was my absolute favorite as a young adult. I read all of them. I still re-read them from time to time. I don't think I have the creative chops to write an actual mystery novel, but I've always wanted to weave a Nancy Drew vibe into one of my books. If you remember *Nancy Drew and the Hidden Staircase*, you will totally get the inspiration for a huge portion of this book. I even gave Channing strawberry blond hair as an ode to Nancy.

There's a fun addition in this book from a reader of mine. I did a Christmas giveaway, and the prize was to let a reader create a character for this story. The addition is mixed seamlessly in my opinion. I won't tell you who it is, but you can try to guess! I'll let you know if you're correct if you ask me...lol Thanks for coming up with someone so perfect for this world, Nicole.

Whenever I pop up with something that's out of pocket for me as an author, I like to leave readers with a bit of backstory. I write what I want, when I want. Sometimes I think that's my superpower in this industry. My own books can still surprise me and leave me wanting more. I can only hope they leave you feeling the same way.

Since this is a step outside of my normal box, I'd love for you to leave a review — good or bad. I know that the ending is gonna be a bit spicy for some readers. However, I'd rather folks be pissed about a cliffhanger than a lame ending that feels forced and rushed.

If you liked book one, believe that I can make book two just as much of a banger.

Acknowledgements

As always, my heartfelt gratitude goes out to all my readers. Be they new to my work or here from the start, casual or die-hard, local or international, any and all forms of reader are the biggest reasons I've managed to live my dreams and beyond for the past decade. So, thank you to each and every single one of you.

Along with my readers, of course, I greatly appreciate all the reviewers and bookish influencers who have given my books a chance over the years. I'm sure it can feel like a thankless endeavor, but know you are deeply revered by the folks writing the words.

Huge shout-out to my beta team. The team I have working on my extremely messy and ugly rough drafts never fails to come through at the zero hour. I'm always amazed and honored to have a dedicated group working on my words under any circumstances. I will forever say that the books that end up in my readers' hands are a thousand percent better because Teri, Pam, Sarah, Alexandra, Cheron, Kelly, and Mel go over them with a fine-tooth comb before I send anything off to editing. They are truly one of my greatest assets as an author.

Mel wears more than one hat in my author world, and there really aren't enough ways to thank her for all she does. Putting her in each and every acknowledgement doesn't seem like enough, but I'll never forget to thank her for just being all-around awesome and super helpful. It's unlikely you would be holding the book in your hand if it wasn't for her keeping track of my squirrel-like brain behind the scenes.

As always, I'm grateful for the professional team I work with. There have been some new faces added to the mix as of late because, once again, I suck and cannot keep myself on a reasonable timeline. Big thanks to Autumn from Wordsmith Publicity (https://wordsmithpublicity.com/) for not only helping make my release days and promo a piece of cake. (I owe Alison Rhymes (https://alisonrhymes.com/) more than one cocktail for recommending Autumn and all her amazingness. Be sure to check out her books if you like BIG angst and some seriously taboo relationship dynamics.)

Along with my new collaborators, of course, my longtime favorites still deserve endless praise. At this point in my independent publishing career, I don't know that I could put a book out without Elaine (https://allusionpublishing.com/), Beth (http://www.bethanyedits.net), and Hang (https://www.facebook.com/designsbyhangle/). I feel like they are as much a part of my books as I am anymore. If you're ever in need of someone to make sure your work is as beautiful inside as it is out, I can't recommend these ladies enough.

Everyone I mentioned is linked at the beginning of the book. Go give them all your pennies.

About the Author

JAY CROWNOVER is the international and multiple *New York Times* and *USA Today* best-selling author of the Marked Men series, the Saints of Denver series, the Forever Marked series, the Point series, the Breaking Point series, the Getaway series, and the Loveless, Texas series. Her books have been translated into various different languages around the world. She is a tattooed gal with very colorful hair who happily calls Colorado home. She lives at the base of the Rockies with her awesome dogs. She can frequently be found enjoying a cold beer and taco Tuesdays.

And if you haven't heard the news, Jay's first book, *Rule*, is being adapted into a movie by Voltage Pictures. It'll be out in 2024!

The following is a list of all the places you can find her:
Reader Group: facebook.com/groups/crownoverscrowd
Bookbub: bookbub.com/authors/jay-crownover
Website: jaycrownover.com
Merch: shop.spreadshirt.com/100036557
Facebook: facebook.com/AuthorJayCrownover
Twitter: twitter.com/jaycrownover
TikTok: tiktok.com/@jaycrownover
Instagram: instagram.com/jay.crownover
Pinterest: pinterest.com/jaycrownover
Spotify and Snapchat: Jay Crownover
Email: JayCrownover@gmail.com

For the *Rule* movie:
#markedmenmovie
Facebook: @MarkedMenMovie

Twitter: @MarkedMenMovie
TikTok: @MarkedMenMovie
Instagram: @MarkedMenMovie

Other books by this author:
Marked Men series:
https://www.jaycrownover.com/markedmenseries
Saints of Denver series:
https://www.jaycrownover.com/saintsofdenver
Forever Marked series:
https://www.jaycrownover.com/forever-marked
Welcome to the Point series:
https://www.jaycrownover.com/welcometothepoint
Breaking Point series:
https://www.jaycrownover.com/thebreakinpoint
Getaway series:
https://www.jaycrownover.com/thegetawayseries
Loveless series:
https://www.jaycrownover.com/lovelesstexas
Stand-alone books:
https://www.jaycrownover.com/standalones

www.ingramcontent.com/pod-product-compliance
Lightning Source LLC
LaVergne TN
LVHW012250070526
838201LV00107B/313/J